Southern
Charmed

D1256643

OTHER BOOKS AND AUDIO BOOKS
BY MELANIE JACOBSON

The List

Not My Type

Twitterpated

Smart Move

Second Chances

Love Unexpected: A Storybook Romance

Painting Kisses

Always Will

Southern Charmed

SHE HAS DEEP HOMETOWN ROOTS.
HE HAS BIG DREAMS.
DOES LOVE HAVE A CHANCE?

a novel

MELANIE JACOBSON

Covenant Communications, Inc.

Cover images: *Beautiful Traveler* © levkr; *Magnolia Flowers* © la_balaur, courtesy istockphoto.com.

Cover design copyright © 2016 by Covenant Communications, Inc.

Published by Covenant Communications, Inc.
American Fork, Utah

Copyright © 2016 by Melanie Jacobson
All rights reserved. No part of this book may be reproduced in any format or in any medium without the written permission of the publisher, Covenant Communications, Inc., P.O. Box 416, American Fork, UT 84003. The views expressed within this work are the sole responsibility of the author and do not necessarily reflect the position of Covenant Communications, Inc., or any other entity.

This is a work of fiction. The characters, names, incidents, places, and dialogue are either products of the author's imagination, and are not to be construed as real, or are used fictitiously.

Printed in the United States of America
First Printing: September 2016

22 21 20 19 18 17 16   10 9 8 7 6 5 4 3 2 1

ISBN 978-1-52440-101-6

For the cousins,
because y'all love Louisiana just as much as I do.

Acknowledgments

I'VE ALWAYS WANTED TO SET a story in my childhood home of Baton Rouge, Louisiana. I moved away when I was seventeen, but my roots are still deep there, and I miss it with an ache. I was blessed by a rich association with colorful characters, faithful Saints, and loyal friends and family. There is no place like it on earth, and I couldn't be more proud of where I came from. Many thanks to my aunt Casey Bennett for patiently answering questions, as well as to my cousins Codey Bennett and Chelsey Roy. Thank you also to my other extended family, Erin and Kelly, and friends Jean Schexnayder, Gwen Hooper, Cynthia Perry, and Emma Perry for poking their heads in on Facebook to answer my silly questions. Thank you to Tricia Moody Hoopes for "checking my Southern" to make sure I remembered right and to Bishop David Lambert of the Baton Rouge YSA Ward for answering my questions. Thank you to Brittany Larsen, Tiffany Odekirk, Rachel Gillie, and Susan Auten for fast but thoughtful reads. It might have been hard for non-Louisiana girls to understand why someone like Lila Mae couldn't just pick up and leave if it hadn't been for the help of these beta readers to make sure her motives were clear even to non-Southern readers. Above all, thank you to my children, James, Grant, and Eden, for their support and patience, and to Kenny for being a gift to me every day of my life.

Chapter 1

I SLAMMED THE CAR DOOR and flinched, not because it was loud but because if Mom had heard it, she was going to give me her "You know better than that" look. Guidrys do not slam doors. But maybe if she'd had a day like mine, she'd know that I had earned a good car-door slam. It had helped a tiny bit, in the way Bible swears did, but what I really needed was a head or two to catch in the slamming. Like, for example, a wedding belle's head. Maybe Jorie's since her wedding was up next and she was therefore driving people the craziest.

Sundays were supposed to be a day of rest, but once the sacrament was passed, it became the most aggravating day of my week, which was saying something for a high school teacher.

I climbed the front porch and inhaled as I passed the jasmine creeping up the columns on either side of the veranda. Purest form of aromatherapy, right there in Mom's climbing vines.

I set my church bag on the antique sideboard in the foyer and called out, "I'm home, Mom."

"In here," she said from the kitchen, but I was already heading there. She always cooked up a beautiful Sabbath dinner, even though it was just the two of us now that Brady was on a mission and Logan was back at BYU–Idaho. I wasn't used to that yet. Since Dad had died two years before, the ritual of the weekly dinners was one of Mom's only anchors, so I ate, even when my throat wanted to close up every time I glanced at Dad's empty chair.

I winced at the serving bowls and dishes covering the counter. It was more than either of us could eat between now and Wednesday. I kissed her on the cheek and sniffed the air. "I thought you were making a roast. I smell crawfish." I eyed the cast-iron skillet on the stovetop and tried not to hope.

"Good evenin' to you too, Lila-girl. I was beginning to wonder if you were going to make it home for supper."

"My presidency meeting ran late. I texted you."

She wrinkled her nose. "Just pick up and call me. You know I hate fooling with texts."

"You'll learn."

"What's the point of being Relief Society president if you can't end those meetings when you want to?"

"It was Jorie. I tried to talk about increasing class participation during lessons, and she started talking about the ballroom dance lessons she and Del are taking for their first dance."

I plucked a warm jalapeño-cheddar biscuit from the bread bowl and popped a piece in my mouth. "It's sad how happy food makes me."

"You wouldn't turn to biscuits if you'd get yourself married."

Jalapeño-cheddar biscuits were the upside to Sunday dinner. Marriage lectures were the major downside. I engaged in evasive maneuvers. "You were going to tell me about the crawfish."

She quirked an eyebrow at me but let me get away with it. "I decided to do a crawfish étouffée."

"Is the bishop coming for dinner?" She usually only made it for him or for out-of-town dinner guests she wanted to give a taste of Louisiana cooking.

"Can't I make it because it's your favorite?"

"Gumbo is my favorite."

"I'm not feeding twenty people," she said, slapping my hand as I reached for another biscuit. "Gumbo's too much trouble for a little ole dinner, and you know it. Take that bread bowl out to the deck. It's nice enough to eat outside." She scooped up the salad bowl and waited to follow me. "Now, if you want a gumbo, find a husband and make me some grandbabies, and I'll cook a gumbo every week to feed all y'all."

"So you're saying rather than make one and freeze the extra in Ziploc bags, the easiest way for me to get gumbo is to raise enough children that we don't have leftovers."

"Yes, sass mouth, that's right."

Sometimes we could go back and forth about this for an hour, but I sighed and told her what she wanted to hear just to get it over with. "Of course I want to get married, Mom." I opened the french door to the deck. She shooed me ahead of her, but I spoke to her over my shoulder so we could be done with this when we sat down to eat. "I want to get married the way LSU wants another football championship, but it's not like I haven't tried."

Someone clearing their throat stopped me cold, and I whipped around to see Max Archer rising from the beautifully set patio table. I nearly dropped the bowl of biscuits. Had he heard me? Because even a non-SEC-dwelling football amateur like himself knew that no one wanted anything more than the Tigers wanted the national championship. He refused to meet my eyes as he looked past me to Mom. Great. He'd definitely heard me. For a split second, I considered walking down to the lake and sticking my head in it.

"Can I help you bring something out, Sister Guidry?" he asked, still not looking at me.

"Oh, no. You're a guest. Sit back down."

"Actually, could you go get the mashed sweet potatoes?" I asked. "They're on the counter in the kitchen."

"You don't have to—"

"Sure he does, Mom. You're always doing too much."

"I'll be right back." He almost sprinted for the kitchen. Smart guy.

"What is he doing here, Mother?" I asked.

"Don't you take that tone with me, Lila Mae."

"What tone do you think I'm taking?"

She marched past me and set the salad on the table.

"Mom? If my tone sounds like I'm trying to figure out the best place to set these biscuits while I strangle you, then I sound exactly like I mean to sound. Why would you invite him here?"

"Oh, I don't know, Lila. Maybe it's because you didn't tell me he was back in town. Maybe if you'd kept me up-to-date on that, I wouldn't need him to come over so I could catch up on how he's doing."

"He's doing fine. Can we give him a biscuit and make him leave now that you know?"

"Oh, I'm not even close to done with that young man." The door opened behind us, and Max stepped out with the crock of sweet potatoes. Mom smiled at him. "Set those on the trivet and have a seat. I'll go get the étouffée. You two go on and catch up while I get dinner."

If Brady had been here, I'd have bet him twenty bucks that she'd take longer than any human had ever taken to transport a pot from the kitchen to the patio. I sat and gave Max my fakest smile. "Don't make fun of the étouffée."

"Why would I make fun of it?"

I only stared at him.

He sighed. "I know you teach history, but you have to know enough math to realize my Louisiana-bashing days are ten years behind me, right?"

"How did you know I teach history?"

"Your mom told me."

Another panic-worthy thought struck me. "How long have y'all been waiting for me?" He could have come over right after church, and who knows what Mom had been telling him while I was gone. I mean, not that she could tell him anything more embarrassing about my desperation to get married than I'd blurted out myself.

"I've been here since five."

"Sorry I made you wait for dinner. She didn't tell me we were having company. I hope she's been making you comfortable," I said. I traced through the sweat on my glass of lemonade, wishing I had a way to ask exactly what they'd been talking about before I'd shown up. Her fears that my ovaries would shrivel before I could produce her first grandchild? How few dates I went on and how much she worried about it? The possibilities were endless. And horrible.

"Of course. Sister Guidry is awesome. She's always been awesome."

"You remember coming over here?" I kept my voice neutral, my biggest life victory in weeks. Dad had been the Young Men president for the three years the Archers had lived in our ward. Because we had a whole acre, plus a boat docked at the lake, the quorums would plan for at least half of their activities to be at our place. The older I'd gotten, the less I'd minded. Except for Max. I'd always minded Max. His family had lived in our ward while his dad was the president of the Baton Rouge Mission. The rest of the Archer kids were pretty cool, but Max had hated it here and made that very clear. He'd been a punk, and from everything I'd seen since he'd shown up in the YSA ward two months before, he was quieter but still a punk.

Unfortunately, he was the only guy near my age whom I hadn't dated, and I'd known Mom would do exactly this if I told her he was back in town, which is why I hadn't said a word. I guess all I could really do was thank my lucky stars that the grapevine had worked slower than usual.

"Yeah. Your dad showed me how to use a jigsaw for my eighth-grade science fair project. He had a cool workshop. I was sorry to hear he died."

"Thank you," I said, even though the word *died* jolted me. Max was always like that though. Where we spoke of someone *passing*, Max used hard words like *died*. Where we said someone had gotten sick after a Church social, he'd flat out say they puked. He'd thought our manners were stupid, most especially our way of phrasing things.

The Archers were from Philadelphia, and even though Baton Rouge had over a half million people, he never missed a chance to tell us how backward he thought we were, like we were a hick town and not the capital of the state. In high school, everything had been about how Philadelphia was better and their teams were better and how Baton Rouge didn't even have pro teams. *That* had gotten him in trouble with the boys.

But the girls . . . Max was a tease, a mean one, making fun of everything from our accent to the way we dressed. He'd talked to us in an exaggerated redneck drawl, a corruption of the soft Southern lilts I'd grown up listening to. He'd been a jerk. And by the time I'd gone to my first stake dance, he'd taken even massive jerkdom to a whole new level.

I didn't have the energy to dredge up that memory. "I don't remember you loving your time here. Why come back?"

"Work."

"Taggart Industries, right? They're huge. Too bad you got stuck here when they have so many other offices."

"I'm not stuck," he said. "I chose this assignment."

"Why?" I asked way more bluntly than I would have in front of Mom.

"It's a good step in my career right now."

"You must really care about your work if you're willing to come back and put up with us hicks."

"I don't think you're hicks."

"Yew shore about that?" I drawled in my best hick voice as Mom stepped back outside with the étouffée.

"Speak like you appreciate the education I paid for, Lila." She set the pot down and didn't see Max's grin at her scolding. But I saw it and dug my fingers into my armrests. He may have fooled Mom with his nice manners, but I'd seen him week after week in sacrament meeting, aloof, refusing to engage with anyone, still acting like he was above it all.

"You've had crawfish étouffée before, haven't you?" she asked him.

"No, ma'am."

Ma'am? Hm. I'd give him one brownie point for that. He'd gotten a truckload of demerits at school for not saying *sir* and *ma'am* because "No one in Philly worried about stuff like that."

"How is it possible that your family lived here three years and you never had étouffée?" I asked.

Light pink dusted the tops of his cheekbones, then faded. "A lot of people offered it, but I was a pretty stubborn kid, especially about food."

"You'll try it now though." Mom didn't phrase it as a question.

"Looking forward to it. I served my mission in Madagascar. That cured me of my picky phase."

"Oh, Madagascar!" Mom loved hearing about mission experiences, especially now that Brady had been out for a year. "Tell us about that."

He did, telling her about a time they'd gone tracting at a house at dinner time and ended up eating *mofo gasy*, which was some kind of sweet fritter thing. While he spoke, he watched me scoop rice onto my plate before ladling the étouffée over the top, the creamy tomato sauce full of juicy crawfish bits. By the time everything had been passed to him, he dished his plate like he'd eaten étouffée a hundred times.

I watched him to see how he liked the crawfish. It was about an eighty-twenty split when the missionaries came over. It sort of depended on how they felt about shellfish in general, but eighty percent of them popped their eyes wide after the first bite, like the étouffée was a revelation, and barely held back shouts of praise. The other twenty smiled politely and powered through it, but you could tell it was a chore, bless their hearts.

I shook my head. I would never understand not loving crawfish. It was one of nature's best gifts.

"Sister Guidry, this is honestly amazing. I wish I could go back in time and slap myself for not eating any when we lived here."

I wouldn't mind going back in time and slapping him myself, actually. I owed him big time.

Mom ladled more étouffée over his rice, even though he'd taken only a few bites. He didn't look like he minded in the least. If he was faking, I couldn't tell. I listened while he answered Mom's questions about his job. It sounded like he enjoyed what he did—something about being a plant operations manager. He ate his whole plate of food, plus two biscuits, a heaping serving of sweet potatoes, and an ear of roasted corn in between answers.

"Well, that's just fascinating," Mom said, patting at the corner of her mouth with her napkin before setting it down and pushing her chair back. "I always respect when someone loves their job. Like Lila. She's such a gifted teacher. You should ask her about it." She stood to pick up the nearly empty bread bowl, and both Max and I rose to help her, Max nearly knocking his chair over in his rush.

"Y'all sit down," she said. "It does me good to fuss over you. Rest a little."

She disappeared into the house, and not even cricket chirps broke the silence she left in her wake. All I could hear was the distant lap of the lake against the shore.

He cleared his throat again, and it reminded me of the same awkward sound he'd made when I'd burst onto the porch blabbing about wanting to get married. I didn't realize I was glaring at him until he gave me a small smile, and I forced my face into a more neutral expression.

"So you got stuck after church today?"

"Yeah. Meetings. I love meetings." I'd recently calculated that I spent roughly twenty percent of my time in meetings, between school and my Church calling. That was about eighteen percent more time than I felt like spending.

"Elders quorum presidency meetings don't tend to go very long. Or at least they didn't when I was in there."

"Good for you." Mine wouldn't go so long either if Jorie wouldn't constantly derail us with wedding chatter. She was a force of nature, specifically a wedding tornado.

He grimaced. "I wasn't implying that I was the reason mine were short. Our president was really efficient. I think he made it his life goal to have the shortest meetings possible."

Was he for real? "Guess I have a new skill to look forward to developing."

He rubbed his forehead. "That didn't come out right either. I meant that in general you girls—uh, women—put way more into your Relief Society callings than I think we do as guys sometimes, so it makes sense that you would have to spend a lot more time planning and . . . whatever." He'd obviously decided he'd better stop talking before he choked on his foot.

I shrugged. Fine. He didn't mean to be insulting. I wasn't going to give him a medal for it, especially since I'd watched his disdain for my city and our ward simmer barely beneath the surface for the last eight Sundays.

Mom stepped back out, intent on getting more dishes to wash. This time I was determined to escape him. "I've got it," I said, lifting the half-empty pot of étouffée from the table. "I mean it. I've sat all afternoon between church, meetings, and dinner. I want to move."

She lifted the pot from my hands. "You two go on a walk. Take Max to the pier. It's a beautiful evening."

The time had changed the week before, giving us an extra hour of daylight, but we weren't even close to long, lazy evenings of mellow sunset. It was already dusk, and lights winked on across the lake every few minutes. "It's too dark," I said.

"Don't be silly. Your daddy and I loved sitting there, watching everyone's lights come on. It kind of reminds me of stars. Go on ahead. I don't mind doing the dishes."

I couldn't stare her down with Max standing right there, so I smiled as I figured out how to get around her. "Would you like to go on a walk, Max?" It was the perfect chance for him to excuse himself to go home.

"Sure."

"I unders—wait, you *do* want to go on a walk?"

"Yeah. Sounds relaxing. When my mom calls tonight, she'll be happy to hear I did something besides work and sleep."

I slid my shoes off and set them beside my chair. "You're probably going to want to do this barefoot. It's muddy down by the water, and I wouldn't want you to mess up your church shoes."

Undeterred, he slipped his shoes off and tucked his socks inside them.

Great.

Chapter 2

WE TOOK THE THREE STAIRS down from the deck to the yard and the brick path leading to the water. My dad had put the path in, and I frowned at the grass poking up between the pavers. Taking care of the property had been the boys' job, but with both of them gone, Mom and I split the work. It was a big yard, and I could see where we had fallen behind, especially since she rarely had the energy to stay on top of her sections.

Max sighed. "Did I do something else wrong?"

I glanced at him, and he imitated my frown. I shook my head. "Do you always assume when someone in your vicinity is annoyed that it's your fault? Because that probably says more about you than you'd like it to."

His eyebrow shot up. "Excuse me if I was off base with that one, but you've been taking everything I say as an insult, so I'm trying to be proactive here."

"Taking everything you say as an insult," I repeated as I picked up my pace so we could get to the pier and get the walk over with. "Can't imagine why I'd do that."

He was quiet, but he stayed right behind me. We were almost to the water before he spoke. "I deserved that. I was a punk when I was a kid. I can promise I'm not like that anymore."

It startled me to hear him refer to himself as a punk, echoing my thoughts from dinner. I didn't know what to say, so I stayed quiet.

"I mean it, Lila." His voice was quiet but so insistent that I stopped and turned to look at him. "I know I was a jerk back then. But that's the thing—I was a kid who got moved to a new place in the middle of junior high. And Louisiana feels more like a foreign country than a state." I tensed, and he rushed to explain. "I mean, that's how I saw it when I was a kid.

I'd never been anywhere besides Philly and Utah, and Baton Rouge is nothing like either of them. I missed my school and my friends and my cousins, and I felt like I couldn't catch a break here."

"You never gave any of us a break either," I said.

"I know. I'm not trying to defend myself. But college, a mission, grad school—that stuff knocks all the stupid out of you if you let it."

Amen to that. "And you let it?" A burning curiosity to know if he remembered and regretted *all* of his jerk moves swept over me, but I wasn't going to bring up the dance. I had a feeling it was the kind of thing that got seared into the memory of the victim while it faded for the perpetrator.

"I tried to."

I considered that and nodded, turning back to the path to pick up our walk, but I was less determined to outpace him now. He fell in step beside me, and I decided I could forgive him enough to ignore him and listen to the frogs instead. It was a step up from the chafing irritation I'd experienced since the first Sunday he'd shown up at church and I'd figured out who he was.

He had been an annoyingly good-looking teenager, and he'd grown into a sexy man. He was a half foot taller than when he'd moved away, and the skinny boy I remembered had become a well-sculpted piece of eye candy with broad shoulders, a strong jaw, and Ian Somerhalder cheekbones. The mess of black curls on his head had been tamed into a well-groomed haircut. If it weren't for his eyes, I might not have recognized him.

Those eyes though . . .

They reminded me of the amber pendant necklace I'd inherited from Mawmaw Bordelon. It wasn't a color I'd seen before or since, so they'd given him away.

I wondered what else had changed about him. In two years of teaching high school, I'd observed that while sometimes a person's better nature could win out, often character was fixed. And I had never cared for Max's character.

Might as well investigate. "You said your mission helped with the rough edges?"

"A hundred percent."

"And what about college? Did you go to BYU?"

"I kind of want to say no because I wish I could surprise people with something crazy like the Sorbonne in Paris or something. But yeah, I went to BYU."

"That's a bad thing?"

"No. I just need a more interesting life story. What about you?"

"I like my life story."

He grinned. "No. I meant where did you go to college?"

"LSU. I guess that makes me locally grown and harvested."

"I did that, in a way. I went back to Philadelphia for grad school."

"Where?"

"Wharton."

"Business school. So you're an MBA."

"I *have* my MBA."

The small correction hewed a little too closely to the old Max, who had spent a lot of time policing people's grammar and pronunciation. I picked up my pace again. "Fine. You *have* an MBA. You *are* kind of pretentious."

"What? No way. That's why I don't like saying I *am* an MBA. MBAs are the worst about that, thinking they're awesome because they went to business school. Wharton MBAs are the biggest offenders." He thought about it. "Well, maybe the Harvard MBAs are the worst. But since we're the top two ranked business schools, guys come out of the program thinking it means something. But I think it's lame for them to say, 'I'm an MBA.' No. False. An MBA is a piece of a paper. As a person, I hope to be more than that. Sorry it came out wrong. I wasn't trying to correct you or anything."

Hmm. Not bad. "You used to do that a lot. Correct people. Do you remember that?"

He grimaced. "Yeah."

"I'm a kind of a jerk for pointing that out. Sorry I jumped to conclusions."

"This might be the highest apology-to-words ratio of any conversation I've ever had. If one of us, mostly me, isn't apologizing every other sentence, I'm not sure we're going to have much else to talk about."

"Sports," I said. "You used to talk about sports a lot."

"Still do. How long are you going to keep baiting me?" He looked like he was fighting a smile.

"I don't know. I was doing it at first because I was having flashbacks of your bad old days, but now it's just funny, so I may not stop."

He stood for a moment and stared out to the water, then back at me. "I was thinking of another apology, like if I pushed you into the water right now, how sincere would I have to sound for you to believe it was an accident?"

I busted up laughing. "You *have* changed. The old Max wouldn't have thought twice about shoving me into the lake. What else is different about you?" Had his attitude toward Baton Rouge changed? I'd been assuming it hadn't based on his body language and blank face at church, but maybe I was wrong about that too.

"I don't know. I still love sports, but I acknowledge that LSU football has earned all its glory, and even though I hate the SEC, it's a good conference."

"Good conference? The *best* conference. Say it's the best conference."

"I admit that it's one of the best. That's all I'm giving you."

"Go Tigers. Can you give me that? Just a little one? Come on, say it. Go Tigers."

"Go . . . jump in a lake."

"Aw, there's the Max I remember. I'm proud of you. Admitting you have a weak conference is the first step. We'll turn you into a Tiger eventually."

"I won't be here long enough for you to try."

"What about your job?"

"I'm hoping to move up through the ranks, and that means moving to a bigger office at some point."

"It's possible I'm biased, but I don't see how anyone could spend two months in Baton Rouge and ever want to leave."

"You're definitely biased."

"I thought you were reformed."

"I am. I'm not making fun of it. I kind of like it here."

That warmed my heart, and the surge of good feeling bothered me; it was hope, because suddenly I wanted to flirt with him as if he were any new guy in the singles branch. But the few new guys who came to the ward were usually at LSU for law school or some other grad program, and most of them were from the South, if not from somewhere else in Louisiana. If I gelled with one of them, our future made sense. They got where I came from and why I'd never leave it. My roots wouldn't survive a transplant. I needed someone else who was rooted here too.

I was so far past dating for fun. I'd thought I would get married way before twenty-four, and I'd tried. But all of my girlfriends from church were married, most with at least one kid, and I presided over a Relief Society full of their younger sisters who were getting engaged.

It was an epidemic. Even the ones who went on missions were getting married within six months of returning. I'd almost say it was something in the water, but I drank that water too, and I hadn't even been on a date in six months. Though I'd never had a lot of options to start. Baton Rouge had only three wards, not counting our small student one, which was nothing for a city our size, so we maybe graduated ten active LDS boys a year from high school. In the *entire* city. And most of them went off to church colleges if they could get in. The ones who stayed for jobs or went to LSU got engaged pretty quickly. The older I got, the more the options narrowed.

Having a hot guy my age with a great career ahead of him show up at church had probably looked like a sign to Mom. It was a bad cosmic joke that it had been Max.

I cleared my throat. "So. Besides my mom's étouffée, what do you like about being here this time? Because can I tell you something about yourself?"

"Uh, go right ahead."

"You don't look like you love being here when I see you in church."

"Is that why you never talk to me?"

"I've talked to you."

"I said hello the first Sunday I came, you blinked at me, squinted, and said, 'I remember you.' And then you told me to have a nice Sunday, and you walked off. And that's been it."

"I thought you were still in your Louisiana-hating mind frame. But if you aren't, what is that bored look on your face every Sunday?"

"You're seeing me feel like an idiot because I'm seventy years older than everyone in that ward."

"Not me. I don't think you've got even two years on me."

"Fine. But everyone else."

"I get that," I admitted. "Last week one of the girls in Relief Society called me Sister Guidry instead of Lila. I'm just Lila!"

"How can I feel old at twenty-six? And somehow every Sunday I do. I'll work on my face though. Make it less mad looking or something. Think you'll talk to me on Sundays now?"

"I think I might." We'd reached the pier. I pointed to Max's pant hem. "You may want to roll those up. It makes the pier more fun." He did and followed me to the end, where we sat and dangled our feet in the water.

"So tell me more about liking Baton Rouge," I said. It had been a long time since I'd felt a tickle of excitement in my chest over a guy, and I prayed that he was going to give me a reason to let it grow.

"It's funny how much my opinion has changed, but it's changed about Philadelphia too. I grew up in the suburbs, and my dad did well for himself, so it was a pretty affluent area. Country clubs, big homes behind tall fences. I didn't go into the city much besides field trips to some of the historical sights. So Baton Rouge was a shock to my system. It sprawls a lot more than Philadelphia does, but it's got a much smaller business district and a lot of old stuff next to a lot of brand-new stuff, and parts are dirty and run-down and totally unlike what I was used to."

"But I'd think Philadelphia would have even more of that."

"Oh, it does. I just wasn't aware of it until we moved back and I realized that Philadelphia has way more problems with poverty and crime than you guys do."

"If you're going to be down here for a while, you'll probably need to drop 'you guys' and practice saying y'all."

"Y'all."

"Sounds good on you."

"Great, except I feel like a fake."

"Just practice. You were telling me about why Baton Rouge rules and Philadelphia drools."

He bumped his shoulder against mine, and heat sprang up between us. Oh, that was not good. Or maybe very good?

"I'm telling you why I like Baton Rouge better than I *used* to. I still like Philadelphia better."

I nudged him back, and my arm tingled again.

"So what's Philly got that we don't?"

He smiled down at me. "You're on a mission to convert me to Baton Rouge, aren't you?"

"Yep, you and everyone else. Every missionary who comes here, every family that relocates here for a job, they all get the Lila Guidry 'Why this is the best city ever' speech. Is it working?"

"Sorry," he said, leaning back on his palms. "Philly still has my heart."

"Then give me the Max Archer 'Why Philadelphia is the best city ever' pitch."

He gazed out at the water. I let him think as I watched the lights across the lake and wondered about the homes and the lives they illuminated. Would someone sitting on the opposite pier have seen our lights two years before and guessed that they burned with fierce grief?

When Max spoke, I'd almost forgotten what he was answering. "Here, people don't push. I can see the value in that, of taking life a little more as it comes. But I'm used to the hustle. I kind of thrive on that, pushing toward what's next, making the deal, breaking through to the next level. I know you're probably about to accuse me of implying y'all are slow-paced because you're unmotivated, but that's not it," he said with a small smile when I bumped him for his y'all. "Do I get a nudge every time I say y'all?"

I nudged him again.

"Y'all are good people, and y'all have a great work ethic. But y'all love it here so much, y'all work hard to figure out how to stay."

I laughed at all the y'alls, and his small smile grew to a grin. "There's nothing wrong with staying," I said.

"Nothing at all. I get it. I also get that I work at a different pace. I'm built more for places like New York or Chicago, where it's constant striving, pushing, climbing the corporate ladder. Which sounds so dry and boring, but seriously, I was born to go to business school and fling myself into the corporate grind. I know it doesn't make sense to a lot of people, but I love this stuff. I'm in Baton Rouge learning the operations side of a major manufacturing plant, and I love it. I accept that there's a weirdo on the pier right now, and it's not y'all."

I laughed again. "*Y'all* is plural. *All y'all* is when you mean a bunch of people. One person is still just *you*. You don't get points for that one."

"Fine. *Y'all* have a great city, I see why *you* love it, but if you came to Philly, you might see why I like it too."

I could hear he loved his job in the same way I loved mine, which was odd given how different our work was. But where normally I responded to that kind of passion, whether it was for food or work or music, his words hollowed out my chest, and the tickle of excitement disappeared in the excavation. I liked him as a person, which was a fast one-eighty from finding him on our deck an hour before, but there was no point in liking him beyond that. He wouldn't put down roots here. Not by a long shot.

We stared out at the water, each with our own thoughts, but it was an easy silence. "This is nice," he said.

"Yeah. I always feel like that when I'm near water. Lakes, rivers, the Gulf. I don't know. Put me near water and it's like someone flipped a switch on my wiring, and I go from wound up to peaceful in minutes."

"You're kind of surprising me."

I tilted my head up to meet his gaze. "How?"

"Whenever I see you, you come across as highly focused, a go, go, go kind of person. I wouldn't picture you relaxing on a pier. I don't know if I could do that if I were in your shoes."

"Why not? Are you intending to do something that should make me nervous?"

"No. I was referring to all the stuff I pulled on you in the past. It's nice of you not to be suspicious of me after that." He scrubbed his hand through his hair and looked away for a minute before turning to face me squarely. "There are probably a lot of people I should apologize to for my idiot teenage years, but I'm pretty sure I owe you the biggest apology."

My muscles morphed from noodles to concrete. The lightness had disappeared between us. "You did apologize. We're good."

"I gave you a general apology. But I owe you a specific one. Do you remember that dance when you were fourteen? I think it was your first one?"

"I remember." I couldn't keep the tightness out of my voice. Max had moved a few months after that night, but the fallout he'd left behind had lasted a lot longer.

He swallowed. "Sounds like you remember it pretty clearly."

I shrugged. I hadn't been angry about it in years, but I wasn't dying to revisit the memory. "Sure. But it's done. Don't worry about it."

"That's the thing. I've worried about it for a long time. I'll drop it if you don't want to talk about it, but I want to make things right."

I straightened and brushed my hands together to knock the specks of dirt off, ready to climb to my feet and leave. "Chalk it up to being a dumb teenager. I teach a few of those now. I get it. You turned out well. It's nice to see some of them have a shot of growing out of it. I accept your apology, and we're good." I drew my feet out of the water, and Max rose to help me up, his expression unconvinced. But I was glad he didn't pursue it. I hated it when someone insisted on making an apology that was more about them than the victim.

Callouses on his palm brushed against mine. Rough skin for a business school pretty boy. He didn't let go when I was standing, and I stared down at my hand, ordering it to let go of his. It didn't. He feathered his thumb across the back of mine, and goose bumps rose along my arm. I pulled away and turned back down the pier.

Having chemistry didn't make someone the right match, but I wished it wasn't Max reminding me how delicious that kind of attraction could feel. We'd shared a few shoulder bumps and a hand up. Easy come, easy go, exactly like Max would be whenever his job moved him again.

We walked back to the house mostly in quiet. A couple of times he asked me what kind of animal or insect noise he was hearing, but he didn't try to apologize again, and I gave him another brownie point.

He stood aside to let me climb the deck stairs first, but when I took the second step, he reached out for my hand, holding me there and smiling up at me. "Thanks for putting up with me tonight."

I smiled back. "It wasn't hard."

"Could we do it again some time? Hang out?"

I squeezed his hand. "Bless your heart," I said, and he groaned.

"I know what that means."

"Bless your heart, but I don't think that's a great idea."

"Can I ask why?"

I thought about how to phrase it. "It's not you; it's me?"

"Is that a question?"

"I'm trying it out to see if you're buying it."

"Do I have a choice?"

"Not really."

"Okay," he said, and I tried to ignore the whisper that wished he had tried to talk me into a date.

Chapter 3

"Liiiiiiiiila!"

I held the phone away from my ear while Hailey Benton squealed into it.

"Did you see? Did you? I put it on Instagram! I'm so happy!"

"I heard. Congratulations!" The Mormon grapevine was operating fine this Monday night. I hadn't even had to check Instagram for this one. I'd gotten three texts telling me Hailey was engaged before she'd called. "Have you talked plans yet?"

"It barely happened at dinner, so we haven't really had time for that," she said. "But I'm pretty sure the reception will be at the Hansens' place, and I think September will be good for that, maybe late September so it's after the worst of the heat but still nice outside. Their yard always looks so beautiful with those white lights strung up. And I think we'll do a Southern-chic menu. I'd love to try to coordinate the food with my wedding colors, but I'm using peach as the main color, and I'm not sure how many foods I can find that would go with that."

"What about peaches?"

"Very funny, Lila. Peaches aren't even peach colored. They're orangey. Anyway, you'll come, of course. And I wondered if your mama would do the flowers? Could you ask her real quick if late September is open?"

"I'll check with her and get back to you." Chances were poor. Mom had opened a floral shop when I was a senior in high school and she'd seen her empty-nest future looming ahead of her. She'd wanted to be proactive about filling her time when all of us were gone. With her impeccable eye, she'd had to do only a couple of events for Daddy's business partners—a private party, a retirement dinner, a baby shower for his partner's much-younger trophy wife—and pictures had shown up in the right Instagram feeds, giving her a steady clientele from the start.

Except that she hadn't gone into the shop more than a couple of times in the last two years, leaving it in her manager's hands, a young widow she'd hired a year after she'd opened, who she'd trained until the woman had as much faith in herself as Mom had. The only flowers Mom arranged anymore were the ones she brought to Daddy's grave.

I didn't bother explaining any of this to Hailey, who was charging right ahead with all the details she "hadn't really had time to consider."

"Lila? Are you listening?"

"Of course."

"Anyway, I know there's lots of weddings coming up, but the Relief Society can help my mother's ward with the food service, right?"

I didn't guess she was going to accept no, so I made a noncommittal "Hmm" sound that she interpreted as a yes.

"I'm so excited!" Another squeal. "I better let you go because I have a lot of calls still to make, but let me know about the flowers, will you?"

"Sure thing." I ended the call and set the phone on the coffee table, then dropped my head back against the sofa, closed my eyes, and blew an exasperated raspberry.

"What a becoming noise, Lila Mae. Long day?"

I didn't even have the energy to open my eyes. "Always. But that was for the call I just got off of with Hailey Benton." For a split second, I considered not telling her that Hailey was engaged, but it'd get to her in the next hour or so anyway, so I filled her in.

"Isn't she marrying a boy down in Thibodaux?"

"Yeah. His daddy's the bishop down there, I think."

She shook her head as she sat in her favorite armchair and picked up the needlework from the basket beside her on the floor. "I hope his mama is fine with him living up this way because no way is Linda Benton going to stand for Hailey moving an hour out."

"They've got a while to figure it out. He's only got a semester done at LSU, so they'll be in town until he's finished with school."

"When did he get back from his mission?"

"Two months ago."

"And already engaged, even with all those cowlicks."

The statement reeked of subtext. *If he can do it, why can't you?*

"Can we not discuss this right now?" I asked, pulling a lacy throw pillow over my face.

"I don't know what you're talking about, sugar."

"Good. Let's move on to flowers. Hailey wants to book you to do the wedding, so I told her I'd check with you and let her know."

"When's the wedding?"

It was a delaying tactic. She wouldn't agree to do it. "Well, she said they hadn't talked about it yet, but she already knows it'll be late September, reception at the Hansens', and there's going to be a lot of peaches."

"Peaches in September? The season will be over."

"Maybe she said peach colors. I don't know." I set the pillow back on the sofa and pushed myself up. "I'm going to bed. Thinking about another wedding makes me tired."

"Don't be like that, Lila. If you won't get married, that's fine, but you can't begrudge those who do."

"I don't begrudge anyone. But I can't say I love the idea that now we have another wedding belle, and they all seem to think our tiny Relief Society is their volunteer staff. I'd much rather be using our energy on other things."

"Another wedding belle. That is the cutest thing. Who thought of that?"

"I don't know. Maybe Becky Robert." She'd been the first, and then two other girls had quickly followed in what had felt like a rash of engagements over the last year. They'd started meeting weekly for lunch to discuss wedding plans so that no one would duplicate anyone else. Apparently it was fine to all have the same photographer, florist, and caterer, but it got touchy quick when two of the brides both wanted an ice cream sundae bar. They'd worked it all out to each other's satisfaction, and somewhere in the discussions they'd begun referring to themselves as the wedding belles. It was sweet enough to make my teeth hurt. Lately it seemed like no sooner had one of them married out than a newly engaged one joined them.

"Beth's a clever thing. Beautiful bride too."

"You only like her because she did peonies."

"That's the truth. If you get married without peonies, I'm cutting you out of my will."

"Yes, ma'am." Like I would ever get married without peonies. The bigger problem was getting married at all. "Mom? I do want to get married."

"I know, baby girl. Your prince will come."

"I don't want a prince. I want a partner. I want to be like you and Daddy."

"Then that means you need a prince because your daddy treated me like a princess. And you'll find that kind of man. Do you get mad at me for being impatient?" She set down her embroidery to study my face.

"Sometimes. I can't do much to hurry up the process."

"You can do more. How about Internet dating? There have to be some single young men within a couple of hours who can appreciate a catch like you."

"I'll sign up for Internet dating when you do, Mom."

Her eyes clouded, and I wanted to snatch the flippant words back. She picked up her embroidery again. "Are you saying you think I should date? I'm not ready for that. I'm never going to be ready for that." Her voice had the distant, hollow tone I hated. It had disappeared during Max's visit on Sunday, but now that it was back, chances were it would linger for weeks.

"I was making a joke. I didn't mean that you should date." Hattie and Jim Guidry had been a seamless whole, and even after two years, the idea of them not being together was nothing short of walking to the Mississippi River levee and staring down at a dry river bed. It was unimaginable, yet it kept being true each day I woke up. I couldn't even imagine what it must feel like to her.

She didn't look up from her hoop, where a magnolia blossomed from the floss. It wasn't fair to call it needlework. It was more like painting with thread. Her flowers looked like oils on canvas. Her work even graced pillow covers in the sitting room of the governor's mansion. She hadn't had time to embroider while running her flower shop before Daddy died, but now that she wouldn't go back to the store, embroidering filled a lot of hours that used to be full of Dad.

"I'm truly sorry," I said.

"I know, honey. I'm not angry. But I think I'm going to work on this piece for a while, and it's probably best if I turn on some thinking music."

I got up and set her iPod to an Andrea Bocelli album before heading up to my room to change into my pajamas. I stuck my hair up in a bun and grabbed a stack of history tests to grade until they put me to sleep. Sometimes my students' essay answers could knock me out better than Tylenol PM. I needed one or the other tonight because the last thing I wanted to do was fight to go to sleep while feeling like a failure because someone else had gotten engaged besides me.

I glanced down at the first question and sighed as I marked it wrong. Well, at least I wasn't about to fail as badly as the captain of the basketball team.

Chapter 4

"Tests are graded," I said, handing them out. "Just a note that while 1865 did technically mark the end of 1864, the correct answer was that 1865 marked the end of the Civil War."

Chauncy Tremonton groaned, and the class burst out laughing.

"Also, Jefferson Davis was the leader of the Confederate States of America, not the leader of the pack, Jamarcus Lloyd."

"Leader of the pack? Dude, why you listening to oldies?" Chauncy asked.

"My gramps likes that stuff. Besides, how you know that's an oldie unless you listening too?" Jamarcus said.

I did a settle-down gesture to stop the catcalls and paused at Sadie Litch's desk. "Highest score. Good job." I kept my voice low. The bright kids didn't always like to advertise their achievements.

"Nerd!"

"Not okay, Jamarcus. Apologize," I said.

"For paying her a compliment? No, ma'am. Hey, Sadie. You ever tutor dumb jocks for fun?"

Sadie grinned. "No, but I don't mind helping a smart one. I'm in the library after school on Tuesdays and Thursdays."

"See you there tomorrow."

We eased into the rest of class, which involved me carrying a suitcase around the room to try to snatch things out of open backpacks and off desks to claim for myself. It was an introduction to carpetbaggers and Reconstruction.

The lesson landed, and I knew it would only get better with each period I taught it during the day, but I couldn't fully celebrate having a lesson go right. Instead, when the bell rang, I called, "You need a rough draft of your

Civil War essays ready for peer review tomorrow!" as they filed out. "Kiana? A moment, please."

She rolled her eyes but sat down and waited.

The whole time I'd been clowning like a carpetbagger, an extra-large sliver of my attention had been drawn to her, my favorite and, not by coincidence, my hardest student in the class.

Kiana and I had navigated a rough first quarter with each other. She would come in sullen on a *good* day. I refused to send her to the discipline office, instead making her come talk to me at lunch, asking questions to understand why she'd been upset. A lot of the time she'd come straight to me in first period after a fight with her mom. Soon I could recognize the expression on her face that told me she hadn't gotten breakfast that morning, and I'd walk past during our opening-bell work and leave a protein bar on her desk. She never said thank you, but she always dropped an empty wrapper in the trash on the way out.

By the end of fall semester, she was drifting into my classroom at lunch time just because. Sometimes she would talk to me. They weren't fluid conversations. She'd sit quietly, fiddling with her jacket zipper or her phone, and then blurt, "Look at this," and show me some YouTube video or meme. Her favorites were obscure pop-culture references or esoteric word play, which meant that the work she was turning in to me, when she bothered to turn it in, was far below the level she was capable of.

"Why you always making me do extra, Miss Guidry?" she complained one day when I returned a test to her ungraded and ordered her in at lunch to complete the essay questions for real. "I did answer these."

"A single sentence is not a long-form answer. You think deeper than you're letting on. Put it down here, and you can spend your lunch period however you want," I said, tapping her paper. She'd grunted, grabbed her pen, and given a thoughtful, well-reasoned analysis of the Missouri Compromise and how she still saw echoes of its effects in her urban neighborhood. It had blown me away.

She still tested me sometimes, probably to see if I was paying attention to her work. Today I'd had to hand back a red D-. That was a warning sign. But worse, she hadn't cracked a smile at Jamarcus's clowning, and when I'd tried to catch her eye, she'd looked away.

"What's going on, Kiana?"

"Nothing."

"You loaded that word up with a whole lot of something. Talk to me."

"Got nothing to talk about."

Students from second period shuffled in. "Come see me at lunch."

She got up and left without a word.

She didn't come in at lunch either. By the end of the day, I was stressed, trying to figure out what the problem could be. I'd pulled her student file the month before, and I could guess some things based on the antiseptic facts it had listed. Her primary guardian was her grandmother, so even though her mom was around, she didn't have custody. That pointed to drug use, probably. A criminal record, possibly. Kiana wasn't the only kid at the high school with that situation by a long shot.

I pulled up her student contact info and tried the home number listed, hoping I could get her grandmother on the phone. It rang several times without going to voice mail. I hung up and tried to figure out what to do next. Would it make whatever was going on worse if I dropped by her house to check on her? Probably, since that would get me fired. I packed up, not able to focus enough to sit and do any grading or prep work.

Mom's car wasn't in our driveway, and I paused to enjoy the quiet when I walked through the door. Every now and then when I had the house to myself, I pretended it was mine and that I got to live alone without any opera on the iPod.

I waited for the wave of guilt that always followed that dream, and it showed up right on time. Living in my childhood home had never been in my plans after my mission. I'd stayed here for a few months while I'd saved up for my own place. I'd been getting ready to move out when Daddy died, and there was no way I was going to leave Mom at that point.

She didn't need me financially. There was no mortgage, and Daddy had always been so smart about saving that she'd be able to live in the house for a hundred years before she'd have to worry about money.

It used to be if I came home to an empty house, it was because she was at the floral shop. Mom had loved that shop right up until the point she'd blamed it for taking her away from Daddy more than she'd meant to be gone and stealing hours she could have spent with him had she known she would lose him early.

It wasn't a rational argument, but I'd had two years of my own irrational grief, so I didn't push her about going back to work. The shop did okay without her, and she had that income too, but I hated thinking about her with too much free time and four thousand square feet of house to somehow fill up with all the things she had lost.

If I had a place of my own, I might not even be able to walk in and appreciate the peace and quiet. Maybe the silence would sound loud and the space feel empty.

I changed clothes and went for a run around the Shenandoah lakes, thoughts of Kiana dogging every step. I called her house again when I got back. Still no answer.

I tried to look at my lesson plans, but after a half hour, I gave up and closed my laptop to pick up my phone and call Kate.

"BFF!" she said, and it felt good to have someone happy to hear from me.

"How's my honorary nephew?"

"Still growing. Doctor says he's right on track."

"Due date still in October?"

"Yep. And he's being nicer to me now. No more morning sickness. I think I might change his name after all."

"That's too bad. Ignatius was kind of growing on me."

"He may earn Ignatius back. We'll see how the rest of the pregnancy goes. How are *you* doing?"

"Rough day."

"Tell me, girl."

Kiana wasn't a new topic for me, and I caught Kate up on my concerns. "Do you think I should try calling again? Do I go over there? I don't know. It's killing me to sit around wondering why she's so shut down right now."

"Of course your worry for these kids is going to last after the bell, and caring so much is part of why you're becoming an awesome teacher, but it might be a bad idea to get too tangled up in their lives outside of school. Then there's no separation for them anymore. Maybe Kiana needs school to be a separate thing from whatever's going on at home, or she never has a place that's not connected to that drama."

I groaned. "You're right. I'll wait and see how it goes with her tomorrow."

"She'll be all right. Try not to worry about it too much. Do you want something else to worry about?"

"Maybe?"

She laughed. "I know I'm months away, but I wanted to ask you something, and you can totally say no, but I will kill you if you do."

"You want me to throw your baby shower? I was already planning on it."

"Oh, thank you, thank you, thank you. You know how Jaimie has been about her wedding, and Mama's so caught up in all that, and I don't want this little man's shower to be an afterthought with leftover decorations from the wedding just because Jaimie's using blue. I know you'll do right by him."

"Of course I will, honey. Don't worry about it. I've got plans already." I didn't, but I would.

"I'm so glad I can ask you that without you judging me for not waiting until you offered."

"That's what best friends are for."

We chatted for a few more minutes while she told me about David's interviews at a couple of local law firms for an internship that summer and how stressed she was about how they were going to handle a baby in the last year of law school and maybe they should have waited. I did some more best-friending, reminding her that a year of law school had nothing on a forever baby.

When we hung up, I wandered into the kitchen for a snack and decided it was probably best I was living at home because I couldn't afford my own rent *and* all the showers I was about to either throw or attend.

I bit into an apple, and the crunch cracked like a gunshot. Too quiet. Always so quiet without Mom.

I didn't have to be home alone. If I'd said yes to Max, I could probably be getting ready for a date with him. And why hadn't I said yes? He was reformed, plus hot, funny, ambitious, and a churchgoer. He was everything I wanted on paper—except for the address line. That would read something besides "Baton Rouge" soon.

I took another bite and went out to the deck. My first instinct when I'd seen him sitting here on Sunday had been the right one. I couldn't leave Mom, and even if Daddy were still alive, Baton Rouge was as much a part of my DNA as he and Mom were. I would never be able to live with the ache of missing it, so there was no point in dating someone who wouldn't stay.

Chapter 5

I ALWAYS LIKED GOING TO my Teachings of the Living Prophets institute class on Thursday nights, but I was especially happy to be walking in after another long day of Kiana worry and a single-serving microwave dinner. They should label that freezer aisle "Sadness."

Kiana hadn't been at school for two days, and the attendance office could only tell me her grandmother had called in to excuse her absences. Mom had gone to Aunt Casey's house all day to help her with some quilting, and I hadn't had the energy to whip up something for myself.

"Good evening, Lila."

I smiled at Bishop Gracely, Kate's dad. Our ward met at the institute building because it felt much cozier than using the church when we didn't need half of it. All we had to do after sacrament meeting and Sunday School was pull the accordion wall down the middle of the main room and we had a perfectly sized Relief Society and elders quorum space. But a big part of the reason the institute always felt so good to me was Bishop Gracely.

"Hi, Bishop. How are you doing tonight?"

"Feeling fantastic, kiddo. Can you stop by my office after class?"

"Sure. See you then." We probably had a sister who needed extra fellowshipping.

Max was already seated, and he smiled when I walked in. I waved, but even though he had the back row to himself, he didn't suggest that I sit by him, so I took my usual seat in the middle row to the side. Brother Linden taught a great lesson, and I wished I wasn't paying enough attention to Max to notice, but I saw him slip out twenty minutes before the end of class. I couldn't follow the rest of the discussion after that. All I could think about was if Max was avoiding me.

When class ended, I walked down the hall to the bishop's office. The door opened as I was fixing to knock, and Max stepped out. I moved out of his way, and he gave me a nod and a look I couldn't interpret. "Talk to you soon, Lila," he said and left.

All righty, then.

"Come on in, Lila. How was class tonight?"

"Awesome, as usual."

"Brother Linden is a good man," he said. "Thanks for staying late to see me."

"Sure. What's going on?" I ran through the list of possibilities of who might be in a tight spot and what they might need. No one jumped to mind, and a ball of worry coalesced in my stomach again, a twin to the one I was carrying for Kiana. A sister with a sudden need often meant an urgent situation, like a health problem or an eviction. Plus, we'd already had one girl end up pregnant a few months before her wedding to her nonmember boyfriend since I'd been in as president.

"You're planning to attend the YSA conference in June?"

"Of course."

"I'm extending a call to you to be the chairperson for the planning committee."

I stared at him, confused. Usually they had someone at the stake level plan the conference. Like actual grown-ups. With grandkids our age. "Why aren't the Duttons doing it?" I asked, referring to the older couple from the Denham Springs Stake who'd been in charge for the last couple years.

"They're serving a mission. They leave in July. They'll be busy preparing for that. You hadn't heard?"

I shook my head.

He sat back and rubbed his eyes. "I'll be honest. The conference fell right off my radar. I need you to save my bacon on this and pull something great together."

"Why can't they assign another couple?" I asked, already feeling over-whelmed by the size of the job.

"The stake sees this as another opportunity for our young people to develop leadership. The whole point of being here is to get y'all married off and ready to serve in a family ward, so I can support that. I know you're fully capable of making this happen."

I shook my head. Managing our tiny Relief Society of twenty-three sisters was one thing. The conferences were a regional event, pulling in YSAs from Mississippi up to Arkansas, and we'd get upwards of two hundred people coming. "I appreciate that, and I'll do it. But I'm already panicking."

"Your setting apart will help, but in case the companionship of the Holy Spirit isn't enough, I'm giving you Max Archer too. He agreed to cochair."

"Why are you smirking at me?" I squinted at him. "Are you match-making?"

"Yes," he said, unfazed. "But I also see this as too big for one person, and you two are perfect for the job. We'll set you apart after church on Sunday. Sound good?"

I swallowed and nodded. "Yes, sir."

He stood and walked around the desk to give me a one-armed hug before escorting me to the door. "Thanks for accepting the call to serve."

I walked out of the office, and he beckoned Jorie's fiancé inside. Outside I found Max leaning against my Civic, grinning at me.

"Hi, you."

I shook my head at him. "We say hey, not hi."

His smile didn't waver. "Hey, you."

"Hey, yourself. So we're in it now, huh?"

"Looks that way. You have time to get some ice cream and talk this new gig over?"

I wanted to. Man, he was cute. I made myself say no. He looked taken aback, and I hurried to soften the answer. "We definitely need to start figuring this out. Three months isn't going to be long enough to pull this together, but I guess we'll make it happen. Just not tonight. I had a distracted kind of day today, and I need to get ready for work tomorrow."

"What distracted you? Wait, you don't have to tell me. I'm not trying to be nosy. I meant to ask if you're okay."

"I'm fine." I should probably have taken my keys out of my purse and let the jingling remind him to get off my car so I could go home, but I left them where they were. "I'm worried about a student, and I shouldn't get so wrapped up in it. But I am. The older teachers say I'll get over that eventually."

"I respect that kind of worry. I bet your students love you." He straightened and stepped away from the car. "I'll let you get home. Want to talk about the conference tomorrow night?"

Get together on a Friday night? I wondered if the bishop had confessed his matchmaking to Max too. I eyed him like he was trying to cheat on a history test, but his expression didn't change, so I shook my head and didn't accuse him of trying to disguise a date as a planning meeting. I wasn't going to take the bait either way. "Sunday after church is best for me."

"Sounds good. See you Sunday. Good night," he said, already turning to walk a few parking spaces down. The lights of a Prius flashed as he unlocked it with his key fob.

I grinned as I climbed into my own car. At least he didn't drive a truck. A good-looking guy in a truck was a lethal combination. A good-looking guy in a hybrid? Slightly more resistible.

But only slightly.

Chapter 6

ON FRIDAY MORNING, EXTRA ENERGY buzzed beneath my skin as I waited for the first-period bell. Would Kiana be here today?

She walked in a half minute after the tardy bell, and I picked up a tardy slip and quirked an eyebrow at her before filling it out.

"Dang, you starting off rough," Jamarcus said.

"Hush, Jamarcus." I finished filling out the slip. *I'm not really writing you a tardy. I just can't let the class think I'm getting soft. You okay?* I set the slip on her desk, and she glanced down at it, her eyes widening before she gave me a short nod. *Lunch,* I mouthed at her. After a long pause, she nodded again but didn't look up for the rest of the period.

The morning classes flew by, partly because the lesson plan worked well but mostly because I'd had a prompting in second period for how to help Kiana even if she didn't confide in me. She might. She did sometimes, but there was no guarantee she would.

She came in about five minutes after most of fourth period had bolted for the cafeteria. It was raining, which meant lunch was inside and everyone would have to scramble if they wanted a good seat. She darted a glance at the stragglers in the classroom and took the desk closest to my mine. I suspected it had more to do with wanting to be away from the other kids than being near me, but I'd take it.

"Hey, sweetie," I said, walking around to take the desk beside her and setting a granola bar down in front of her. "How are you?"

"I'm fine."

"Really? How come you didn't grab lunch in the cafeteria before you got here?" Most of the kids qualified for free lunch.

She shrugged and picked up the granola bar, unwrapping it with the meticulousness of an archaeologist on a dig site. "Too much noise."

"What's going on? I tried to call your house a bunch of times, but no one answered."

Another shrug.

"Kiana," I said, keeping my voice gentle. "I was ready to drive over to your place to check on you."

Her head shot up. "Don't do that."

"Tell me I don't need to."

"You don't need to."

"Tell me why."

She worked at the granola wrapper a little longer, but once it was off the bar, she couldn't stall anymore.

"Kiana."

She rolled her eyes. "My mama showed up after being gone for two weeks. She wasn't in great shape. She wanted to try telling me how to get my little brothers ready for school and say something about what I was wearing. I've got it locked down. She just makes stuff harder. I told her that. It got ugly."

My heart broke for her as I heard the story she wasn't telling me behind the story that she was. She wouldn't appreciate my sympathy, so all I said was, "I'm sorry that was a rough day, but if I tell you to come in for lunch, you need to come in. Do you understand?"

She nodded, no resentment in her face. I didn't have a ton of experience with these kids and their tough home situations yet, but I'd done a lot of reading on how to help at-risk students, and so much of the educational literature emphasized firm consistency. I hoped the experts were right.

"Good. I have something I want to show you." I grabbed my tablet, pulling up the webpage I'd bookmarked for her. "Have you heard of Madame CJ Walker?"

"Nope."

"She was the first female millionaire in the United States, and she was from right here in Louisiana." Kiana's eyes showed only mild curiosity, so I dropped the boom. "And she was African American."

Kiana's eyebrows rose. "The first lady millionaire was black?"

I nodded and handed her the tablet. "Read through this website for a while. I'm going to check in with you at the end of lunch. I have an idea for you."

She took the tablet, and I sat at my desk, trying not to show my excitement at her interest. Kiana had average grades. No F's but no A's, not even in PE. Her standardized test scores, on the other hand . . . they were high. Really high. She didn't have the overall GPA she needed to get into LSU yet, but with the right extracurriculars and teacher recommendations, plus a strong personal essay, she could do it, and I could help her find the grants to pay for it. But the kicker would be the history project I was fixing to pitch her.

A few minutes before lunch ended, I sat beside her, trying not to look giddy that she'd stayed on the Madame CJ Walker page instead of Internet surfing. "Interesting, right?"

She handed me the tablet. "Why you showing me this?"

"Have you ever heard of Kiwanis Club?"

"Those them dudes with the goofy hats?"

"It's a group of businesspeople with philanthropic goals, but they don't wear fezzes."

"Wear what?"

"The funny hats. Those guys are the Shriners. Anyway, the point is that the Kiwanis are sponsoring a local competition for high school students. It's kind of like a history fair, but they want students to focus on an element of Louisiana history, a person, place, or event. I think you should enter it, and I think Madame CJ Walker might be the perfect subject for you."

The prompting I'd gotten had been clear: Kiana needed to make the acquaintance of Madame CJ. She needed to see a woman who'd been born into rough circumstances who had overcome them without any advantages except her own cleverness and determination.

"I don't like that kind of stuff," she said, but it wasn't convincing.

"Hear me out. If you win the local competition, first prize is $500. Think about that for a minute. What could you do with that? You don't need to tell me. But think about it."

She chewed on her bottom lip. "What am I supposed to do? Make one of them goofy backboards with a bunch of paragraphs printed out about Madame CJ?"

I leaned forward, not bothering to hide my excitement. "No! It's more of a showcase, so you have a lot of latitude for how you present what you've learned. I mean, you could write a tuba solo that tells the story of the Battle of New Orleans if you want." She snorted, and I grinned at her. "The point is that they don't want a backboard with immaculate hand lettering. They want performance pieces or original fiction. Multimedia experiences or dramatizations. On Monday I'm assigning this as a semester assessment to all my classes, but I want *you* specifically to think about it in terms of the Kiwanis competition, not your class grade."

She squinted at me.

"$500, Kiana."

She shrugged again.

"And total freedom to present whatever you choose however you choose."

The squint narrowed, and I hid another smile. I'd gotten through. I could feel it.

She left without a word, but I didn't mind. I could read her too well to be fooled. Her wheels were turning, and this would be on her mind all weekend. By Monday, she'd be hooked.

When my last class filed out for the day, I leaned back in my desk and propped my feet up, tired peace settling around me. Mom and Bishop Gracely might look at my life and see the big marriage-shaped hole in it, but I had a job I loved, teenagers who often broke—but always filled—my heart, a home I loved, and a feeling that my Heavenly Father knew and heard me.

Not a bad haul.

The fact that the first marriageable guy to come along in more than a year was Max—who wasn't a prospect at all—was no doubt God teaching me something, and I'd just have to hurry up and wait until I learned the lesson. In the meantime, I would practice appreciating everything I did have and not resent what I didn't.

Chapter 7

I COULDN'T REMEMBER IT BEING so hard to sit in the middle row during sacrament meeting before. I couldn't pay attention to Cecily Moore in the best of circumstances because her nerves made her giggle. And today was not a "best circumstance" since I needed eighty percent of my brain capacity and all my willpower to keep from turning to stare at Max on the last row. The back of my neck had itched from the second he'd taken his seat after blessing the sacrament. The one time I'd turned to look at him, he'd been watching me with a thoughtful expression. He'd smiled when he'd caught my eye, and I'd smiled back but turned around quickly before I'd blushed.

I mumbled my way through the closing hymn and counted it as another blessing that it wasn't my month to conduct Relief Society. I was off my game, although I had a better grip on myself once we pulled out the accordion wall and shut Max on the other side.

When class ended, the click of the wall opening again made my stomach flip. So stupid. There was no reason to be nervous about a planning meeting with Max. *Get it together, Lila. Get. It. Together.*

Max didn't rush over, and Hailey caught me for a few minutes, full of more wedding details and several messages to pass along to Mom about flowers. By the time she let go of me to join the rest of the wedding belles for some gabbing and note comparing, my stomach had twisted into a stupid knot. The stupidest knot. *Why, stomach? Why? What do you have to be nervous about? Nothing, stupid stomach. Nothing.*

Max was listening to a conversation about March Madness brackets, but even though it didn't seem like he was contributing to it, he still didn't excuse himself to come talk to me. I hitched my church bag over my shoulder and walked over. "Hey, Max," I said, during a lull.

"Hey, you."

"Still have time for some conference planning?"

Surprise crossed his face, then a smile. "Your mom didn't tell you."

"Tell me what?"

"I'm coming to your house for dinner again tonight. I figured we could talk it over there."

I didn't know what to say next. But since I wasn't about to bad-mouth Mom, I smiled back. "Sounds good. See you for dinner."

I drove straight home and headed for the kitchen. She stood behind the counter, a pile of chopped vegetables beside her, and I dropped my bag and glared.

"I guess you heard we've got company coming." She didn't even have the grace to sound guilty.

"Stop, Mom. I don't want to date him."

"I think you do want to date him. I know your type, Lila. He's it."

"My type is a guy who wants to buy a house in this neighborhood and see the same faces at church every Sunday for the rest of our lives. Max is not that guy."

"You don't know what he wants."

"Yes, I do, because he told me after you tried to throw him at me last week. He's leaving town as soon as he gets another assignment."

"Then he doesn't know what he wants."

"He's very clear about it."

Instead of getting flustered, Mom sliced another onion, calm as could be. She wasn't listening. "I mean it, Mom. I'm done investing time and energy in relationships with guys who don't want to stick around."

"You act like they're loving and leaving you, but every last one of them has wanted to take you with them. I love you like my own daughter, but you are half the problem in those relationships."

"Ha ha. And I know that. Which is why I'm not going to contribute to the problem anymore. I'm not breaking hearts, and I'm not getting my heart broken. It's a solid plan, so no more Max for Sunday dinner after tonight."

She finally set the knife down. "You want to live with me forever, sugar?"

"Yes," I said.

She smiled. "No, you don't. Don't put your life on hold because you're worrying about me."

I slid into one of the kitchen chairs. "Would you really want me to date one of these guys if it meant I'd end up in Montana? Or Arizona? Or New York?" I said, thinking about my conversation with Max on the pier.

She didn't say anything, but her knife flew over the onion, the rhythm speaking louder than words. No, she didn't want to see me go.

"I'll get changed and come down and help." I stopped and sniffed the air. "Gumbo, Mom?"

Her cheeks flushed. "I haven't made one for a long time."

I let it go and climbed up to my room, dithering over what to wear like an idiot. But I had my pride. I may not want to go out with him, but that wasn't a reason not to look good. I settled on a pair of leggings with a geometric print and a long cream sweater, a thin one warm enough for a spring night in case Mom tried to make dinner more romantic by moving it outside again. I wouldn't put it past her to make us eat by candlelight.

She'd been a relentless optimist until Daddy had died. I would have been happy to see her optimism come back if it didn't center on a future for Max and me.

I checked myself in the mirror. I looked good, and I immediately pulled the outfit off and grabbed my most broken-in jeans and LSU T-shirt. I wouldn't let her fall into the trap of false hopes. I couldn't make it any plainer that I wasn't interested in impressing Max than to walk downstairs in my grubbies. I pulled my hair into a sloppy topknot and padded barefoot back down to the kitchen to help her cook.

She frowned at me. "I told him to come over at five. You're going to have to change again in twenty minutes."

"I'm not changing."

"You're a hot mess."

"I'm comfortable."

"What's he going to think when he sees you looking like this?"

I stared at her, waiting for it to click.

She went after the vegetables when she figured it out.

"The gumbo is already cooking," I said, realizing what was wrong with this picture. "What are you chopping now?"

"Bridger told me today that Coleman isn't eating well. I told Bridger I'd bring dinner tomorrow, but I'm going to Casey's again, so I'm putting something together now."

"Oh, that's sad. How are they doing?" Coleman Lewis's wife, Debbie, had died right before Thanksgiving from cancer. She'd been pretty young, about Mom's age. Of their four kids, only Bridger, a high school senior, was still living at home. Their second daughter, Phoebe, was a year younger than me, and she was living over in Walker, so she helped out when she could, but she had a two-year-old and was pregnant with her second, so it was hard for her to keep an eye on her dad like she wanted to. She'd begged the ward to step in, and they had tried, but Coleman had been insistent that he was fine. Mom taught Bridger in Sunday School, so sometimes she wiggled the truth out of him and brought over a few meals for them to eat throughout the week.

"I don't know how they're doing, exactly. They both have that zombie walk. You know how it is."

I hugged her before I dug out a second cutting board. Now that I'd lived with grief, witnessed Mom slog her way through it, seen each of my brothers handle it—or not—in their own way, I knew the zombie walk. Some people reacted to grief by working through it, keeping themselves busy, insisting they were fine and that they liked the work, whether it was a job or a calling or both. That had been me. Some people disconnected from the world around them, shuffling through the motions so they seemed all right, but if you took a closer look, it was obvious their minds and spirits were off somewhere else. That was Mom. Before Max showed up last week, the only thing that had roused her were Brady's weekly missionary e-mails.

"What are we making?" I asked.

"Casseroles. I've got a tray of enchiladas in the freezer, and now I'm doing a King Ranch and a poppy seed chicken. This is the last of the veggies, but you can chop the chicken. It's in the oven."

I pulled it out and laid the breasts on the cutting board so I could cut them into bite-sized pieces. "Better let these cool. What else can I do?"

"Throw a cobbler together for dessert?"

I went straight to the pantry for the peaches she'd canned last summer. I loved cooking, and I understood why she made so many meals for ward members. She missed cooking for Daddy and the boys. I did too. She'd taught me to make huge spreads with love in every detail.

I gathered the few ingredients for the simple cobbler; when it was dripping with as much butter as this one took, you didn't need fancy, just cholesterol meds. I measured and mixed while I told her about my new calling with Max.

"Planning the conference? That's kind of short notice, isn't it?"

"Yeah, but I already have a ton of ideas. That's the easy part. Trying to find available venues will be the headache. I did some legwork on this yesterday, but it's going to be a pain."

We brainstormed ideas, the cobbler coming together as we talked, until the doorbell signaled that Max had arrived.

"Why don't you go ahead and get that?" Mom said. "I've got chicken hands." She grabbed a piece of chicken from the cutting board to make her words true.

I shook my head but rinsed my hands and answered the door.

"Hey," I said, trying not to stare. He'd changed into a black V-neck sweater and gray jeans. The black made his eyes more intense, and I blinked at him. He blinked back, and I cursed myself for dressing like I was about to clean out the garage. Then I cursed myself again for caring what he thought. But only Bible curses.

"Smells amazing," he said.

"Seafood gumbo. My mom is spoiling you."

"She will never have a more appreciative audience." He followed me to the kitchen. "Hey, Sister Guidry."

"Hey, Max. Good to see you. I'm finishing up a casserole for later this week, so I'm sorry I can't hug you, but come say hello anyway." She paused and tilted her head.

Confusion crossed Max's face.

"Give her sugar, Max. Between this and the gumbo, it means she's practically adopted you. Drop a kiss right there," I said, tapping my cheek.

His face lit up in delight, and he hurried to kiss her upturned cheek.

Mom went back to chopping and issuing orders. "Pop the cobbler in the oven, Lila Mae. Max, move every dish you see on the stove to the table, would you, darlin'?"

"Yes, ma'am."

"Yeah, adopted," I murmured to him as he passed me coming from the stove on the way to get the rice.

Five minutes later, we were all seated, and Mom had already gotten more out of Max about his job than I had in our entire walk the week before. She had a way of making everyone talk.

"What does an operations manager do, exactly?" she asked. "That sounds like one of those jobs like consultant that can mean just about anything."

He laughed. "Sometimes my job feels like it covers everything, but I guess that's why I like it. You know Taggart is an energy company, right?"

Mom nodded. "Right. Oil business."

"That's mostly what it's been, but about eight years ago, they expanded their clean-energy efforts. I'm pretty interested in that field, so I interviewed with them and got hired."

"But what do you do with them, exactly? Walk around with a clipboard taking notes and . . . what?" she pressed.

He hesitated. "You really want to know about this? It might sound boring to anyone else."

"I really do," she said. Listening was one of her super powers. I was glad since I was curious in spite of myself.

"Right now we're trying to figure out how to maximize solar energy in rainy climates like Louisiana," he said. "My job is to monitor the operations side of things, so it basically means I'm constantly trying to streamline the processes to get the most out of the work our people do. I have to watch everything from how they clock in and out to the materials we order for our solar cells to the way our researchers gather and compile data, constantly watching the whole process to make sure every step of it is as efficient as possible. Aren't you sorry you asked?"

"No, I am not," Mom said, patting the back of his hand. "What do you plan to do with all of this efficiency experience?"

"Operations is a really good place to start when you want to climb through the executive ranks," he said. "I want to be running a boardroom of a major corporation by forty."

Mom sighed. "You remind me of Jim. He was a go-getter too."

All through dinner, she kept him talking, and Max looked like he enjoyed the grilling. By the time he finished his third bowl of gumbo, Mom's questions had led him to entertain us with a string of mishaps from his mission and give us a comprehensive overview of his final project at Wharton.

When Mom stood to collect our empty bowls, Max's face fell. "I'm so sorry. I can't believe I spent all that time talking about myself. My mom would be so embarrassed."

I burst out laughing. "Don't worry about it. It's called the Hattie Effect. It freaks the elders out the first time she does it to one of them too."

"Oh, stop," Mom said, not sounding particularly upset. "There's nothing wrong with being a good listener."

"You're right, but you're a devious interrogator, and you should apologize," I said.

"Lila Mae, say you're sorry right now," Mom demanded, laughing.

"For telling the truth? No, ma'am. Now let me help you clear the table."

Max climbed to his feet too, and we all took the plates to the sink. Mom handed him a rag to wipe down the counters while she and I put the leftovers away, including three days' worth of gumbo for Max to take home.

"I guess y'all need to work out all your conference details," Mom said as she placed Max's leftovers inside a paper grocery sack. "I'm going to work on my magnolia, but holler if you need me." She gave each of our arms a squeeze before she headed into the living room.

"She's working on her magnolia in the living room? Like bonsai?" Max asked.

"No, like embroidery."

"Ah. So, hey, now that you know more than you could ever want to know about my job, will you tell me about yours? Is it hard?"

"So hard, but I love it. The bad thing about teachers is that we won't shut up about our jobs once we get started, so I better not even get going. Let me grab my conference binder, and we can jump in. Is the table okay?"

He glanced out the window. "Do binders have to be involved? Because if not, I think we should have this planning meeting on the pier."

I pointed to myself. "Teacher, remember? Of course there has to be a binder. But only because it works better for me to organize this visually instead of in computer folders."

"Makes sense," he said. "Any time I have to do something with our supply chain, I have a million software options, but nothing makes it click like working it out with pencil and paper."

"Exactly," I said. "Hang on." A minute later, I was back with the binder I'd fished from my church bag after ignoring Mom's hopeful "How's it going?" look as I'd passed the living room.

"Do you have any hard-and-fast ideas about this conference?" I asked as I took the seat across from him.

"Let's start with your ideas."

"I've been to a few of these now"—heck, I was probably the stake record holder for number of YSA conferences attended—"and the main draw is time to socialize. So I think we plan a marquee event for Saturday night, pick a theme that ties into it, build in plenty of chances to mingle, including a service project, sprinkle in some awesome speakers, and that's it. We've got a conference."

"What's an example of tying a theme to a marquee event?"

"I went out to Central yesterday to look at this elderly guy's property. Brother Samuelson. He's in the Pride ward with my aunt, and he's independent enough to live alone but hasn't been able to keep his place up too well. He's got about five acres, and the priesthood does regular service projects there, so the land's in okay shape, but they mainly do the regular upkeep, like mowing. Other things have gotten kind of run-down. Like he has this barn there, a good-sized one, and it's structurally sound, but it needs paint and a good interior cleaning and some purging."

I flipped to a preliminary conference outline I'd roughed out the previous night after touring Brother Samuelson's place. "My aunt Casey thinks his adult children would love to come over and supervise a Friday service project where we help him whip the barn back into shape. Then we could talk to the Denham Springs Stake Relief Society and have them decorate it on Saturday while we're in workshops for a barn dance that night. Service project and dance venue all in one, come up with some scriptural farm-sounding theme about harvesting, and boom, done. Shouldn't be hard."

Max skimmed the list. "Sounds like a good place to start."

"Why don't we divide up tasks? I can put you in touch with Brother Samuelson's oldest son to talk about muscle and equipment and which jobs everyone can do."

He gave me the "slow down" hands. "I meant it's a good place to start for ideas, but we should talk about other options too."

Great. He was going to take his cochair job seriously instead of taking orders? There's nothing like someone else trying to actually do their job to get in the way of you doing yours. "Options like what?" How long did I have to let him brainstorm before I navigated us back to the perfectly integrated barn plan?

"I think we should look at going with something less . . ." He trailed off. He must have realized there was no inoffensive way to finish his sentence.

"Less what?"

He shrugged. "Obvious."

It was an irritating assessment after I'd spent three hours scoping it out yesterday. "What do you want instead? Enchantment under the sea and tying it into fishers of men or something?"

"No, but fishing for men as a singles conference theme might be the funniest thing I've heard in a while."

"I didn't mean it like that," I said, smiling even though I was annoyed.

"I know. But as far as a barn theme, is that something you guys do a lot down here? Like country western dances or potlucks and stuff like that? I remember having a few dances and activities like that. Maybe a barn dance isn't going to feel like a marquee event."

"You think it's hokey."

"You're putting words in my mouth."

"No, I'm reading tone." My temper rose, but I took a deep breath and decided he was doing me a favor to remind me that he was an outsider who thought anything "down home" was corny. "We don't do a lot of barn dances. Most of us live in the city, and that's not a thing."

"Maybe the tone you're hearing is frustration that you went out and decided on a venue without including me in that decision. Can we back up and talk about our roles first?"

I frowned. "That's fair." It hadn't once crossed my mind to call and invite him to go see Brother Samuelson's place. "Okay, division of responsibilities."

"Let's back up further to leadership philosophy. I'm not one of those guys who thinks it's my job to show up the night before to set up chairs and tables and call it good. I want to help for real. Can you live with making major decisions together and handling details our own way?"

I turned his words over, trying to read his intent. It was so much easier when I could run with a plan without any interference. I couldn't tell if Max was really thinking in terms of partnership or if he wanted to hold all the reins. "Fine. Let's discuss all major decisions. Theme?"

"I like your idea of letting the venue dictate it. Focusing on a marquee event is smart. How would you feel about checking out more venues to see what ideas we get?"

He definitely wanted the reins. "Is the right venue the one that feels right to *you*?"

"Nope. We'd have to agree. I think we have such different tastes that if we find something we're both excited about, it's a good chance the other people are going to be stoked too."

"You're using voodoo business school psychology on me."

He gave me an "if you say so" look.

"It worked. That's a good plan."

"And another thing. We should check out venues together."

It was a bad idea to spend that kind of time with him but a good way to approach venue selection. "Fine. What else should we file under 'major'?"

We added a few more things to the list. "I think venue stays at the top," I said, reading it over.

He saluted. "Agreed."

We moved on to brainstorming more classes than we could ever fit, narrowed them down, and still couldn't whittle the list as far as we needed to. "You have too many good ideas," I complained.

"I'm not just a pretty face."

No. You're awesome shoulders and a nicely sculpted chest and sexy arms and great legs. But I kept my mouth shut and rolled my eyes at him.

"Hey, y'all," Mom said, walking in to get herself a glass of water. "How's it going in here?"

"We're getting a lot of planning done."

"Sounds like y'all make a great team. I'm going to check the cobbler and get out of your hair again."

I could have sworn Max's ears perked up. "Cobbler?"

"Lila made it. She's a good cook."

I wondered if she would offer to let Max take me out and kick my tires next. She pulled it out of the oven, set it to cool a bit, and wandered out again, satisfied that her work was done.

Max and I went back to figuring out speakers, dividing up a list of bishops to ask for suggestions. By the time Mom came back in again to dish up the cobbler, we'd started in on the venues. Max had Googled a few things, and I'd added my native knowledge. We talked through the list while Mom scooped ice cream.

I don't think Max even realized she'd come in until she set a bowl down in front of him. He jumped and blinked at it, then at her, a huge grin spreading over his face. "You've made this for me before. I remember once when we came over for dinner. We had cobbler for dessert, and you gave me an extra scoop of ice cream, and then I got a crush on a married lady, and I wasn't even sorry."

"It's as easy as ice cream, huh?" she said.

"Of course not. Even two scoops of ice cream wouldn't have done it without the cobbler."

She laughed and patted his back before setting mine in front of me. "You'll have to thank Lila for making this one." She winked and left us alone again, and I took a bite.

"I know it's wrong to say this since I made it, but this is perfection."

He nodded but didn't stop eating to answer. When his bowl was empty, he leaned back and watched me, which made me hyperaware of the way I chewed. Did I do it right? Were my lips supposed to be all the way closed when I chewed or did I look stupid like that? How did other people do this? Why couldn't I remember the right way to chew?

"Do you remember that? When we came over for dinner?" he asked.

"Yes."

He cleared his throat. "That was a fun night."

It had been, but given everything that had followed, it was hard to look at it as its own event and not part of a chain that led to my total humiliation.

"We played Sardines, right?"

"Yeah." It had been one of our favorite night games, a reverse hide and go seek where one person hid and, one by one, the searchers found and joined the hider. On that night, Max had found me first. Those were still ten of the most intense minutes of my life.

I finished the last bites of my cobbler and reached for his bowl. He held it down on the table. "Uh, sorry," he said when I withdrew my hand. "But on a scale of one to ten, how bad are my manners if I ask for more?"

I smiled. "I don't know, but mine are worse since I should have offered. Let me go dish you up some."

He was determined to wander down memory lane while he ate. "One of the weirdest things about being back here is that I remember being so upset about moving here and being so happy to leave, but I keep remembering awesome stuff, too, that somehow I didn't notice then."

"Why did you request the Baton Rouge office?"

He shrugged. "It's bothered me for a long time that I had such a hard time adjusting when I was a kid. I see it as a massive character flaw."

"Me too," I said.

"Watch it." He pointed his spoon at me. "Anyway, I had several options for field offices, but I wanted to come here to give it another shot."

I hated that my heart rate accelerated. He wanted to like Baton Rouge. *That's not a sign*, I lectured whichever part of my brain controlled hope. "And it's better than before?"

"Louisiana didn't need to improve. My attitude did."

"Why'd you hate it so much? You knew it would only be three years."

"That's an eternity when you're thirteen. And Baton Rouge feels like other big cities, but then it's like it's surrounded by a foreign country. And I don't mean that as an insult. The food and the music and even the religion is different from other parts of the South, much less the rest of the US. It's hard to explain if you haven't traveled a lot."

"You think I love Baton Rouge because I haven't been other places to know any better?"

"It sounds bad like that. I only mean sometimes it's hard to truly appreciate and understand your hometown until you have to live away from it, and then you get another perspective on it."

I wondered if I should explain to him exactly how much experience I'd had traveling outside of my home state. I decided to let it go on the grounds that I wasn't supposed to be trying to impress him. "So now you think Baton Rouge isn't so bad, but you don't exactly love it."

"Are you going to kick me out if I say yes?"

"No, I'm taking it as a challenge. By the time we're done with this conference, you'll be able to write a book about why Louisiana is awesome." I picked up the list of venues. "Let's put together a tour list now."

He groaned and closed his eyes. "Have mercy," he said, cracking one eye open to look at me. "That's a thing you say down here, right?"

"Sure, Elvis."

"If we're going to do any more conference stuff tonight, I'm going to need to get up and move around first. I demand a walk to the lake."

Despite a sneaking suspicion that he was trying to poke at my personal boundaries, I could use a walk too. "Let me grab a jacket." I snagged a hoodie from the laundry room. Max already had his shoes off and his pant legs rolled up when I came back. A minute later, we were trekking to the water.

"Do you remember the lightning bugs?" he asked.

I stumbled over a paver, and he steadied me by grabbing my elbow. The night we'd played Sardines, someone had left an overturned rowboat on the bank to repair. It was a gift from the hide-and-seek gods: a brand-new location outside of our usual spots. I'd ducked under it, knowing it wouldn't be too long before Brady or Logan thought to check it out, but when the first set of sneakers came walking up to the edge, it had been Max's beat-up Adidas. He'd ducked down and slid beneath it without a word when he saw me.

Silence was key in staying hidden, but I couldn't have spoken if I needed to. I'd just turned fourteen the week before, and at Mutual, they'd called in all the teachers and Mia Maids at the end of the night to wish me a happy birthday. The Mia Maids had baked me a cake, and when they'd finished singing, everyone was calling for me to make a wish. When I leaned forward to blow out the candles, my hair fell forward too, nearly trailing in the icing, and I'd jerked my head back, making it harder to blow out the candles. Five of them still flickered.

Max reached over and gathered my hair in a loose ponytail. "One more time," he said. "Lean closer." And even though I'd never had such a violent outbreak of goose bumps across my scalp and neck before, I managed to blow out the rest of the candles. He let go of my hair when I straightened, and each strand felt alive. I stood there registering almost nothing else around me, totally confused about why I had a sudden radar for Max's every movement.

On Sunday, he stuck his head into our classroom looking for something, and I felt the air around me stir when his eyes skimmed over me before he ducked back out again. I recognized the symptoms—he wasn't my first crush, but he was the first one to spring up so violently. The weight of how much I liked him sometimes made it hard for me to breathe, like there wasn't room for anything else inside me besides my feelings, not even air.

It was the most confusing thing that had ever happened to me, and it had baffled Kate when I'd confessed it to her the day before by her pool. "I thought we hated him," she'd said.

And I thought we had too. But some switch had flipped inside of me, and I'd felt the uncertainty of it in the dark beneath the rowboat. We sat next to each other, both of us facing the side of the boat instead of each other until I heard a soft, "Whoa." I looked at him, and between us, a lightning bug glowed.

We'd both watched it for a minute, and then another one joined it, then another. Before long, a dozen of them filled the space between us. It was the closest thing to magic I'd ever experienced, before or since. Aidan, Max's older brother, had shown up then, and the lightning bugs had drifted away.

"I haven't seen lightning bugs since we moved away. That's one thing I always missed about this place."

"Just the lightning bugs?"

He stopped at the water's edge and pretended to think. "And king cake. That's it."

"You should be sad that Mardi Gras is over. My mom always picks up the cream-cheese-stuffed king cake from Gambino's on Saturday so we have it for Sunday dessert. You missed out."

"Oh man. How hard do you think it would be for me to start Mardi Gras in Philly?"

"Maybe you should give in to the bayou magic and stay here so you can have it every year without trying to export our culture."

He laughed. "You don't pull punches."

"Not for you."

"I like that."

We walked in quiet the rest of the way to the pier and settled on the end, feet in the water.

He spoke first. "I swear I'm about to start talking conference again in a second, but can we soak this in for a minute?"

I leaned back on my hands as an answer, my feet doing a slow swish in the water. He hummed, and I leaned closer to make out the tune. He smiled, his eyes drifting closed as he sang some Otis Redding. "Sitting on the Dock of the Bay." I almost committed my first swoon listening to his soft tenor.

He was killing me. He had to be, because I was about to die.

The last notes faded, and it took me a minute to find my voice. "I had no idea you could sing. That was great."

"Thanks."

"What other hidden talents do you have?"

"Well, Sister Guidry, that sounds like a date-type question, and this here is a planning meeting."

I kicked water at him, but I was too lazy to be accurate.

"I'm not afraid of water. Sorry. You can't avoid a venue discussion."

"What do we think our top five are?"

"The riverboat and the Capitol Park Museum."

I nodded. "Maybe White Oak Plantation, but I'm not sure we can afford it. Leonard's Cajun Dance Hall could be great, and I still think you need to check out the Samuelson property barn before you veto it. I demand that it round out our top five." I splashed water in his direction again.

"If you demand it, then sure. But I can't see myself signing on to a country theme. We need something super dope."

I folded my arms like a gangster to mock him. "Super dope?"

"I was going to say we should think outside the box, but I hate business clichés, so I went for something different."

"I'd keep your business expressions. Stay inside the box. Like smack in the middle of the box. And make it a small box. So small you never think of saying 'super dope' again."

"Noted. Can we still do outside-the-box conference activities though? Like could we go to the potato chip factory and have a competition to invent the best new flavor?"

"The problem is whether they can accommodate two hundred people. And shut down regular production while we play around."

"Maybe we offer four or five of those kinds of activities and people pick one. One group can go to a catering hall and do a big old cooking class. Or go to a plant nursery and learn how to grow something. Or go to a lumber store and make something."

"I don't know." It was too far outside of people's expectations. "We need more familiar activities so everyone's anxiety doesn't shoot up."

"No, we need something crazy so that everyone can bond over being in unfamiliar territory."

"No one's going to register for the conference if they're going to spend half of a day looking like idiots."

"They'll love it. They'll expand their horizons."

Somehow it felt like the argument had quit being about conference activities. I took a minute to clear my head. "We don't have to solve that part tonight. Let's go look at a couple of the dance venues this week and see where that gets us."

"Wednesdays are great for me. Want to shoot for that?"

"Yeah. Want to start with the riverboat?"

"Sounds good. I'll call and set it up. When should I pick you up?"

My heart rate quickened at the date-like words. Stupid, stupid, stupid. "Don't worry about it. I'll drive over from school."

"Lila, I promise not to treat this like a date. I figure driving there and back together would give us more time for planning."

I climbed to my feet, tired from the whiplash movement of my emotions. *He's trying to make this into a date. Yay! Wait, no. Boo!* "It's not that. I'd be going out of my way to come home from work first. It makes more sense to go from school."

"Where do you teach, anyway? I went to University Academy when I lived here."

"I know. Anyone with two extra cents sends their kids to private school, but I'm one of those idealists that teaches in a public school. Lincoln High."

He was on his feet now, and it was too dark to see his expression clearly, but surprise tinted his words. "Oh. That was a pretty rough school."

"Still is."

I walked down the pier, sorry to see the night coming to an end but achingly aware that this was exactly why it should. We discussed some minor conference details on the way back to the house. When I closed the front door behind him, I darted for the stairs so Mom couldn't ask me any questions. The only answer I would be able to give her was that I had no idea what was going on. And I had no idea how I felt about that.

Chapter 8

ON MONDAY MORNING, KIANA CAME in ten minutes before the bell. "I read more about that competition on the Internet. Did you know if I win the parish competition, I go to state?"

"Yes."

"Do you know what I win at state?"

"Yes."

"A $5,000 scholarship."

"Pretty awesome, isn't it?"

She drummed her fingers against her thigh. "I don't know about college."

"It's the thing after high school."

Her shoulders tensed. Obviously she wasn't in the mood for joking. "I don't know if I can go."

"Your grades are borderline, but winning this competition will put you over the top with any Louisiana college you're interested in, except maybe Tulane."

"Miss Guidry, you the one teacher I count on to remember I'm not dumb. I looked into college. But my life is complicated. Going ain't as simple as up and saying that's what I'm going to do."

I took my time trying to step through an answer for her. "Did you read about Madame CJ this weekend?"

"Yeah. If I did a project, it would most definitely be about her."

That warmed my heart. "I brought her to your attention because I see you as the same."

"Because all black people look alike?"

I gave Kiana a level stare.

"Sorry, Miss Guidry. I know you're not like that."

"I see in you what I see in her: strength of character, cleverness, determination. Maybe you don't want to start a business to earn a million dollars, but there has to be something you want. What is it, Kiana?"

Her face stayed blank beyond a quirk of her lips that communicated a careless "Nothing" without any words.

I didn't buy that for a second. I tried a different tack. "Let's pretend you wake up tomorrow and someone is granting you a year of life to spend however you want without any obstacles. Money, time, other responsibilities—none of that's an issue. What would you do with it?" I could count on one hand the number of kids who would answer seriously, and Kiana was one of them.

Her response was instant. "I'd be a veterinarian. Or . . ."

"You can tell me."

She shrugged. "Maybe a writer."

"So there you go. Read more about Madame CJ. Look at previous winning projects in the competition archives. Think about how to present Madame CJ. And then think about how much you want the future you would have if there were no obstacles. Think about her obstacles and if they were harder than what you're facing. Think about whether you want your dreams as much as she wanted hers. Then come talk to me on Wednesday and tell me what you've got."

"Yes, ma'am." She turned to take her seat but paused. "Why you giving this to me but not the whole class?"

"Why would I waste their time when I know you're going to win? They can all do their regular projects for class. You're the one that's right for this competition."

She smiled and went to her seat.

Monday was a very good teaching day.

* * *

Wednesday afternoon I walked out to the faculty parking lot with a smile on my face but lost it as soon as I reached my car. I bit back my favorite Bible swear, but I did let it echo through my head a few times as I stared at my back left tire, which was so flat that my Civic looked drunk.

I did not have time for this. I had the jack, tire iron, spare, and knowledge it would take to replace it, but I most certainly did not have the time. I was already fifteen minutes late because I'd gotten caught up talking to Kiana again about her project. Ideas poured out of her mouth almost faster than my ears could keep up.

I loved hearing them. Kiana's mood swings could be so extreme that early in the year I'd wondered if she was possibly bipolar, but patience and careful questioning had made it clear that her low ebbs were directly connected to incidents with her mother. Fights, broken promises, extended absences. I was pretty sure she was dealing not only with normal teenage moods but with far more extreme circumstances than most kids too. Just to be sure, I'd pelted the school psychologist with an earful of questions, and she'd confirmed my instincts. Kiana didn't have bipolar disorder so much as a bad mom, which was an equally heavy weight to carry.

But while I wouldn't take back a minute of the extra time I'd spent watching her fizz with ideas and fascinating tidbits about her new hero, it had left me no margin for a flat tire.

I stared down at my black wide-leg linen trousers. They might survive, but I was pretty sure my pink silk sweater would be a goner. I'd felt the need to redeem my wardrobe choices in front of Max after Sunday, but I regretted it now as I considered the flat.

I pulled my phone out to text Max. He'd texted me earlier that morning. *Got your number from LDS Tools. Confirming for our boat thing that it is not at all a date so don't even try to back out.*

I'd laughed when I'd read it, but I could only sigh now as I tapped out an update. *Walked out to a flat tire. May be late. If I don't make it, go ahead without me.*

His reply was instant. *Where are you? I can YouTube how to a change a tire and be an expert by the time I get there.*

Ha. I know how to do it. Just takes time.

How about I pick you up now and help with the tire after the boat?

I hated to make him drive over, but it was probably the most efficient solution. *I'm at school. I'll be the one in the teacher parking lot looking ridiculously peeved.*

I'll be the guy in the Superman suit looking way too excited to have a mission.

You're a dork.

Yes.

He pulled up behind me not ten minutes later and rolled down his window. "You're kind of on my way home from work. I don't know why that makes me happy."

I didn't know why it made me happy to hear it, so I frowned at him. He left the car idling but stepped out to scoop up my school bag so full of essays it looked like it was vomiting loose-leaf. "Is this coming with us or staying with your car?"

"My car, I guess." He reached around me to open the back door and set my bag inside.

"We'll only be about five minutes late if we take off now. You good?"

"I'm good." He opened the passenger door for me before getting in on his side. "You know, here in our elementary schools, they teach us about how you Yankees are cold, soulless robots who don't believe in manners, but you handled that whole door thing nicely."

"We're soulless, but they did program us to open doors, so I can only take so much credit." He said it in a flat robot voice.

"Your programmer did good work."

"Thanks. Her name is Catherine Archer, and she spends a lot of her time wondering how she got all her childrens' coding so wrong, so I'll pass along your compliment."

We'd reached the exit to the parking lot, and he stopped to let a group of students on the sidewalk cross before he pulled out. A loud bang on the hood made us both jump, and I glared out at Jamarcus's grinning face, his hands flat on the car where he had slammed them. "That your boyfriend, Miss Guidry?"

I lowered the window and stuck my head out so I could give him my dirtiest look.

He lifted his hands and held them up in the air, backing away until he reached the sidewalk. His grin didn't fade one bit.

"You got him to do that with a look?" Max asked. It was like I'd performed a perfect gymnastics vault or something.

"That's nothing. I can shut down a whole mob of teenagers in a movie theater the same way."

"Good trick. I should always have you come to the movies with me to handle the mobs."

Nice try. "Or I can teach you how to do it."

"My way's better."

"For you."

He grinned. "So. Tell me about your day."

"It was great until one of my kids tried to embarrass the snot out of me. I guess he'll be sorry when I flunk him."

"Somehow, I'm betting this is not the first time he's given you a hard time. And I'm betting you don't mind him much."

"I don't," I confessed. "I have to walk a line with them as far as how much they're allowed to joke around with me, but mostly I like my little weirdos."

"Is it hard?"

"Hardest thing I've ever done." His questions about work kept us occupied all the way to the boat landing.

"I'd love to see you in action in the classroom sometime," he said when he came around and opened my door for me. "Except it would make me regret you weren't my teacher."

Was that a "hot for teacher" innuendo? It was funny how many guys thought that was original, but Max's expression was truly wistful.

At the *Creole Belle*'s gate, we gave our name to the ticket taker, who checked his list and made a call. "Mrs. Chapel will be down in a minute."

We sat on a bench to wait. "Names that are also things are goofy," I said.

"Like chapel?"

"Or Baker. Or Archer." I kept a straight face.

"Hey!"

"Oops, sorry."

He narrowed his eyes. "You *should* feel bad. When I was a kid, I used to imagine what it would be like if you could only do the job that matched your last name. So since Guidry isn't a charm that means anything, in my alternative universe, you wouldn't even have a job. Now you're sorry for real."

"I take it back. Please don't exclude me from your imaginary reality."

He shrugged. "Too late. You're cut off."

"That's sad. Do you have a different imaginary world I could join?"

He gave me a long, thoughtful look, like he was assessing my worthiness for admission. "There's the one where everyone is only allowed to do jobs that rhyme with their names. Like I could do something with taxes. Or faxes."

"Lila. I could do something with . . . aisles?"

"*Lila* doesn't rhyme with *aisle*."

"It rhymes with *aisle a*. Like *aisle a soup*. So grocery manager?"

"Don't limit yourself. What about the Isle 'a' Man? You could be a tour guide."

"That's it! Where is that? Ireland? I'm moving to Ireland! Enjoy your faxes. I'm going where the action is."

"Are you saying that faxes and taxes are boring? That's slander. Probably."

"If you thought of all this stuff as a kid, why are all your scenarios about work? Like jobs people can have?"

"Never thought about that part. What kind of thing would you make up about names?"

"Something way cooler than rhyming jobs," I said. "Like that everyone has a karmic namesake so you have a direct connection to a famous dead person with your name. It appeals to my inner historian."

"Which dead person do I get?"

"You're Maximilius Severus reincarnated. Dude was a homicidal Roman general."

He stared at me. "You made that up."

"Yeah."

"I spend a lot of time thinking about shoving you off of docks and piers. Maybe I do have some Maximilius Severus in me."

"Hey, y'all." A middle-aged woman with a name tag reading Linda Chapel had walked up during our bickering and stood smiling at us. "I understand you're interested in checking out the *Creole Belle* for an event. A wedding, I assume?"

"No, ma'am," I said, not looking at Max, who gave a laugh-cough. "Our church is looking for a place to host a dance for about two hundred singles, ages eighteen to thirty, but mostly they'll be under twenty-five."

"Oh, I'm sorry," she said. "Y'all have such an easy way with each other that I assumed. Forgive me and my big mouth. Pretend I never said that, and let's go tour the boat. If you like what you see, we can talk dates and rates."

She was full of facts about the history of paddle-wheel boats on the Mississippi, the origin of the *Creole Belle*, and its romantic past. "If you book with us, that's the angle y'all want to sell," she said. "Lots of fraternities and sororities like to hold their formals here because once we leave the dock, it's like stepping into another world. People tell us all the time how magical it is. There's nothing as beautiful as the moon shining down on the Mississippi while the shore lights slide by."

Even though we still had plenty of daylight left, I could imagine it. An inky black sky, the splash of the river against the boat, the sound of laughter drifting toward the banks, everyone dressed to the nines and hoping for a fairy tale. And it would happen. People would meet and marry because of this conference.

We stopped in the bow while Mrs. Chapel explained the possible setups they could do. I pictured it in my mind's eye, and my chest twinged like I had jalapeño heartburn. Yeah, magic would happen for some couples on this very deck. But not me. I by no means *felt* old, but a guy my age would have already been off his mission for at least three years. There were not a lot of those single guys around who were active in the Church.

I surveyed the deck again, following as Linda's finger pointed to where the refreshments would be set up, then to the deejay station. I was imagining myself as an observer, someone who would be monitoring the levels on the cookie trays and making sure it all went smoothly. I wouldn't be dancing my feet off, giddy over a new face.

Max's hand brushed against the small of my back, and my spine tingled. They were waiting on me to answer something.

"Sorry. Thinking about the possibilities. What was the question?"

Max gave me a funny look, but he didn't say anything as Mrs. Chapel repeated herself. "I wondered if you would be interested in a full dinner option before your dance so you can keep the group together longer?"

"We'd like to see your price for both."

"Wonderful. Is there anything else you'd like to see before we finish?"

Max and I exchanged glances, and he shook his head. "No, ma'am. I think we have a good feel for the venue. We still have other places to look, but price will be a big factor in our decision."

"If you have a few minutes, you can explore some more while I work up a preliminary quote."

Max lifted an eyebrow at me.

"That works for me."

Mrs. Chapel smiled and headed back to her office.

"What do you think?" I asked when she was out of earshot. "Too traditional and Southern?"

"No. I thought it would be, to be honest. But it's pretty awesome. I like the idea that we're on the water for two hours and people can't duck out until *we* say the dance is over."

"Really," I drawled. "Is this a manifestation of some latent control-freak tendencies?"

He blinked at me.

"Were my words too big?"

His cheekbones flushed the tiniest bit as he opened his mouth to deny it, but my mouth dropped open first. "Max Archer. It honestly surprises you when I use big words? Or is it just that I use them correctly?"

"I didn't say that!"

"It's written all over your face. Are you seriously not over the whole 'Southern accent equals stupid' thing?"

"That's not what I was thinking." His cheeks were still red, but he reminded me of my littlest cousin, Luke, who had once worn the exact same expression before he'd confessed to setting a garter snake loose in my bedroom. "I'm not at all surprised at how articulate you are. But it made me think about how much I used to tease you before. I had a flashback to some of the dumb stuff I said. I can't believe you didn't smack me upside the head."

I leaned against the boat rail, and he joined me. "If my mother wouldn't have killed me for it, I would have."

"I don't think I'm going to be able to apologize enough."

I stole his shoulder bump move to let him know it was okay. "I don't need it. You're forgiven."

"What about confessions? Can I make confessions?"

"Um, yes? Should I sit down for this?"

"Nah. You'll probably want to stay on your feet so you can take off running." He made a quarter turn toward me, and I did the same, so now we were leaning on the rail facing each other.

"Confess," I said, and I meant it to sound like an order, but it came out as the most flirtatious invitation I'd ever made.

A slow smile spread across his face. "I teased other kids about Louisiana because I hated it. I teased you about it because I liked you."

So I hadn't imagined it back then. The way it had felt beneath the rowboat, the looks he'd sent me all the way until the night of my first dance. "If you liked me, why . . . ?"

"Why did I like you? The same reason I like you now." My heart gave a hard knock against my ribs. I'd meant to ask him why he'd humiliated me at the dance, but I wasn't about to correct him until he finished this fascinating thought. "Fifteen-year-old boys fall for girls for dumb reasons. You were so pretty. I couldn't think straight around you."

"Max." I cleared my throat. "I'm not trying to ruin your moment here, but you just said you were really dumb for liking me."

His smile only widened. "That's not what I said at all. I said my reasons were dumb. That was past tense. I know you don't teach English, but try to keep up."

He slid closer. It would take only the barest lean in for our lips to touch. I rested my hand against his chest for a moment before I stepped back. "We need to go, Max. Because I want you to finish that thought way too much, which is not smart. I'm going to walk away and see if Mrs. Chapel has anything for us. Then I need you to drive me to my getaway car because I have got to get away from you."

He straightened from the railing, his smile now looking satisfied. "I'm getting to you, Lila."

"I'm getting away from you, Max." I headed toward the business office, and he followed with a soft laugh.

Mrs. Chapel was waiting for us with an envelope when we got to the gate. "There's a printout on the prices, and here's my business card. We'll look forward to hearing your decision soon."

We said good-bye to her and walked toward the car. As Max opened my door for me, he caught my eyes. "I'm wired to tease, but I don't ever want to do it in a mean way again. Let me know if I ever step out of line, okay?"

"Sure. And, Max, I know you were teasing on the boat, but to be clear, we're a bad idea."

I sat in the passenger seat and shut the door. He started the car but looked at me before putting it in gear. "I disagree. Have I made *that* clear?"

I did not like bossy men. I should have hated everything about what he was saying and how he was saying it. But heaven help me if it didn't flip my stomach faster than the *Creole Belle's* paddle wheel.

"*Vámonos* to my car, Romeo."

He grinned and started the engine, getting us onto I-110 and on the way back to Lincoln in no time flat. I let out a long sigh.

He laughed. "Am I getting on your nerves that much?"

"Surprisingly, no. I was thinking about how much I'm not in the mood to change my tire."

"I told you I'll help."

"You said you don't know how to change a tire."

"We did it in Scouts once. Good enough?"

"Good enough. Thanks."

For the rest of the drive, we discussed possible themes if we went with the *Creole Belle* for the dance. By the time we reached the turnoff for Lincoln, we decided on "Stay in the Boat," from Elder Ballard's talk about sticking to what you believe.

As we pulled into the parking lot, I spotted a set of yellow lights flashing. "Is that a district vehicle? That's kind of weird to have one here this late in the day." The mystery grew when I realized it was parked by my car. The side read "Pilcher's Towing," and I groaned. "Why would they tow me?"

"Better find out." Max cruised into the neighboring space.

I was out of the car before he could get out to open my door. "Excuse me," I called to the driver in the idling tow truck. "Are you towing me?"

"Hey, Lila?" Max said.

I held up a hand to indicate I'd be with Max in a second, another teacher habit. "Because I don't think I'm parked illegally."

The driver blinked at me. "You're not. I'm here to change a tire."

It was my turn to blink. Max cleared his throat. "I made a call. I have Triple-A, and I can use it for any car I want. I figured we might as well get your flat fixed."

"I thought you said you learned how to fix a tire in Boy Scouts."

"The Scoutmaster started by telling us we'd make our lives much easier if we got Triple-A."

"Smart Scoutmaster," I said.

The driver climbed out of his truck, which I could now see had the distinctive AAA logo under the tow company name.

"Do you have a spare?"

I nodded and popped the trunk. Max rummaged around under the carpeting to find it. I knew I should be a modern-enough woman to insist I could do all of this myself, but Max was doing it exactly how Daddy would have, and it was good to be looked out for this time. Maybe a lot of times.

Fifteen minutes later, I had my spare on and a reference from the tow guy on where to get a replacement. As the tow truck drove off, Max jingled his keys. "What else do you have on your list to check out?"

"Leonard's, the Cajun place over in Port Allen." It was a bar, and somehow I didn't think the stake would go for a dance at a place with flashing Abita Beer signs on the walls. But I very much wanted to drag Max through the full Louisiana experience, and nothing would be better than Leonard's.

To his credit, he didn't question me. I wondered how hard of a fight it was for him to keep an open mind about this purely ridiculous suggestion.

"All right. Leonard's it is," he said.

"Can you do Friday right before the supper rush so he has time to talk?"

"That's fine. Should I pick you up for this one? I solemnly swear I won't think it's a date just because we have to do some conference research in suspiciously date-like circumstances."

"Are you accusing me of something?"

"I'm too afraid of you. What time should I pick you up for this non-date trip to a restaurant and dance club on a Friday night?"

I punched his arm. "Very funny. Five o'clock. Leonard says dinner service doesn't start hopping until seven. That should give us enough time."

"Five, then. See you Friday." He almost took a step toward me but stopped and changed direction.

Had he been about to hug me? I wanted to call him back so he would do it. Instead, I got in my car and drove home, listening to NPR and refusing to think about Max, except I had to shove him out of my brain about a hundred times. I wished it was like exercising, where the muscle in question got stronger with every rep. But Max only proved harder and harder to push away.

Chapter 9

"ARE YOU SURE ABOUT THIS?" Max's eyebrows tried to climb into his perfect hairline and hide there.

"You don't trust me?"

"I did until we pulled into this parking lot."

We stood in front of the dilapidated building, "Leonard" spelled out in peeling paint above the door. Neon liquor signs flashed in the blacked-out windows.

"You ready?"

"No."

"Great. Let's go in."

We pushed through the door, the smell of stale alcohol and warm cooking grease washing over us. A bartender glanced up from behind the bar, but there was no one else inside.

"Hey," I said. "We're looking for Leonard."

"He expecting you?"

"Yes."

"All right, have a seat, and I'll fetch him."

We chose a table in front of the bar, and she disappeared into the kitchen hollering "Leonard!"

Max studied the space, from the stage in the corner to the well-worn dance floor. "It's bigger inside than I thought it would be."

I loved that he was trying hard to give a fair chance to a clearly terrible idea. "Plenty of room, even if everyone hits the floor at the same time."

He nodded, no expression on his face. The kitchen door opened again, and a short, wrinkled man emerged. He was eighty if he was a day.

"Welcome to my place," he said, reaching our table in the fastest shuffle I'd ever seen. He flipped a chair around and straddled it as he joined us.

"What questions can I answer for you?" He had a distinct Cajun accent, and I loved it.

"Have you ever had church groups rent your place for a dance?"

His eyes twinkled. "Church? No. Plenty of biker groups though."

"What church are y'all from?" the bartender called. "Sounds like one I want to go to."

"We're Mormons, and we'd be glad to have you," Max said.

The bartender set her rag down and stared at us. "You're yanking my chain. Mormons don't dance."

"Oh, they do, Donna," Leonard said before either of us could defend ourselves. "Back in the fifties, some of the best dancing I ever did was with a pair of Mormon sisters who snuck out of their house every Saturday night to come in here and cut a rug. Didn't drink, but they tore up the floor like they were possessed."

Max looked like he was caught between laughing and cringing. I made a note to ask Mom if she knew which two scandalous sisters Leonard might be referring to.

"Now tell me about this no-drinking thing," Leonard said. "That's going to cost me money. It's some health thing y'all have, ain't it?"

"Yes, sir. It's a code we live by because God asked us to. But don't you love the idea of having at least one night where you don't have to bust any heads because your patrons got too rowdy?" I wheedled.

He waved that off with a chuckle. "Rowdy keeps it interesting. And it's all that alcohol that pays the bills. I'd have to charge you for an average night's drink sales to make it worth my while."

"That's going to be out of our budget," Max said.

"That's too bad," I told Leonard. "I was hoping to show our out-of-towners what it looks like to have a good time, south-Louisiana style." I crooked my head to indicate that Max was not schooled in the ways of *laissez les bon temps rouler*—let the good times roll—the semiofficial state motto.

"Didn't think you sounded like you was from around here." Leonard cocked his head. "You ain't seen it done like we do?"

"I guess I ain't," Max said.

Leonard grinned at Max's imitation of his grammar and showed a mouthful of blinding dentures. "I'm sorry to hear we can't reach a business agreement, but y'all need to let me treat you to a little taste of Leonard's. Delmond!" he called, and a huge black guy stuck his head out of the kitchen door. "This guy here had the great misfortune to grow up above the Mason-Dixon line. Probably ain't ever had a decent meal in his life. Set him up with somethin' good and show him what he's been missing."

"Yeah, boss." Delmond disappeared.

Leonard smacked the table and cackled. "This is going to be fun, Yankee. Sit tight. Good things are coming your way." He pushed himself up from his chair and tottered toward the kitchen, calling out something about boudin.

Max watched him go and blinked at me. "Two questions: First, do you really call non-Southerners Yankees down here?"

"Only when we're messing with people."

"That's what I thought. Second, boudin. Is this one of those things where I don't want to confirm the ingredients?"

"Absolutely."

"That's also what I thought."

"You're taking this well. I've seen people's faces prune right up at the idea of eating boudin."

"I guess Madagascar broke me in. I'm game to try anything once."

"What theme would you have gone with if we'd had the dance here?"

Max snorted. "What about another Elder Ballard classic? Rais—"

"Don't say it!"

"Raising the bar?"

I fell out laughing, and the suggestions only got worse.

When Leonard made his way back to our table, he squinted at us. "Y'all sure Mormons don't drink? Because y'all are exhibiting all the signs."

"No, sir, we don't. We know how to act a fool all on our own," I said.

He smiled and set down some fragrant bell peppers. "These here are boudin stuffed, and if you want to know why it tastes so good, it's 'cause I passed my hand over it."

"That sounds exactly like something my granddaddy would say," I told him.

"Then your grandaddy must know how to cook. Now, y'all need to come back on gumbo day. I make it with a secret ingredient."

"If I ask nicely, will you tell me what it is?" I said.

He winked at me. "I'll tell you just for being pretty. I stir it with my finger!" And with another cackle, he headed back to the kitchen.

Max snatched up his fork. "Nothing that smells this good could taste bad, right?"

I was already cutting into my own bell pepper. "Take the leap." Even my eyes widened at the rich flavor.

"Oh man," Max said. "I want to shovel it all in, but then it'll disappear too fast."

"You're always in too much of a rush, Max. Savor it." I took another bite, and a happy sigh escaped me.

A few minutes later, Leonard shuffled back. "How y'all like it?"

"So good," I said.

"Amen," Max said.

Leonard laughed. "I'll send out more. Where you from anyway, son?"

"Philadelphia."

"They got anything good to eat there?"

"Philly cheesesteaks. They're sandwiches."

"Heard of them. Don't sound too bad. But I'm going to go you one better. Sit tight." He disappeared toward the kitchen again, and we finished our green peppers in silence.

I was too in love with the food to use my mouth for talking.

Leonard came back bearing two full plates, and when he set them down, Max's eyes nearly bugged out. "I brought y'all my special sampler platter. It's so good it'll make you jump up and slap your mama. That means," he said, with a pointed look at Max, "that it's going to be the best cooking you've had in a while. Delmond don't mess around."

"Did you pass your hand over it?" Max asked.

"I did." Blinding white grin.

"Then I believe you."

"Good. I never lie about food. You got some collard greens, red beans and rice, fried catfish, hot links, hush puppies, smothered chicken, and fried okra. It's a little bit of everything, and I expect y'all to finish them plates off, you hear?"

"Yes, sir," I said.

"I'mma be watching you. I better not see them forks stop for too long," he said, turning toward the bar. "And what do y'all drink, anyway? Can you have a Coke?"

"Yes, sir," I assured him.

"What kind?"

"Sprite."

Max looked perplexed at my answer.

"We call everything a Coke here," I explained.

"Which kind you want?" Leonard prompted him.

"An actual Coke?"

"You got it." Leonard nodded at the bartender and disappeared into the kitchen.

Max held up his fork, and I tapped it with mine. "See you on the other side," he said.

I started with the catfish. He went for the smothered chicken, and we both moaned at the exact same time.

"I can't even talk to you until all of this food is gone," he said, bliss all over his face.

I only nodded since I was already working on another bite. By the time we finished off our plates, several tables had filled, and a five-piece band was setting up on the stage. I pointed at them taking out their instruments. "Check it out."

An upright bass was now resting against the back wall, and a middle-aged woman with big hair was strapping on an accordion. An older gentlemen took out a fiddle and tuned it. As the noise drifted out over the diners, heads turned, and the energy in the room shifted from relaxed to a coiled-up waiting, like horses behind a starting gate.

"Where's the drummer?" Max asked, raising his voice to be heard over the tuning and mic checks.

I shook my head. "Traditional Cajun bands use the bass for rhythm, no drums. No brass either. Those are for jazz."

He took his last bite of red beans and rice before he twisted in his chair to watch. Three servers now worked the tables, busing empty plates and glasses back to the kitchen at a faster clip.

Leonard reappeared at our table. "Sugar, you know your two step?"

"I was raised right. Yes."

He grinned and held out a hand. "I'm stealing your girl," he said to Max, winking. Then he nodded at the band, who swung into a cover of one of my favorite BeauSoleil songs, and we were off, Leonard guiding me around the floor with strong hands and a toothy grin for the regulars, who hooted. Our second time around the floor, more couples joined us. When the song finished up, the crowd hollered, and the band went right into a jitterbug while Leonard escorted me back to my table.

"You ain't bad, sweetheart. You ain't bad at all."

"That's only because you made me look good." I kissed him on his cheek, which set off another cackle.

"You hear that, son? And now your girl is kissing me too! You better take her out on that floor before I steal her away from you." Leonard shuffled off before Max could even get all the way to his feet.

"I mean to respect my elders," he said, holding a hand out for me to take.

"You know how to Cajun jitterbug?"

"I took ballroom at BYU. It's close enough that I think I can follow."

We stepped out on the floor. He put his right hand on my waist and bounced with the beat a couple of times, getting the rhythm but watching me, not the other dancers.

"Might be easier to start with the waltz," I called over the music.

"Have a little faith." Then, with a gentle touch, he guided us into the circling dancers and matched my steps easily.

Oh, he was good. Just the right amount of pressure on my hand and waist, confident without making me feel like I was being manhandled.

The song finished, and a waltz started. He pulled me into a waltz hold. "Is this okay?"

"It's not a date," I blurted. Because I needed reminding.

"Okay," he said and kissed my forehead. "Will you still waltz with me?"

I followed his lead instead of answering, too dazed from the touch of his lips to think much.

He pulled me into a close hold, closer than he needed to, but I didn't care. We floated around the dance floor again, only separating when he spun me before pulling me close again. The blood pounding in my head muted the band, the music coming at me through a haze. The whole dance hall shrank down to become just us somehow. A dim awareness that the music was slowing filtered through the tension between Max and me, and I willed the band to do another verse. I didn't want to stop.

But we did, at the edge of the dance floor near our table, only Max didn't let go. He pulled me closer and settled my head beneath his chin, swaying with me in a slow dance that had nothing to do with the two-step playing now.

I closed my eyes, time melting away, people melting away, until Max asked a question, soft in my ear, and delicious tingles rocketed down my spine.

"What are we doing?"

We swayed for several more measures before I answered. "I don't know."

"What is this? Because it's something. To me, it's something."

I leaned back enough to meet his eyes. "Me too."

He stepped back but kept my hand in his, drawing me over to our table only to find the waitress clearing it. "Can we get the check?" he asked.

"Go on with you." She shooed him off. "Leonard said it was on the house. Pay us back by telling your friends if you liked it."

"We will," he said. When she headed toward the kitchen with the last of our silverware, Max left a big tip on the table. "You ready to go?"

I nodded, even though I wasn't. Part of me wanted to stay on the dance floor with him. Part of me wanted to avoid the discussion that was about to happen. But mostly I wanted to freeze time and walk around in this moment some more, just feeling it without considering what it meant.

We walked out to his car in the nearly full parking lot. He leaned against the door. My heart did a weird skip beat. "Max—"

"I know," he said. "You don't want to date. But why? It feels like we have chemistry. Do you feel it? Tell me you don't, and I'll drop it."

I couldn't meet his eyes.

He reached out for my hand, tangling our fingers together. "Go out with me. For real. The kind of date where we see what can happen between us."

"There's no point. What if it's amazing?" I could barely get my voice above a whisper because they were words I didn't want to say.

"Then it'll be amazing," he answered. "Why is that bad?"

"Because you're leaving Baton Rouge as soon as you can, and I never will."

"I've never felt this kind of a pull toward someone before." He hesitated, like he wanted to add something, but he swallowed and fell quiet again.

I didn't have anything to say. All I wanted to add was words I had to hold back. *I want this.*

He straightened and pulled me into a hug, settling my head where it had been when we were dancing. "If you're right, and there's no way for us to work out, it will fall apart pretty quickly. At least neither of us will have to wonder ten years from now what might have happened. And if we're supposed to work out, we will." He pulled back, and I glanced up to find him watching me. "I'm not trying to pressure you, but it feels wrong in every part of me to let you go. Am I coming off like a total head case right now?"

I shook my head. "Not a head case. Or I'm one too, I guess. Can I think about this?"

He smoothed back my hair. "Whatever you need." A car door slammed, followed by the bright babble of voices heading into Leonard's. He rested his forehead against mine, and his next words were quiet, but I could *feel* them all the way through me. "I'm fighting all my instincts to give you more to think about, to make this decision harder." He turned his head the tiniest bit, brushing his lips against mine. It wasn't even a kiss, but it nearly buckled my knees. "But not here, and not now." He let me go and stepped back.

"You play dirty," I said when I thought I could keep my voice even. It almost worked.

"I play honest," he said. "I'm being as clear as I know how to be. I'll get you home."

When he dropped me off and waved at me before walking back to his car, it occurred to me that it was a gesture that could mean both good-bye and hello. And I didn't want to say good-bye anymore.

Chapter 10

KIANA WAS WAITING BY MY classroom door Monday morning. "Why so early?" I asked, but I was fighting a smile. I'd seen her wound up before, but usually it was stress. This was different. This was a nervous, twitchy energy that betrayed excitement even though she was trying to keep her face blank.

"Nothing I had to do at home, so I came in."

I nodded and unlocked the door. "Have a good weekend?"

"Yeah."

"What'd you do?" I settled my bag on my desk.

"Research." She shot me a look to see my reaction.

I didn't gloat. Barely. "On Madame CJ?"

She nodded.

"Interesting stuff, isn't it?"

"Yeah." She sat in her desk and pulled out a notebook, pretending she needed to write something down, but her pen never moved. Finally she spoke again. "How I'm going to do something original about her? Everything needs saying already been said."

"You think so?"

She shrugged.

I sat back in my teacher chair and studied her for a long moment. "Do you think if you stood up and read what you found online about her to the class that they would get why she's so interesting?"

"No. Jamarcus would probably be talking some mess about how he wants to be a millionaire and not get why it's such a big deal how she did it back then."

"So maybe if your peers wouldn't get why it's a big deal the way it's currently been explained, it hasn't been said the right way. Maybe there's a way to say it so people like Jamarcus would get it."

"That's what I'm supposed to figure out how to do?"

I grinned at her.

She eyed me. "It ain't that easy."

"Of course not. But you can do hard things, Kiana. And this one is going to pay off for you."

"How do you know that?" she said, sounding more curious than angry.

"You see connections between things other people don't. If you can figure out how to explain them to other people, you have this in the bag."

She looked back down at her notebook for so long that I left her to her thoughts and turned to my computer to enter scores for the essays I'd graded all day Saturday.

"You gonna help me?"

I glanced up at her, her question asked quietly but with that same hard, protective edge I'd had to chip at for the whole first semester. "Yes, Kiana. I'm absolutely going to help you. But it has to come from you, so I can't do any of it *for* you."

"Then how you going to help?"

"Advising. Like this. Tell me what got you so pumped about Madame CJ this weekend?"

Kiana shifted around in her seat. "She didn't just make something up and then a bigger company came and bought it from her and made her a millionaire. And she didn't come from money either. Her parents were slaves, but she was born after Lincoln freed them. But they still didn't have nothing, really. She was smart though. Paid attention. And she made this whole business that didn't just make her rich, but it helped all these other black women too. She gave them recognition for having good sales but also for doing good things for their neighborhoods. I like that. Don't seem like that's how most people are trying to make money these days."

"Sounds like you went beyond the Wikipedia article."

Another shrug. "I went to my cousin's house. They got Internet. I did some looking."

"Great historians ask one question over and over again to uncover truth: why? Why did people do what they did? They ask until they find answers. If you can dig into Madame CJ Walker's life story and figure out the why, that's good. If you can figure out how to present it to other people so they understand the why too, that's better. If you can do it in an unexpected way, something fresh and creative, that's best. Make sense?"

"Yeah. I mean, yes. But I don't have no idea what kind of project to do."

"Don't worry about that. Focus on digging into Madame CJ's why. I'll see if I can find some extra resources for you to read." I had privileges at the LSU library; it was all I could do to refrain from logging into the system to search right that second. If Kiana was this excited from basic Internet research, she was going to lose her mind over the scholarly research.

"Ask yourself hard questions. Why did she do what she did, Kiana? Why did she do it the way she did it? Why did it work? Why is she not as famous today as other people who started beauty product lines, like Estee Lauder? Why should she be?"

Kiana squinted at me. "That's a lot of whys."

"Cool, right? Should give you plenty of scope for your project."

"So you're saying go read right now, and some kind of project is going to come to me?"

"Yes."

"You kinda crazy."

"No. It's just experience. As you learn more and more about this woman's life and you're thinking about how to make other people understand her and why she matters, inspiration will strike."

The squint returned. "Now you being mystical."

"Yes."

She shrugged. "All right. I can do some more reading and wait for some idea to come hit me over the head."

"Good. Except for one thing. Thomas Edison has a pretty famous quote about inspiration. He says that success is ninety-nine percent perspiration and one percent inspiration. What do you think that means?"

"You gotta work?"

"You gotta work," I agreed. "Besides reading up on her, keep looking up projects from years past. And look for history projects from all kinds of competitions, not only this one. If you need Internet access, wander in here whenever you need to, okay?"

The door opened, and a couple of kids came in. It would be a steady trickle for the next few minutes with a final flood right before the tardy bell. I was extra glad to see their faces today. I hadn't only been happy to see Kiana because it was fun to see her excited; there had been a significant part of me that was grateful for the distraction of something to think about besides Max.

I'd seen him at church yesterday, suffered that same impulse to constantly look back at him during sacrament meeting and Sunday School. By the time Relief Society had started, my neck had been downright stiff with the effort of not turning around. It didn't help that the few times I couldn't resist, I found him watching me. The first three times, he looked thoughtful. The fourth time he caught me, he flashed me a tiny knowing smile. That was the last time I turned around.

He had found me after church, waiting for me to untangle myself from the wedding belles so he could walk with me out to the parking lot. "You look pretty today," he said.

I had blushed. Dang it. I hated that he could do that to me. But I'd put on the dress with him in mind, hoping he'd like it. It was pale yellow and swishy, with tiny red flowers on it, like spring woven into fabric. "Thanks."

"So, have you had any time to think?"

I've done nothing but think. You won't get out of my head. "I need more time."

He drew me into a hug. "Call me when you figure anything out," he said, releasing me and walking off toward his car. No, sauntering off. Sauntering! Like this was not the most stressful situation in the world.

When I had gotten home and realized Mom had cooked for an army again, I accepted it as a sign that my stomach did an excited flip. But it was for Brother Lewis and Bridger, not Max. Still, it had been good to watch Mom fussing over someone besides me.

A wad of paper went sailing toward the trash can. "Marcus Brown!" I called and shook my fist until he picked it up and dropped it in. Facing a classroom of teenagers, their noise and energy, forced Max into the background, but they couldn't push him out of my thoughts completely. Was that even possible at this point?

Oh, man.

Chapter 11

Tuesday night, Mom called as I was driving home.

"Where are you?" she asked. "In a ditch?"

"What? No. I'm on my way home."

"You're so late I thought the only reason I hadn't seen you by now is because you'd driven yourself into a ditch."

"No, I stayed to get some things ready for my lessons tomorrow."

"We have company for dinner, and we've been waiting on you almost fifteen minutes. Hurry up. But not so fast that you drive into a ditch."

"Yes, ma'am," I said. "But you didn't tell me we were having company. How was I supposed to know you wanted me home?"

"I only decided on company this afternoon. Pedal to the metal, darlin'. But don't—"

"Drive into a ditch. Got it. Bye."

Wait. What if the company was Max? I was torn between speeding home or speeding in the opposite direction because . . . Because. Just because.

It was a Prius parked in front of the house, and I got an instant case of butterflies. Max's voice drifted from the kitchen when I opened the front door, and my nerves hummed. "Hey," I said, walking in.

Max stood on a chair, fiddling with a lightbulb hanging over the table. He paused and grinned down at me. "Hey yourself." He wore black dress pants and a gray-striped button-down shirt, like he'd just come from work. He looked good. Really good.

"I had him come over and help me with a few things," Mom said. "I offered him dinner, and he couldn't say no."

"I'd have done it for nothing," he said, climbing down from the chair and giving her a peck on her cheek. "I happen to like the Guidry women. Dinner is a bonus." Mom looked as pleased as if one of my brothers had given her sugar.

"How are you?" Max asked, rounding the table to pull me into a hug. I'd seen it coming and hadn't bothered getting out of the way.

"Tired," I said. "Glad to be done at work."

"Hard day?"

"They're all hard days," Mom said before I could answer. "She puts her whole self into her job, no holding back. Wears herself out, but it makes her a good teacher."

"Thanks, Mom."

"Of course, sweetie. We're having meatloaf. I threw it together while Max worked."

I glanced at the clock. It was six thirty already. "How long have you been here?"

"An hour. I stopped by on my way home from work."

"What exactly has she had you doing?"

"All the stuff we never get to," Mom answered. "He changed four lightbulbs, put some boxes up in the attic, and rearranged my office furniture."

I almost said, "I could have done that for you," but the fact was that I hadn't. Instead, I smiled at Max. "You shouldn't let her con you into anything else. She's got a good home teacher, and the Young Men in her ward are always begging her to let them come do service projects."

She made a dismissive sound. "I'm a project because I'm a widow now. This is the kind of thing I'd make your brothers do if they were around, but there's not nearly enough to keep a quorum busy, and there's too much to pull Brother Campbell away from his own family to fix. So Max is the perfect solution. You're a good boy, Max."

"Thanks, Sister Guidry."

"You can call me Hattie."

MISS Hattie, I mouthed at him.

He nodded. "I'm glad to do it, Miss Hattie. Call me anytime."

"Let's eat," she said. "I believe the meatloaf is about done."

I crossed over to the cabinets and took out plates to set the table.

"I'll help," he said right behind me, and I whirled, nearly dropping the dishes. He took them, and as his fingers grazed mine, I could swear the light-bulb he'd replaced flared brighter for a second.

"Let Max do the table, and you throw together a green salad," Mom said, pulling the meatloaf from the oven.

"Yes, ma'am." I changed course to the fridge. A few minutes later, we were all settled in and eating.

Max took a bite and chewed slowly, then nodded. "Magic."

Mom laughed. "Have you talked to your mama lately? How is everything?"

"She's great. She's busy getting ready for Samantha's baby to come."

"Where's Samantha now?" I asked. She was a year younger than me, and I remembered her pretty well.

"She's in Kansas City. This'll be her second. My mom always goes and stays with my sisters for about a month when they have a baby. She'll do it for the daughters-in-law too, if they'll have her, but Aidan's wife doesn't like having her for long. She says it stresses her out to make my mom do her housework."

Mom's face had softened as she'd listened to all the baby chatter, and even though she didn't look at me, I could feel her grandbaby hunger simmering beneath the surface. She decided to embarrass Max instead of me. "Are you the only one who's still single out of all the kids?"

"Yes, ma'am."

"So even your youngest sister is on child number two, and you're still unattached."

He shifted in his seat. "Yes, ma'am."

"Leave him alone, Mom," I said, my voice light. She had the impeccable manners of any well-bred Southern woman, but the older she got, the more she did that other quintessentially Southern-woman thing: she claimed the right to mother anyone a decade or more younger than her, up to and including getting into their private lives to offer unsolicited advice.

"It's okay," he said.

I scooped up another forkful of meatloaf. "It's your funeral."

"You hush, Lila Mae. So tell me, why aren't you married yet?"

"Mom! Too much. Let him eat in peace."

"It's fine, Lila." He pushed his meatloaf around for a minute. "I haven't found the right woman. As simple as that."

"Are you too picky?" she asked. "That's a problem more and more with young people these days. Too many options, so they don't choose. It's decision paralysis." I almost intervened again until I noticed her expression. Clear, focused. Present. It was so good to see her—all of her—no fog in sight.

"I don't think I'm holding out for a fairy tale or a dream Barbie. My mom always told us that you marry the person who makes you see forever. I've only been able to look a few years down the road and see trouble with anyone I've dated so far."

Mom shook her head. "I don't like the sound of this, Max. What do you mean, trouble?"

"I've dated a couple girls where it started getting kind of serious, and I would try to imagine married life in twenty years, and I couldn't imagine having enough things to talk about to fill up that time. Seems important."

Mom didn't argue or lecture him. That was a shocker. Instead, her expression grew thoughtful. "That's a good thing to consider. But I can tell you the real problem."

"Watch out," I said. "She's playing love doctor now."

"Diagnose me," Max said. "I'd like to be fixed."

"You've been dating the wrong kind of girls."

"My mom says the exact same thing," he said.

"Then date the right kind of girl," Mom said, spearing a piece of meatloaf with an air of triumph, like she'd single-handedly figured out how to marry him off.

"I'm trying," he said, his voice even. His eyes locked on mine, and my mom's gaze sharpened, but she didn't say anything except, "Good," and went back to her meatloaf.

When dinner ended, Max didn't try to finagle a walk out to the pier. He only helped clear the table until Mom shooed him off. He laughed and stepped out of the way. "I guess that's my cue to leave. I have to catch up on some work, and I should probably give Lila a chance to relax."

"See him out," Mom said, already zeroing in on the dishes.

I did, walking him out to the veranda. "What kind of work do you have to bring home?" I was kind of curious but mostly looking for a way to keep him a few minutes longer.

"Tonight, it's risk assessment reports. We've got a slight increase in minor on-the-job injuries, and I want to see if I can figure out why, maybe bring the numbers down. Next week, it might be reports on opening up a market for our stuff in Canada."

"Workplace injuries and new-product markets seem like two very different things."

"They are. And neither of them is technically my job, but how am I going to run the world if I only understand one corner of it?"

"Run the world, huh? You think big."

"Only metaphorically. I'm not planning global domination anytime soon, just corporate. Working in operations helps me see how the different systems in Taggart work, and that's a major plus for moving up through the ranks."

"So today, operations manager; tomorrow, CEO?"

"It's more like a ten-year plan, but yeah, basically."

It depressed me to think about how following that path would lead him right out of Baton Rouge, so I dropped the subject. "Thanks for helping my mom out. You didn't have to do that."

"Sure I did."

"Because you're trying to impress me?"

"A little. But mainly because I wouldn't be the man my dad raised me to be if I didn't."

Okay, *that* impressed me.

"I'm going to get on the road. See you Sunday?"

"Definitely."

He walked to his car, and I cringed the second his back was turned. *Definitely?* I didn't even know what I meant by that. It was something you said when you wanted to flirt, like if someone asked if you were going to a party or something and you said "definitely" because you wanted them to know you were going to be there for *them*.

Ugh. He was so confusing he was making me subconsciously flirt. I watched him drive off. If he could read minds and he had half a grain of common sense, he should be running as far and as fast as he could from the train wreck of conflicting needs happening inside my head.

Wait. Maybe he just had.

Good!

Then why did I feel so bad?

Chapter 12

THURSDAY ON MY LUNCH BREAK, Kate called. "Can you talk?"

"Yes. Is Ignatius okay?"

"He's fine. We're calling him Jellybean right now. What are you doing? Do you have students in there?"

I glanced over at Kiana on one of the classroom computers in the back of the room, and a small knot of my honors students huddled around a cell phone watching anime. "Yeah, but they don't need me right now. What's up?"

"Nothing. I'm feeling a teeny bit queasy and looking for a distraction, so I thought I'd see what you're up to."

"Max. He's all up in my head." I kept my voice low so my kids couldn't eavesdrop on my love life.

Kate's voice took on the tone she got when Dillard's clearance went an extra fifty percent off. "What kinds of thoughts are you thinking, Lila Mae? Thoughts about how much you want to kiss his face?"

"Thoughts like how he's probably already out of patience with me. I don't even make sense to myself right now. I told him to give me time to think, and then I'm totally bummed that he did. Oh no."

"What?"

"I sound like every third conversation I hear in my classroom at lunch time."

Kate burst out laughing. "How about you and I go to dinner tomorrow night, and you can tell me all about it? We should probably fix you."

"I'm not broken."

"You are, but don't worry. I know what to do."

"Tell me? I'll do it."

"You need *Max*imum exposure!" She laughed harder when I groaned.

"I'll pick you up at six tomorrow, but no puns."

"Yay! Take me somewhere with garlic bread. That's what Jellybean needs."

We hung up, and I spent the rest of lunch marking papers and keeping a tally of every time I caught myself thinking about Max. I was up to thirty-seven by the time I packed up to leave for the day. I'd kind of hoped seeing the hard evidence of how ridiculous my brain was being would make me stop, but by the time I got home, I'd easily doubled that number.

My phone went off as I was parking. It was Max, and my cheeks burned even though he couldn't know how much he'd been on my mind. I almost let it go to voice mail to prove that I could, but I picked up on the last ring possible instead. Because . . . Max.

"Hi," I said.

"Hey. I want to run something by you. I know you are a popular woman who is highly in demand, who would never be sitting at home on the weekend, but are you free tomorrow night? Because I found a venue we should check out."

"On a Friday night again?"

"Best time to see the place in action."

"I do have plans already." Although Kate would kill me for keeping them if she knew Max had called.

"Oh." He sounded the way my tire had looked after the riverboat last week, but he didn't stay down for long. "How about Saturday?"

"I can do that. Which venue?"

"It's a surprise. Can I pick you up and drive you over?"

No. Terrible idea. "Yes. Sounds good. What time should I be ready?"

"How about seven thirty?"

I agreed, and we hung up, but it seemed kind of late in the day to be checking out venues.

I spent Friday making tally marks for Max thoughts. By lunch, my Post-it full of hash marks looked like I'd been counting down every day of a twenty-year imprisonment on a dungeon wall. I accepted that he'd staked out a long-term rental in my brain's real estate and threw the Post-it away.

Kate didn't help over dinner. She tried to Facebook stalk him on her phone. "He's set to private. Jaimie says he's hot. He was always cute though. I want to see him. Why aren't you Facebook friends?"

"We're barely real-life friends."

"Take a picture when you go out tomorrow."

"We're not going out. We're checking out a venue."

Kate set her fork down and stared at me. It was the only reason her chicken alfredo didn't disappear in world-record time. "All right, let's be real here. Do you *want* to date him?"

"No."

Her stare didn't waver.

"I don't! He's leaving soon."

"How soon?"

"I don't know. When he gets a new assignment for work."

"And you don't know when that is? Maybe that's in a year."

"It doesn't matter if it's in three years. He's leaving, and I never will. And I don't see a point to getting involved."

Kate went back to her alfredo, but even though her mouth was too busy for words, her expression still said lots of things. She swallowed and let the words out. "Forget if he's leaving, forget that he was a punk teenager. Based on Max in the here and now, everything else factored out of the equation, do you want to date him? Just based on how you feel when you're hanging out with him, nothing else."

She would see right through a lie, so I didn't bother. "Yes."

She took another bite, and this time her face was purely about the cream sauce.

"That's it?" I asked. "You're not going to lecture me or get on my case about it?"

"No. I'm going to let you think about that for a while."

"I don't want to."

"But now that you've admitted it to yourself, you will. So, really, I don't need to do any work. You'll do it for me."

"I don't like you right now."

"You love me. And I'm right. You don't know that he wouldn't stay here for you, so you may as well see where this all goes."

Kate would never try to talk to me about leaving Baton Rouge for Max because she wouldn't have done it under any circumstance either. I had a lot of doubts, an eighteen-wheeler full of them, as to whether Max would ever stay here. No, I didn't even have doubts. I had an absolute certainty that he wouldn't.

That wouldn't matter if we dated a few times and fizzled out, but the spark between us scared me. Ten years ago, that had ended in public humiliation. Now the spark was bigger, and so was my fear. It was like when I'd gone cliff-jumping with some cousins on a Lake Powell vacation one summer. The first two days had been a blast until a boat had pulled up and this old guy had told us about his grandson who had been paralyzed while he was cliff-diving. I'd stood on the edge of the cliffs for the rest of the week with a different perspective, the sure knowledge of how fun it would be to go soaring off the side tempered by the awareness that pain wasn't an abstract possibility.

Jumping into something with Max was bad odds.

I went to bed wondering if Kate was truly seeing the whole situation more clearly than I was, and I woke up without an answer. I saw more warning flags flying than at Biloxi Beach in hurricane season.

Mom was working on her magnolia when I came downstairs at seven thirty, this time with Bonnie Raitt playing in the background. It had been one of her and Daddy's favorite albums. She glanced up at me, the familiar fog back on her face, and gave me a vague smile that made my heart sink. But then she blinked, and her gaze turned sharp. "You look good. Going out with Max?"

I'd curled my hair and put on a gauzy shirt and my best jeans. "It's just conference stuff." The doorbell rang, and I snatched up my purse and stepped out onto the veranda, shutting the door firmly behind me so she wouldn't try to call him in to grill him. "Hey," I said, smiling at him. "So where are we headed?"

"You'll see."

"I feel like that might be what kidnappers say when they lure victims into their car."

"Hang on." He did a quick one-eighty and ran back up the porch steps, stuck his head in the door, said something to Mom, disappeared into the house for thirty seconds, and came back. "Your mom knows where we're going. And I paid my tax," he said, tapping his cheek to show where he'd kissed her. "Do kidnappers do that?"

"Guess not."

"How'd your week go?" he asked after we'd gotten in the car and he was steering onto the main road leading out of the neighborhood.

"It was good."

He shook his head. "I know I keep saying this, but I really admire what you do."

"I bet I'd think your job was hard too. Doesn't it wipe you out some-times?"

He shrugged. "The stakes aren't as high. What you do matters. Me? Not so much."

"Then why do it?" I asked. This was a conversation I'd had with my brother Logan, who was majoring in business. He'd talked about people who were mission driven versus task driven or something like that. The gist was that there were people who felt lost when they didn't see a greater purpose for their work, some way in which it made the world a better place. That was me.

Logan saw work as a means to an end, and as long as he found the process satisfying, it didn't matter if it changed the world or the community. To him, there was honor in a job as long as he could provide for a family. That was where he felt he'd do his changing the world.

"Why do it?" Max's tone was thoughtful. "I like a challenge. I like going in each day and figuring out how to untangle a puzzle, how to make an objective happen. There's a certain amount of winning and losing that happens in business, and I like to win. Sounds shallow, huh?"

"Not really." It might have without my conversations with Logan. "Maybe if you'd said you liked making money or something, that would sound shallow. But liking a challenge doesn't sound shallow."

"I like making money too," he said, a slight smile on his face. "It's one way to measure how well I'm doing what I do. Every raise, every promotion, it all points to one kind of succeeding. But in my mind, I separate the paycheck from success. That's something my dad taught me. The pay will reflect how well I'm doing my job, but success is about something else."

"Like what? What's success to you?"

"Probably the same thing it is to you. Comes down to family, really. Right now that's about the family I was raised in. Maybe someday it'll be about raising my own family."

"Maybe someday? Sounds so far away."

"I know." His smile fell away, and I felt like I had stolen it.

"Sorry."

"No big deal. So Baton Rouge is a lot different than when I left it. Does all the change bother you?"

I accepted the change of subject. "Some of it. I don't like how the newer neighborhoods squeeze the houses together, but I guess that's the same everywhere. And every time I see a new shopping center open, I get a little depressed. Most of the changes are good though. I wish more change would happen in the areas that really need it, but I'll take progress over being stagnant."

"Why would a shopping center depress you?"

"Watch up here, when we get through this light. Look at the shopping center on your left."

As we crossed the intersection, Max studied the area I'd pointed out. "What about it?"

"That's probably about twenty years old. See all those empty stores? And whoever owns the property doesn't try to keep it up or modernize the look. I wish people would think, because once you cut down a bunch of trees and slap up a bunch of buildings, they're never going away. It's not like you can be like, 'Oh, I guess this shopping center isn't working. Let's put everything back the way it was.' You changed it, and it stays changed—no do overs. Run-down strip malls isn't progress."

"But when it works, it means jobs and tax revenue. Don't you think cities need developers to take risks so they don't rot?"

More scenery slipped by, mostly tall expanses of trees broken up by turn-offs into subdivisions. "Maybe we shouldn't change until we're uncomfortable. *Really* uncomfortable. Like getting to the point where every time you go to the store, they're almost always out of what you need because everyone else needs it too. Maybe that's when you say, 'We need another one of these.' But I don't think building something so it'll be a mile closer for a few people to drive to is a great reason."

"Then define good progress."

"New schools, libraries, police stations."

"That's a very public-school-teacher thing to say," he said, and I heard a smile in his voice.

"Yeah. But those are new things that are always needed, and there's never going to be enough of them. That's what I mean to say: I don't have a problem with Baton Rouge changing, but I wished we focused more on developing neighborhoods that need it, not building more bright, shiny things where everyone's doing all right anyway."

He smiled again as he moved into the turn lane. "I kind of like the way you see things."

I didn't know what to say to that. I turned to look out my window for another change of subject and wrinkled my forehead as he pulled into a parking lot. "This is the movie theater. This is where we're going?"

"Yes."

"Where are people supposed to dance?"

"Let's go in, and I'll explain what I'm thinking."

We walked in with the rest of the Saturday-night crowd, but instead of asking to speak to a manager, Max steered us to the ticket line. Something didn't smell right here. "Max."

"Yes."

"You're trying to sneak a date past me ninja-style."

"That's dumb."

"Really? What are we seeing?"

"*Swipe Right.*"

That was a new romantic comedy. "That's a date movie."

"For other people. For us, it's the movie showing in the theater I want us to check out."

Uh-huh.

He got in line for refreshments.

"We don't need popcorn to check out a theater."

"Shh. We're doing this incognito. I want to see what the service is like when they're not trying to win an extra theater rental from us. We need popcorn to blend in."

"We don't. We can go sit like we're going to watch the movie. Lots of people do that without popcorn."

"Only weirdos don't get popcorn at the theater. I don't want to blow our cover by making people ask questions."

Five minutes later, we walked away from the counter with a heaping bucket of popcorn, two sodas, and a box of M&Ms. I held a soda and watched him juggle the rest. "You spent $4,000 on movie food. Can you make rent this month?"

"It's worth it if it keeps up the disguise."

I shook my head but followed him to the theater printed on our ticket. He climbed halfway up the stadium seating and took a seat in the middle of the row. I stayed in the aisle and waited for him to notice.

"What are you doing?" he asked when he realized I hadn't followed.

"Checking out the theater. What am I looking for? It's an auditorium. Verified. Now what?"

He walked back to me. "Now you sit and get the full experience. I picked the best seats in the house. Please, enjoy one." He took my hand and pulled me down the row. *Hand holding now?* Busted.

He sat, but I stayed standing, which forced him to let go of my hand. The lights dimmed for the previews, and I could see him frown. "It's about to start."

"I'm not sitting down until you confess that you're trying to ninja date me."

He stood again, so close I had to look up to meet his eyes. The theater went swirly, and I gulped.

"If I tricked you onto a date, I would be dead meat, wouldn't I?" His voice was soft, but the people in front of us shushed him anyway.

"Yes."

"Then this is definitely not me tricking you. Sit, watch the movie, think about the theater, and I'll tell you my idea for it afterward."

"Shhhhhhh," the woman behind us said.

I couldn't blame her.

I sat and watched a couple of the previews in silence. When the opening credits for the movie came on the screen, I reached over and slipped my hand into his. He turned to look at me, and I could feel the weight of his unasked question. "Don't want to stand out too much," I murmured.

"Got it," he whispered. He lifted the arm rest between us and pulled me closer to his side.

It was the best movie I'd seen in a long time.

Actually, I had no idea what happened in the movie. But all theater seating should be like that forever.

When the movie ended, we sat all the way through the credits. The lights had come up, and I should have been rustling around, picking up my handbag, helping Max collect the trash from our movie treats, but credits had become the most important thing in the world; every name needed to be read and considered while I coincidentally stayed tucked against Max's side.

When the screen went blank and the theater employees began their cleanup, I sat up and scooted toward the edge of my seat. Max's arms closed around me and pulled me back. "I'm going to buy two more tickets."

"Are you going to try to convince me that it's so we can get a true feel for the theater?"

"Duh."

"Nice try," I said, pressing lightly against his arms to break his hold and stand. "I'm not trying to brag or anything, but I'm on to you."

"Oh, really, smarty pants? Because here's my whole pitch for the theater, which I wouldn't have even thought of if this was a ninja date. We should do a morningside in here with a keynote speaker and then show a Mormon movie, a fun one, like that comedy about girl's camp. Cool, right?"

I crossed my arms, annoyed-teacher style. "You had to bring me here to pitch me that idea? I call shenanigans. Just admit you ninja-dated me."

He climbed to his feet, which forced me to look up at him again. "No way. This would never be the first date I took you on."

"Good, because if someone were to do a movie first date, I would feel so bad for their date-planning skills, I might be moved to do something about it."

His eyes were slits. "I respect that, but there might be a reason someone would do a movie for a first date. Like maybe a guy was trying to show you how normal everything could be and not scare you away with some big production. Speaking hypothetically, of course. Because it's possible you put out a major scaredy-cat vibe."

"Excuse me?" I said, and my right eyebrow shot up. Every time it happened in class, the kids would go, "Oooooh, you gonna get it," to whoever had earned the eyebrow.

"I said it"—he crossed his arms to imitate me—"and I'm not taking it back."

"Oh, it's on, friend. We're going on a date. Tomorrow. Be ready by eight o'clock."

"Tomorrow is Sunday."

"I know. It's kind of perfect, right? Here you had a whole Saturday night and whiffed it, and I'm going to work with a Sunday morning and still put together a better first date."

He tried to keep a straight face. "Whiffed it? Do you want to leave any of my ego intact?"

"No. You deserve it. I told you no to a date a million times, and you did it anyway, screwed it up, and now I have to fix it. If we're going to have a first date, we're going to do it right."

His arms snaked out, and he looped a finger through each of my front belt loops, drawing me to him. My hands flew to his shoulders to keep my balance. "I'll let you show me how it's done on one condition," he said, resting his hands on my waist. "Let's call it what it is: a second date. Because I don't think you're a kiss-on-the-first-date kind of girl. And I'm most definitely going to kiss you."

My mouth dropped, and he smiled down at me and brushed his thumb against my bottom lip. And even though he'd just caused a near-death experience, he stepped back, claimed my hand, and led me out of the theater.

Chapter 13

I PICKED UP MAX BECAUSE he lived closer to our destination. While I waited in his parking lot for him to come down, I leaned against the car and tried not to fidget. I straightened when I saw him walking across the parking lot dressed in his church clothes, like we'd agreed.

He looked good. So good. Light-blue shirt, a narrow black tie, sleeves rolled up to his elbows, hair still damp. He hugged me, and I wanted to burrow against him, breathe in his fresh starch smell. His arms tightened around me for a second before he cleared his throat and stepped back. "What's on the agenda, boss?"

"A picnic and some exploring."

"Sounds good. I don't want to sound sexist, but can I still open your door for you even though you're driving? If I don't, it's going to feel like I'm starting off this date with only one shoe or something."

I moved to the side, and he opened the door for me, then went around and climbed into the passenger side.

"Oh, man, it smells amazing in here." He sniffed. "Bacon. That's all I need to know."

"That's my air freshener. I only brought granola bars and some bananas because they're easier to pack. Sorry about getting your hopes up."

"The only thing that could improve a morning with Lila Mae and bacon is Lila Mae wisecracking about bacon."

"I'm feeling inadequate that I'm not enough on my own."

"Hey," he said, reaching out to run his finger along my jawline until I smiled at him. He dropped his hand and sat back. "You are all the things, Lila Mae. All the things."

"Thanks." My heart did a Cajun jitterbug.

It was about fifteen minutes to the state capitol. We talked conference most of the way until we turned onto the capitol grounds and he realized where we were going. "I haven't been here since my eighth-grade Louisiana history field trip."

"It's a good place for a picnic," I said. I could have probably picked a few different parks for us to go to as well, but those would be busier with families as the morning wore on. The capitol had only two other cars in the parking lot, and the lawn stretched out empty, unbroken, and inviting.

"You know what's funny?" he asked as we climbed out. "Since eighth grade is when you do state history in Louisiana *and* Pennsylvania, I actually know more about your state than mine."

I smiled, even though, stupidly, it bothered me that he called Louisiana "my" state. It drew a line between us, a line as invisible and real as the Mason-Dixon line itself.

I opened the trunk and reached in for the picnic hamper and blanket, but Max lifted the basket out of my hands. "Let me."

"You're trying to get close to the bacon, aren't you?"

"Guilty."

We followed the sidewalk through the manicured grass lined with low green hedges to a live oak tree I liked.

"Does this look good?" I asked.

"Looks perfect."

I spread the blanket out and positioned us so we could see the statue of Huey P. Long and the capitol building behind him. Max sank down beside me and eyed the basket. I laughed and produced a foil-covered casserole dish. I handed it to him to open while I removed the plates and cutlery strapped to the hamper's top. "Don't get too excited about that," I said as I handed Max a plate. "It's a hash-brown, egg, bacon thing I used to make for my brothers, so it's nothing fancy, but it travels well."

He took a bite. "Between you and your mom, I have to run a bunch of extra miles to keep from blowing up like a puffer fish."

"Glad you like it, but save some room. I have orange rolls. Home-made. They're kind of my specialty."

"You haven't made anything that wasn't awesome yet, so it must all be your specialty."

"Keep talking. You're doing good."

"No talking. Eating."

We spent the next fifteen minutes joking as we finished off the food. "I have to admit that your first date is better," he said as he slid his empty plate into the plastic grocery sack I'd brought for trash.

"We're not even done yet. I thought we could go for a walk."

"Yes, ma'am."

He helped me to my feet and insisted on carrying everything back to the car himself. When it was safely stowed, he took my hand. "Where to?"

"You okay with wandering?"

"That works."

We started at the statute. "If we came here in two more weeks, this whole place would be full of azaleas."

"It's pretty cool as it is." He read the statue's plaque. "Louisiana has some interesting history."

"Most interesting in the whole United States."

"Way to show your pride, but don't forget Philadelphia kinda had a lot going on there."

Good point, dang it. "But is it as *colorful* as our history?" I pointed at Huey P. Long. "You remember that he was called the dictator of Louisiana, right? It doesn't get much more colorful than him."

"We have a statue of Rocky. Also, remember that we had Ben Franklin? I can go toe-to-toe with you on colorful historical figures."

"Does your state capitol or mine win?"

"Uh . . . mine is a national historic landmark, and it's based on the design of St. Peter's Basilica in Rome. So mine does."

I scowled at him. "Ours is an Art Deco masterpiece. And it's the tallest capitol in the US. And if the azaleas were blooming, mine would definitely win."

"I remember the azaleas. You're right. If they were blooming, you'd win."

"You're just saying that to be nice."

"Yes."

"Fine. But our food is still better."

He opened his mouth and snapped it shut. "I feel guilty that I can't argue with that."

"I should have brought you to the Old State Capitol. A bunch of movies have been filmed there. Oooh, we should look at it as our next venue. Now *that's* a marquee-event kind of place."

"I don't want to talk about the conference or why you're having a competition about Baton Rouge versus Philly."

"Then what are we supposed to talk about?"

"Nothing. I don't want to talk." Instead he cupped the back of my neck and let his thumb dance over my wild pulse. He bent and kissed me, and every sound stopped except for his soft exhale as he lifted his head. He watched me, gauging to see if I was okay with it. His hand stayed where it was, and since my hammering pulse was telling him everything I might want to deny, I didn't bother to try. I rested my hands on his chest, glad to feel his heart pounding as hard as mine, and tilted my head in an invitation. He leaned down for another kiss, longer this time, and impossibly, it was even better.

He straightened and laced his fingers through mine, guiding us back on the path to wander again.

When my pulse had calmed down, I heard a chorus of birds perched in the live oaks. "Want to hear a nerd confession?"

"Hit me," he said.

"I think bird watching would be cool."

He shook his head. "It will never be cool. But it might be fun. Making a mental note for our third date."

Third date. I didn't have the faintest desire to resist. "We're only an hour into this one, with four to go until church. I might have been ambitious. I'm not sure what else to do."

He grinned down at me, and I pinched him for the look in his eyes. "What was that for?" he asked.

"You know." I used my disapproving teacher voice.

"No, Teach. Spell it out for me."

"Y-o-u-b-e-h-a-v-e-y-o-u-r-s-e-l-f."

"Yes, ma'am. But to tell you the truth, I could do this all morning," he said, squeezing my hand.

"We'll probably do about seven hundred laps of the grounds. It's not that big."

"How do you feel about a Sunday drive?"

"Where?"

"Hey, I'm not in charge of this date."

"Then let's follow the river two hours one way and see where we end up before we have to turn back around."

"On one condition. Does your teaching credential certify you to tell me facts about the Mississippi River that I didn't get in eighth-grade history?"

"Yes."

"Then I'm in."

"What if I don't want to teach you about the Mississippi?"

"I was bluffing. I'll sit in your car for no reason at all."

I stopped in the middle of the sidewalk and grabbed hold of his collar to pull him down to kiss him. "You are unfairly good at this," I said when I let him go.

He stole a kiss back. "It's because I'm playing to win," he whispered against my lips.

Oh, man.

Chapter 14

"Where are we again?" Max asked.

"Natchez, Mississippi."

"I can't believe you took me across state lines."

"I regret nothing. Want to climb the levee?"

"As much as Cajuns want crawfish."

There was no fence separating the road from the upward slope of the levee, and it was an easy walk to the top.

We sat, and Max stretched his legs in front of him, leaning back to watch the river. "I remember when the levees broke during Hurricane Katrina. It was before we moved here, and I thought a levee was much different than what it is."

Most levees were earthen embankments built high so that it would be harder for the river to flood over them. "The ones in New Orleans are different. They're built out of concrete."

"We should do that for another field trip—go down there and check them out. I haven't been to New Orleans, and it sounds like a cool town."

"I'm surprised you didn't do that when your dad was mission president."

"We didn't travel with him on Sundays much, remember? He went with his APs, and Mom would bring us to your ward."

"Right. How could I forget that little black rain cloud in the middle of the chapel every Sunday?"

"I don't know why you're so mean to me." His eyes widened. "Wait. Yes, I do. It's because you had the biggest crush on me of all time back then."

I clapped my hands over my face and shut him out. "Shut up. We're never going to talk about that again."

He laughed and peeled away enough of my fingers that he could meet my eye. "The only crush bigger than yours was the one I had on you."

He let my fingers go and covered my face again. "You had a crush on me?"

"Going to have to look at me if you want an answer."

I peeked out at him. "Hey."

"Hi."

I cleared my throat. "So?"

"I was crazy about you, but it always seemed like I only drove you crazy. Then one day it seemed like you were feeling it too."

I let my hands drift down. "I was both. I loathed you and wanted you to like me all at the same time. It was confusing."

"Yeah. To put it mildly." But his smile was self-deprecating. "That's why—" He broke off with another wince.

"Why what?"

"You said not to bring it up. I'm going to respect that. I don't want to upset you."

"It's all right. Now that I teach high school, I know you were just being sixteen."

"I wasn't sixteen! Fifteen-and-a-half, actually. Fifteen is so much dumber than sixteen."

"Fair point. Fifteen isn't great for boys." I stared out at the river and sighed. "All right, I'm Sunday mellow. Hit me with whatever you want."

"When I asked you to dance, I never meant for it to end like it did."

I'd been so excited about that stake dance I'd been almost nauseated. What if no one asked me to dance? What if Max didn't? What if he did? It had been scary walking into the building, but I'd tried to remember Mom's advice: "If you're always dancing your heinie off during the fast numbers, everyone will assume you're dancing the slow ones too, even if you're not. But honestly, no one will be thinking about whether you're dancing or not except you."

I'd gone into that stake center prepared to dance like I was going for a gold medal in the sport of Whip Nae Nae, or whatever we were doing ten years ago. Max stayed against the wall with a couple of other boys in the teachers quorum who'd decided he wasn't so bad. A couple of times I'd caught him glancing my way, and I'd looked away and done an extra shimmy.

When the first slow song came on, boys who had been on the sidelines the entire time trickled onto the floor to ask girls to dance, but no one asked me.

I fled to the water fountain, pretending not to notice Max hanging out about five yards from the door. I didn't want him to see how much I wanted him to ask me to dance. I wasted more time until I was sure the slow song was over and went back into the gym, where Kate pounced on me. "Where'd you go?"

"Bathroom. No one asked me to dance."

She looped her arm through mine and dragged me out to the dance floor, shouting, "I'm asking you now!"

We danced until the next slow song played and two short guys came up and asked us to dance. My partner told me he and his friend were in a competition to get girls' phone numbers, and he wanted to get mine.

I thought I would feel flattered the first time someone asked me for my number, but being a statistic in someone's bet with a friend didn't sound so cool. I said, "No, thanks."

He shut up for a painful minute and then started talking about how many he'd gotten so far and how his older brother was the most popular guy at their high school and how he was going to pass him up.

I yanked my hands out of his. "I think it's pretty rude to ask for a number to win some dumb bet." I walked off the floor and waited for Kate.

"Good for you," she said when I told her what happened.

"This dance isn't what I thought it would be. Can we go home?"

"Because Max hasn't talked to you?"

He was talking to the guy I'd just danced with. "Max? No way. I don't care."

Kate told me I had to prove it and dragged me out to dance again. We got only three songs before the next slow one, and I didn't even have time to panic when Max appeared and asked me to dance. We kind of did the deacon shuffle, and a few silent seconds went by.

"So, this is your first dance, huh?"

"Yes."

"You like it?"

"Yeah." *He* was trying to talk to *me.* I relaxed a little.

"What do you like the best so far?"

Dancing with you, hands down. "The cookies. What about you?" *Say dancing with me.*

He didn't answer. Instead he leaned down a little. He had only about three inches on me back then. I moved a tiny bit closer to him, so tiny only I would notice I had done it, but I felt brave.

He pulled me in closer, letting go of my hand to hold my waist instead, fumbling where his hands met behind my back, like he couldn't figure out exactly what he was supposed to do with them.

We were doing "I like you style" dancing on our very first dance together! When the song ended, he let go and stepped back. "Thanks for the dance," he said with that smirk that used to drive me bad crazy. Suddenly it was crazy cute.

"You're welcome," I said, and he walked back to his friends, who were all grinning and fist-bumping him. I found Kate in the corner, and she grabbed my arms and squealed.

A couple of guys walked by and checked us out, elbowing each other and grinning. Kate smiled back, and they kept going. "I think this is one of those situations where you guys hated each other so much that you were doomed to fall in love," she announced.

A couple of girls walked past and giggled. One of them stopped and watched us, but the other girls pulled her along with them. I wanted to jump up and down, but I stayed cool. "So what do I do next?"

Her eyebrows rose when her older sister walked up to us. "What's up, Emery?"

"You have toilet paper hanging off you, Lila." Mortified I shot a glance down at my shoes, but there was nothing. "Not your shoes. Your waist."

I tried to peek over my shoulder, but I couldn't see anything. Kate whirled me around and squeaked. She tugged at my waistband and held up a four-foot-long piece of toilet paper in her hand.

I glanced over at Max, and he smirked again, not even breaking eye contact with me when one of his friends gave him a "good job" punch on the shoulder. I turned my back on him and everyone else who was laughing at me and stared at the accordion wall past Kate's shoulder, the one that separated the gym from the chapel, wishing I could slip past it into the quiet beyond.

"Why did he do that?" I asked.

"I don't know. Because he's Max," she growled, her fists balled.

"But I thought—" And my throat closed up, crowding in around the sob that would have come out next.

Kate had gotten permission from one of the chaperones for us to sit in the Primary room until the dance was over while she tried to cheer me up with a game of hangman on the chalkboard in which every answer was an insult about Max. I'd seen him when we'd joined the flow of people out to the parking lot, and it had made my stomach hurt. I'd never spoken to him again, and his dad had been released a few months later.

And now here I was, sitting on the bank of the Mississippi with the perpetrator whose prank had led to the boys in my ward making toilet-paper jokes about me until I'd graduated high school. Where other guys might call girls angels, they called me Angel Soft. Among other things.

Max's brow was furrowed, and I smiled at him. "If this was five years ago, I might be tempted to push you into the river," I said.

"I should probably throw myself in. I deserve it."

"Maybe back then you did. I've been over it for a few years, so we can move on."

"Could I explain something, and then we'll drop it forever?"

Mom's training to always be gracious asserted itself, and I smiled again. "Sure, explain."

"I thought you were being mean to my friend, and I decided to teach you a lesson." He winced. "I was such an idiot. I wanted to impress my buddies because I was starting to fit in with them, and I wanted their approval. As soon as I saw your face when you found the toilet paper, I wanted to rewind time and not do it."

"It's okay, Max. Like I said, I watch stuff like this play out between high school kids all the time. That's what it was—high school. Don't feel bad."

He turned and sat cross-legged so he was facing me. "You're kind of great."

I held out my arms for a hug. "Come on, then. Squeeze the Charmin."

He groaned and collapsed back on the grass. "I take it back. You're the worst."

I broke up laughing. "Well, worst or not, I'm your ride to church, so we better get on the road if we want to get there on time."

"Will you sit with me?" he asked, sitting up again.

"The ward will have us engaged by the end of sacrament meeting, and by the time I get home, my mom will have had five phone calls asking her when the wedding is."

"Is that so bad?" he asked. "To have people get all crazy with their speculation?"

I forced a smile, a "haha that's a funny joke you told" smile, and climbed to my feet, offering a hand to pull him up. "I try never to be the ward news," I said.

"Chicken. Let's go back and not face the music."

It was a slightly awkward moment, and I worried it would mean a long, awkward ride back to Baton Rouge, but it didn't. He made it fun, testing me on my Louisiana history and making up facts of his own.

I gave him a real one to counter his nonsense. "Here's an interesting fact: there are only a hundred cities in the whole state with populations greater than five thousand."

"So you're saying there are a lot of small towns to make up stories about?"

"I didn't think that's what I was saying, but now that you mention it, yes, I guess that's what I'm saying."

"Cool. Whoever makes up the best story about each town we drive through wins." He pointed to a sign for Morganza. "Have I ever told the story of how good ole Morganza got started?"

We laughed the whole way back. My side hurt by the time I pulled up to his apartment complex. We still had thirty minutes to spare before church, so that meant plenty of time for him to get his car and drive himself over. "Lila Mae," he said, when the car was in park. "Thank you for the best Sunday morning I've ever had. I'll see you at church?"

"See you at church."

When he climbed out of my car, it was the first I'd ever noticed that such a small car could feel empty with only me inside it.

Chapter 15

MAX DIDN'T COME FOR SUNDAY-NIGHT supper because he'd gotten an invitation to eat with some of his parents' old friends from their mission days. I tried not to be freaked out that it already felt odd for him not to be at our dinner table after church. It helped that Mom had invited the Lewises. Brother Lewis had deep, tired lines etched around his eyes and mouth. He was probably only a little older than my mom, maybe in his early fifties, but he looked as if he'd lived a lot harder in the handful of extra years that separated them. I guessed it was the difference between losing your spouse in an instant, like the way Daddy went out, versus nursing your spouse through a long, brutal illness.

I wanted to hug Brother Lewis and tell him it would be okay, but how would I know? I hadn't lost anyone the long way. And if my grief had taught me anything, it was that "It will be okay" was the wrong thing to say. Grieving people only resent hearing it. It would never be okay. It would only be something you learned to live with.

So over dishes, which Brother Lewis insisted on helping with, saying his wife would be ashamed of him if he didn't, I put an arm around his shoulders and gave him a light squeeze before picking up the rag to dry with. "I'm sorry it hurts so much. Would you tell me about Debbie? I knew her a little bit, but I'd like to know more."

Brother Lewis swallowed, and a small smile crept over his face. "Sure. Debbie was great. She ran a tight ship." And I listened while he told me all about her. Bridger was out in the work shed with Mom, who had invited him out to show him some of the birdhouses Daddy had made over the years. He'd gone from simple lines in the early birdhouses to some so beautiful and complicated that no bird could have figured out how to actually get inside one of them.

The Lewis's company made it easier to get over the fact that Max hadn't called or texted. Maybe he thought it was overkill after spending the whole morning together or something.

Monday he redeemed himself when I checked my phone between classes and found a text from him. *Much rather be driving to Natchez.* He'd followed that with a bomb emoji.

So work is going that well?

He answered with three more bombs, which made me laugh, and I started third period with an extra burst of energy. By bedtime I hadn't heard from him again, and I screenshot his morning text and sent it to Kate with a demand to explain what it meant.

He had a bad a.m. at work.

I rolled my eyes at her answer. *Thanks, Sherlock. I meant abt Natchez part.*

Long pause, then, *That Natchez is better than his work?*

I growled in frustration and called her. "I meant that he didn't say he wanted to be driving to Natchez with me, just that he wanted to drive to Natchez instead of work," I said when she answered. "What am I supposed to think about that?"

"I know what I think, which is that you have it for him so bad," she said, satisfaction oozing through the phone.

"I don't. He confuses me, that's all."

"Nope. You're analyzing his word choice in texts. Admit you're smitten, and go with it."

"I can't talk to you," I said and hung up the phone.

It lit up twenty seconds later with a text from her. *Hahaha. Love you.*

I flopped back on my bed and stared at the ceiling. Was she right? I'd been trained as a historian. I should know exactly how to look at the facts of a situation and understand what they pointed to.

Fact: A morning *without* a text from Max felt like my old early-morning seminary days. A morning *with* a text from Max felt like the last school bell before Christmas break.

Fact: A round-trip to Natchez with him had made me laugh harder than a week of Fallon episodes.

I texted Kate again. *He feels like a cold Dr. Pepper in July.*

Her answer was lightning fast. *You're toast.*

I pulled my pillow over my head and screamed. I totally was. Now to figure out how not to be the burnt kind.

* * *

When a wadded-up paper ball went flying across my classroom the next morning, I knew I had to snap out of it. I had a pretty good handle on my classes, but they were still kids who took a mile for every inch they were given, and my distractedness had given them a few inches today.

Max did not help when he texted me during my lunch break. *Do you want to grab some dinner tonight?*

YES. But I stayed strong. *Can't, sorry. Have to do a massive classroom makeover plus grading. Will be here forever.*

Got it. Raincheck?

Definitely.

As much as I hated saying no, it was for the best. Next time I saw him, I needed to know what I wanted from him. It was time to make some big decisions.

By dinner time, I was wondering if anyone ever outgrew their need for their mamas. As I stood on a table in the back of my classroom with a giant piece of butcher paper trying to attack me, I decided that I most likely never would because all I wanted to do at the moment was whip out my phone and beg her to come help me—help me with my bulletin board, help me with Max, help me with dinner.

The classroom door opened, and I heard a chuckle that was both too soft and too deep to come from any of my students. Something thumped down on a desk, and footsteps came to my rescue.

"Hey."

I recognized Max's voice, but the paper trying to eat my head blocked my view of him. "Max?"

"Tell me how to help."

"Could you climb up here and hold this paper up so I can staple it?"

The table jostled as he stepped onto it, and a few seconds later, he was smiling at me as he lifted the mutant butcher paper and pressed it to the wall.

I whacked it with the stapler.

"Way to show it who's boss."

"Small but mighty." I flexed a bicep. "Also, it's therapeutic. Try it."

He took the stapler and tacked his corner up with a grunt. "Yeah, I can see the therapy thing. Feels pretty good to do this a few dozen times, I bet."

I pounded a completely unnecessary staple right into the middle of the newly covered wall. Max hopped down and held up his hands to help me down too. I could have climbed down easily, but I let him swing me down, his hands on my waist guiding me to land directly in front of him. "Thank you."

"Sure." He didn't move his hands. "Hi."

"Hi."

"Hi." A slow grin overtook him. "You should probably let me go before I get the wrong idea," he said.

I gave a pointed look at *his* hands on either side of *my* waist.

"Right," he said, still not moving. "Hey."

I rose to my tiptoes and pressed a kiss against his mouth, a teasing brush against his lips, before I stepped out of his grasp and headed toward my desk at the other end of room. "What are you doing here so late? What are you doing here at all? And how did you find my classroom?"

He walked to the second desk from the door where he'd set down a duffel bag. "I decided it was my turn to do a picnic. The food is in here, which is not my gym bag, and you shouldn't be afraid to eat anything that comes out of it." He pulled out white paper bags with Raisin' Canes, my favorite chicken chain, printed on the side. "Also, finding your class was easy. The baseball team was coming off the field from practice, so I asked where your room was, and about five of them told me."

I groaned. "They're going to bust my chops tomorrow."

His forehead wrinkled. "Why?"

"You forget you're in a high school."

"Oh, right, the 'Miss Guidry has a boyfriend' thing." He sounded unconcerned as he worked on arranging our dinners.

But the word *boyfriend* embarrassed me, and I rushed to cover it up. "That's if I'm lucky. I mean, I'm not saying I'm lucky because you're my boyfriend." *Oh, help.* "And I'm not saying you're my boyfriend. I mean I'm lucky if that's all they say. Probably they'll be worse because they'll think it's funny."

Max had paused about halfway through that barrage to stare at me. "They might be right."

"Oh, kill me now. It's not going to bother you if I eat under my desk and don't make eye contact, right?"

He walked over and kissed me so thoroughly my knees buckled and I plopped onto my desk. It didn't break the kiss, and when he did straighten, he smiled at me. "Yes, I mind if you eat under there."

He guided me toward his picnic. I shouldn't have been doing any of this until we talked, but there had been something about watching Mom last night, her eyes twinkling as she'd talked to Bridger and Brother Lewis, about hearing her laugh a couple of times out on the deck as she and Bridger had fussed with the birdhouses. Life had stirred in her voice the same way life had begun to peek out in the yard, where buds were forming on azalea bushes, ready to break into a riot of color in a few short weeks. That feeling of life about to happen laced every molecule of the air between Max and me, and it had since Leonard's.

He made a table of two student desks, and each seat had a warm Styrofoam takeout box, thirty-two ounces of blessed caffeine, and a stack of napkins.

"Go ahead," he said, opening his own box and letting the smell of garlic and fried chicken fill the air. I opened my own and gave a happy gasp. "Texas toast and extra dipping sauce!"

"Of course extra sauce. Isn't the sauce the point of the chicken?"

I'd already dug in, so I only nodded. When I'd finished half of my tenders, I sat back to rest. "Is it possible that food you eat with your hands tastes better than fork food?"

"No, because you can't eat gumbo with your hands, so it can't be a fact."

"Good point."

"Ready for round two?" He reached into the duffel bag he'd set on the next desk and pulled out another to-go box. "I've eaten here before. I never underestimate how much I'm going to want."

It made me laugh, but that quickly changed to grabby hands when I realized he'd also brought more Texas toast. We talked about high school sports (he'd played soccer; I'd been more into theater) and whether we would go back if we could (not for any amount of money). When the food was finally gone, he jerked his head toward the bulletin board. "So have you been working on the walls all afternoon?"

I shook my head. "I had a batch of essays to work through. I've only been working on the wall for an hour, so I have a while to go."

"What's the bulletin board going to be?"

"I'm about to launch spring projects with my juniors. They're a massive deal, and I want to kick it off in style, get them excited about it."

"So we're going to do an epic bulletin board?"

I liked that he made it sound like spending hours on a bulletin board was totally reasonable. I loved that he used *we*. "If you want to jump on this crazy train, then yes, that's what we're going to do."

He rubbed his hands together. "Tell me the plan." I explained my vision for a giant smart phone screen where every app would correlate to a concept, event, or historic figure we'd be learning about, and his eyes grew wider. "I'm seriously impressed," he said. "I should have guessed after all your ideas for the YSA conference that you're insanely creative."

I leaned forward and plucked at the front of his shirt to pull him toward me. When our lips were nearly touching, I leaned the tiniest bit more until I could whisper in his ear, "Pinterest."

He planted a kiss on me.

"I can't think when you do that."

He kissed me again. "Then no more until this board is done."

I jumped up. "What are we waiting for?"

An hour and a half later, I was massaging a crick out of my neck and Max was rubbing his lower back, but we were doing it in front of an awesome cell phone full of apps the kids would be dying to explore, and I was fine with the pain for the payoff.

I pointed to a seat near our abandoned picnic setup. "That belongs to Kiana in first period. She keeps me up at night. But she's got an idea for her project that she can't let go of, and that's a beautiful thing to see. Maybe this board will spark a few more of those."

"What's her project about?"

"The first female millionaire in the US, who happened to be from Louisiana and who also happened to be black, which Kiana is."

"I didn't know that."

"Yes, Kiana is totally black."

"Ha ha," he said, nudging me with his foot. "I meant about the first female millionaire. How did she make her money?"

"Beauty supplies for other black women. Hair pomades especially. But the cool part is that she also focused on trying to make each of the women who sold her products successful too."

Worry crept across his face. "Uh, is this where you tell me you have a great business opportunity that can improve my life?"

I snorted. "Funny, Max. Wait, no. Not actually funny."

"It was."

"A little bit."

"I'll take it." He turned back to the board. "So how's she going to do her project?"

I sighed. "I don't know yet. She's still gathering information, but she hasn't had a breakthrough idea, and that's where I can't help her. It has to come from her so that she'll execute it with total passion. She's meant to be great. I can feel it."

"There you go being amazing again."

"I'm not. This isn't about me. She doesn't see her own potential. Every Sunday after I turned twelve, I stood up and said I had divine nature and individual worth. Nobody's telling her that, and if I tried, she'd give me her "okay, crazy white girl" look, but I've been trying to *show* her since August. I realized I was running out of time, and I have to make these last two months of school count, so I'm making her enter this big history competition to force her to step up her game. Achievement breeds self-esteem and all that. If she can tap into her natural grit and throw herself into this, she'll rock. I know it."

"You really love this, don't you?"

"No, I kind of hate doing bulletin boards."

"Funny," he said with a shoulder nudge. "Seriously, you must love coming here every day."

I glanced around at the classroom, the other walls covered in posters of some of my heroes, favorite quotes, examples of student work. Bookshelves lined the wall beneath the bank of windows, and bins sat on top of each shelf, overflowing with assignments that would take me hours to grade. Small bits of paper littered the floor around Kendyl Harris's desk, as usual, because she picked the ragged edges off her notebook paper and dropped them on the ground when she was bored in seventh period, and I always forgot to make her stop and pick them all up.

The classroom walls probably should have been repainted in the last couple of years, and scuff marks and sun fading marred different sections. But I smiled at all of it before I turned back to Max. I loved it so much it never left me. I carried these kids around with me wherever I went, the weight of their problems, the joy of their successes pressing on my mind or nestling in the corners of my heart, always. "I do. I love it."

"That's really cool."

His complete admiration was evident, but I only shrugged. I wasn't going to take credit for being a good human just because I was lucky enough to love my job.

I suddenly felt too awkward to meet his eyes. I reached over and smoothed down a corner of the bulletin board instead. "I'm trying to do right by these kids, that's all."

"You are. You matter. And they're going to love your board."

"All hail Pinterest."

He shook his head and pulled me close to him, leaning down to steal a kiss but faking right at the last minute to whisper "Pinterest" in my ear. I pinched his arm, and he stepped back with a laugh. "You mad, Lila Mae? Is it because you want me to kiss you for real?"

I grabbed his shirt and pulled him down for the kiss I wanted before he could tease me again, and when it wrung a small growl out of him, I smiled against his lips. "I win," I whispered.

He answered with another kiss.

When he let go, he took a step back and looked around the classroom like he needed to reorient himself. He gave his head a tiny shake. "Hey, sorry to be unsuave, but is there a bathroom nearby?"

I pointed the direction down the hallway. "Halfway down on the right."

"Be right back."

I picked up bits of paper from our decorating efforts, but the silence in the room was deeper than usual, and I stilled, trying to figure out why. The reflection in the wall of windows caught me, a vignette of me next to our dinner trash waiting to be thrown away. Two of everything.

That was it. Ever since my mission, I'd dreamed of what married life would be like: quiet nights at home, cooking together, or Saturday mornings sharing sections of *The Advocate*, arguing over who got the sports pages first. I'd pictured neighborhood walks and listening to my husband talk about work. I'd show him hilarious test answers or share my frustrations when I couldn't get through to a kid or brainstorm ideas for lessons. Those dreams had overtaken visions of wedding dresses and bridal bouquets a long time ago.

This feeling, these last two hours of being in it together, the ease, the way the work went faster—this was the dream. Warmth spread through my chest, and I knew a prompting when I felt one. I closed my eyes and sent up a quick prayer that I would understand what to do with this insight, and as I finished, Max walked back in.

"Hi," he said, pausing at whatever it was he saw in my expression. "Something changed. What's up?"

I took a deep breath. My mind had changed. My heart had changed. They'd changed a while ago, but I was only now accepting them. I'd never clearly seen the face of the guy in my daydreams, but looking at Max, I could see it now. "Nothing's wrong. I'm going to clean up this dinner mess."

He hurried over to help me, scooping up most of it before I even reached the desks.

"Thanks again for bringing this," I said, dropping a crumpled napkin into the trash. "So you love their food too?"

"Definitely. It takes a lot of willpower not to eat there every other night." He caught my skeptical look. "Fine, not to eat there every night."

"What about the rest of it?"

"The rest of what?"

"Everything. Your job. The city. Do you love those too?"

"Sure, it's been a good trip back."

A tightness crept into my chest. "*Trip* sounds really short-term. You've been here a few months already, and you could be here for a while longer."

"I mean, yeah. I could. It's hard to say. They move me when they think I've proven myself and they're ready to put me into a bigger office."

"So it could be a while," I pressed him. I needed it to be a while.

He shrugged. "Yeah." By now, he'd gathered up all the trash, and he stood still, watching me, his eyes scanning my face like they were looking for a hidden latch to a secret door.

"That's not really a trip. You're living here. In Baton Rouge. You live here," I repeated.

"That's what I meant."

"But you said trip."

Another shrug. "I didn't mean anything in particular."

"You meant that this is temporary."

He sighed and leaned on the desk behind him. "I never said it wasn't."

"I know." I knew it too well, but his words ate away at the warmth I'd felt moments before, termites that fed on happiness, stripping it down to nothing. "I guess I was hoping your perspective on being here had changed." *Like that you love it and you can't leave my city or me until we've figured us out.* I held those words back. Barely.

"Perspective is a funny thing. Baton Rouge is your whole world. This city will never have a better spokesperson. But if you had more experience outside of it, it wouldn't feel so much like the end of the line for you." He winced. "Wait. End of the line has a negative connotation, and I don't mean anything negative. I mean that I wonder how strongly you would feel about spending the rest of your life here if you had more time in other places."

"You think I only love it here because I haven't been to enough other places to know better?"

"No! I mean, yes, I mean those words but not in that tone."

"Did my tone sound condescending? Because that's how your words sounded."

"Are we about to have a fight?"

"That depends on if you're willing to walk back what you just said." I wasn't mad yet, but I could feel it coming on.

He scrubbed a hand through his hair. "When you have a chance to live outside of your hometown, you come back to it with new eyes. Sometimes you think it's as great as ever, and sometimes you decide it's not so great when you see what else is out there."

It was a punch in the stomach. "You're saying that Baton Rouge isn't that great compared to other places?"

"No! It's so much better than I let myself believe it was when I lived here. But here's an example: I was in this little village in Keliloha, and I met this kid named Haja. And he had no desire to live anywhere else but Keliloha, even though he didn't have much of anything there, including opportunities. It was what he knew, and it was enough. Then his mother got malaria and Doctors Without Borders arranged to have her transported to the city, which had an actual hospital where she could get the help she needed. But she was terrified and wouldn't go unless Haja went with her.

"They were there for three weeks, and as she got better, he got to explore. Suddenly his village was too small to hold him. For the next two years, he did everything he could to get admitted to the technical school, and a couple of months ago, he sent me an e-mail telling me he was about to get certified as an X-ray technician at the hospital and how happy he is in the bigger city of Madirovalo. But he'd thought he was happy in Keliloha until he saw more options."

"Basically you think if I went anywhere besides Baton Rouge, I'd change my mind about wanting to live here." It was unbelievable. Somehow the smug, arrogant boy I remembered from years ago had reappeared, even though his tone was kind and thoughtful. The underlying thinking was *so* messed up. "Here's the thing, Max. I served a mission. Did you know that?"

Surprise crossed his face. "I didn't. How come I didn't know that?"

"I don't know. Didn't come up, I guess. But I served in London, which is not a bad gig. I got to have a completely cosmopolitan experience there. And then I decided to do a study abroad in France for a semester because I knew the language and LSU sponsors a great program for history majors there. So I spent time in Paris and in the countryside, and I got that whole experience. So basically, I lived in Europe for two years. Then, on top of that, I've gone on two Habitat for Humanity trips, one to Haiti and one to Columbia for a month each. I've truly and fully experienced the world, Max. I loved all of it, but all it did was deepen my appreciation for what I have here." I wrestled a desk back into place so it faced the front again. "Thanks for helping me tonight. It's probably time for me to get home. I need to check on my mom."

"Wait, Lila. I'm sorry."

"It's okay."

"No, I mean it. I'm sorry. I was being insensitive."

"It's fine. There's nothing to apologize for." It would be like making him apologize for being who he was. His whole Haja story showed that he was more of his teenage Max-self at his core than I had realized, the guy who still believed Baton Rouge was a backwater, just less of a backwater than the rest of the state. But it was a backwater I was never going to leave.

The warmth in my chest was long gone, replaced by tight, prickly misery. How had I read that so wrong? I had talked myself into believing I'd had a spiritual prompting because I liked Max so much. But I loved Mom too much to ever leave her, to rip my roots out of the soil and walk away. So what was I going to do with these feelings for Max when he saw no place here for himself to grow?

Chapter 16

I WENT TO BED MISERABLE, even after a long prayer to try to figure out what I was supposed to be doing. I kept thinking, *It will work out.* Obviously I needed to sign up for meditation classes; maybe if I learned to block out the voice in my head telling me what I wanted to hear over and over again, I could hear what it was that God wanted for me.

I woke up exhausted after a long dream about failing to make red beans and rice. I had always thought that was a dish I could make in my sleep: nope. In my dream, I'd been soaking the beans, but no matter how often I checked them, they were never ready to cook. It was one of the dumber stress dreams I'd had.

Work started off rough too. Jarrod Cole laid into me as soon as he walked into the classroom. "Miss Guidry has a boyfriend, y'all. I saw him trying to find her last night."

"Was he fine?" Keisha Brown called from the back of the room.

"I don't pay attention to that," Jarrod said, looking offended. "He look rich though, like he got on some high-dollar suit pants and Sunday shoes."

The kids all catcalled, and Keisha hollered, "Yeah, Miss Guidry, reeling in her sugar daddy!"

"Stop with that mess," Kiana said. She had her eye on me, not Keisha, and she must have seen the thunder brewing in my expression. "You really think Miss Guidry is going to date some fool because he got pricey shoes? Maybe you, Keisha, but not her."

That earned a chorus of "Ooohs" and "Burn!"

"Yeah, you right," Keisha said. "I like a man that look good."

"I look good, baby," Jamarcus called.

"You wish you did," Keisha said, to laughter.

"I'm serious, Keisha," Kiana said, not looking like she found any of it funny. "Don't you think any guy coming around Miss Guidry is going to be lucky if she gives him the time of day?"

"Truth!" Keisha's best friend Georgia said. "That's the truth."

A half dozen shouts of "Amen!" and "Word!" followed, and I winked at Kiana for turning my morning around. "Two-point bonus on the next test," I said, and she smothered a grin before she busied herself looking for something in a binder.

Ten minutes before lunch, my classroom door opened, and a city marched through it.

No, really.

A scale model of Baton Rouge on a piece of wood about four feet wide was coming through the door at an angle. I couldn't see who was carrying it over the tall buildings of downtown Baton Rouge, but I recognized the shoes Jarrod had mentioned. The city floated toward me, and I moved out of Max's way as he set it on my desk. His face was flushed, and he had to wipe some sweat from his forehead when he straightened.

"Who's that, Miss Guidry?" at least twelve kids said on top of each other.

"This is Mr. Archer. Um, why are you here, Mr. Archer?"

"I wanted to see you," he said, setting off a flood of catcalls.

"Y'all, he doesn't even like Baton Rouge," I told the class. "He's probably here to set that thing on fire." I examined it more closely. It was a professional-looking model, except for the homemade construction paper flags on toothpicks stuck in different spots. One flew at the state ‘capitol, one at the riverboat dock . . . Wait a minute.

"I don't hate Baton Rouge," he said. "This is my proof. Is it okay if I steal a few minutes to offer a review of some modern city history here in your history class?"

I gave him a "have at it" wave and took an empty seat in the third row, my arms folded while I waited to see what he was up to. It wasn't like I was going to be able to get the class to focus even if I kicked him out now. Also, I was dying to know.

"I'm learning to like Baton Rouge a lot. For example," he said, pointing to a flag, "this is a place by my house that has the best boudin balls. I don't get boudin where I'm from. And here," he said, pointing to a flag that looked like it was on the Shenandoah lakes, about right where my parents' house would be, "is where I almost kissed my first girl."

More catcalls sounded, and my face lit on fire. He meant me, but he meant the night under the dinghy when the lightning bugs had woven a spell around us. He wasn't done. "Here is where I learned that your city's history is as long and as rich as my city's history"—pointing to the state capitol—"and here is where I figured out that Baton Rouge high school football is way more fun than Philly high school football." That flag was University Academy. He pointed out other flags, including places where he'd discovered a favorite milkshake or fishing spot.

The kids seemed to like it, but when the bell rang, one of the boys stopped by the model and squinted. "That was better than taking notes, dude, but it didn't exactly sound like history." And he walked out.

I waited until the kids had all left before I shut the door so my students would know I wasn't available for lunch. "Where'd you get this?" I asked, walking over to peer at it more closely.

"Hey." He slid his hands into his pockets and waited.

"Hey."

"Sorry I interrupted your class. I tried to time it so I would be here for lunch, but I was afraid if I didn't get here before the bell, this thing would get bumped by giant high schoolers stampeding for food, and it's on loan."

"Who has a giant model of Baton Rouge lying around?"

"An architectural firm, for one." He rested his hands on my shoulders and pulled me toward him enough to drop a light kiss on my forehead. "I'm sorry. Forgive me?"

"Yeah. To be honest, I was putty by the time you got to the first-kiss flag." I stepped back, aware that kids might come gawking through the window at any moment.

His hands disappeared into his pocket again, and he glanced back at our cell phone display. "How did the kids like it? I was bummed they weren't all staring at it when I walked in."

"They might have been if you hadn't been carrying a city when you showed up."

"Good point. Still disappointed."

I smiled. "They loved it, actually. We spent the first half of class talking about it. I think most of them aren't dreading their projects now."

"So mission accomplished?"

"That bulletin board is so yesterday. Let's talk about today. Why are you here with Baton Rouge? You said you were sorry last night. I appreciated it. And I'm not mad at you."

"But you seemed mad, and I would be too if I were you. I want to make it right."

I had to give him another smile. "By bringing me a city?"

"I couldn't sleep last night. I knew I blew it. Bad. So I got up and Googled architectural firms and sent e-mails to several of them asking if any of them had anything like this. I told them it was vitally important—"

"Vitally, huh?"

"Yes, vitally. And I attached a résumé plus a bunch of Internet links to prove I'm a trustworthy guy, and I offered to pay a big deposit if they would let me pick this up and borrow it until the afternoon."

"And someone went for that? Called you up and said, 'Hey, come get this super expensive city model off of our hands for a few hours based on the strength of your résumé'?"

"It may have involved a little more than that."

I thought I'd seen Max looking uncomfortable on the banks of the Mississippi in Natchez when we had talked about the dance, but now he was squirming.

"This I have to hear."

"Maybe another time. It's not really the point now. What *is* the point is that I want you to know I'm sorry. I like you. A lot. I think about you constantly. I want to be with you all the time. I don't want to be the reason you're upset or angry, ever. I want to know how to make this up to you so you won't be mad at me."

I melted and ached at the same time, and that seemed the best way to describe what trying to be with Max was like. "I'm not mad at you, Max. I'm mad at myself."

He took one of my hands, brushing his thumb across my knuckles. "Don't be. I'll take on anyone who's mad at you, including yourself."

I turned my hand over to tangle my fingers with his, aching all the more that it was so easy to do, to wrap up bits of myself in him. "I'm mad at myself because I like you too, and I don't know why." That won a laugh out of him, and I squeezed his hand. "I didn't mean it like that. You are so worth liking. But you're also leaving sooner than later. And so this makes no sense," I said, nodding at our clasped hands before I slid mine out of his.

"I want to talk about this, but I don't want to make it awkward for you with your next class too. Plus, I stayed home from work all morning to put those flags on, and I need to return the model and check in at my office. Can I come over later? Or tomorrow, maybe? I'm going to have to work late tonight to make up for being out all morning."

"I don't know."

"Lila Mae, please don't make me call your mother and tell her that I want to come over and you won't let me."

I burst out laughing. "That's playing dirty."

He stood there with a half smile that said he was only half joking.

I rubbed my forehead, still smiling. "Okay. But not tomorrow. Just come for Sunday dinner, okay?"

"What about conference sites. We still have more to check out, right?"

"Do we?" I asked.

"We're doing the boat, aren't we?"

"Yeah."

"It's a good call, even if it means I can't talk you into going anywhere before Sunday. I can live with that, if that's what you need. But why don't you let me handle booking it so I can free up more of your brain cells to think about us."

"Max . . ."

He winced at my tone. "I know you're thinking about all the reasons why we can't work. Will you try thinking about the reasons we can? This is too important not to give both sides equal weight."

I hesitated but nodded. It felt like agreeing to go to the Cheesecake Factory in the middle of a three-day fast, but he was right. It was important enough to be sure about this that I'd let myself imagine a relationship with him working out.

He sighed, and if I'd had it on video, I could have turned him into a gif of pure relief. "Good." He grinned. "I can work with that. And now I'm going to get Baton Rouge back into my car before the halls fill up again."

I held the classroom door open while he maneuvered it out like he was handling a live bomb. He paused in the hall to look back over his shoulder. "I won't drop by until Sunday, but you're still going to hear from me."

"Maybe I won't answer."

"Doesn't matter. Unless you tell me to go away, I won't." He headed down the hall, drawing curious glances from the few kids who had trickled back in from lunch early.

I sank back down in my chair, staring at my new bulletin-board display. How on earth had he sweet-talked his way into borrowing an entire city? He had some mad persuasion skills.

Then again, I already knew that.

* * *

I couldn't decide if the number of times Max kept popping into my head was a blessing or a curse, but by Friday afternoon, I decided it was a blessing. Kiana had been particularly difficult in first period, no better behaved when I made her come in for lunch, and as I eyed the clock twenty minutes after the last bell, it looked as if she'd bailed on coming in after school like I'd requested.

I was shoving another pile of essays to grade into my school bag when I heard a cough and looked up to find Kiana standing there, her face closed off, an air of waiting surrounding her.

"Let's sit," I said, heading toward her desk. When she was in trouble, she sat in front of my desk to talk. When we were talking but she wasn't in trouble, we sat near hers. I hoped it would help her let her defenses down some. She took her usual seat, but everything about her was an inward curve, from slumped shoulders to her tipped-down chin.

"What's going on, Kiana?" It was the same question I'd asked her at lunch after I had called her in for mouthing off to me twice during class. She'd only answered me with a mumbled, "Nothin'." This time she sighed, but she still said nothing. "Kiana? Talk to me." It was a request, as gentle as I could make it, and her chin rose a fraction.

"Is your mom back?"

Her shoulders tensed.

"Is she coming around more than usual?"

"I can't hardly get a break from her now." It was a spew of frustration. "Twenty-three hours a day she act like she the kid, but the other hour she keeps trying to step into what I already got going, and it messes everything up."

"That sounds hard." The words were cheap Band-Aids for a deep wound.

She shrank smaller, like her confession had occupied a space that was collapsing in on itself now that she had pushed it out. "That's not even all of it. Mama is a pothole. I got sinkholes to deal with too."

"This is exactly why I gave you Madame CJ for your project."

She glanced at me, her eyes too tired to be angry. "I know, so I can win and rise above this all. Ain't going to happen."

"No, not so you could win. So you can see what's possible. Have you been reading up on her some more? Found anything new? Thought of what you want to do for your project?"

With a sigh so deep it was almost a groan, she straightened. "Am I in trouble?"

"That's not what this is about—"

"Then I need to go," she said, standing up. I scrambled to my feet too. "Look, Miss Guidry. You're nice, but you have no idea. Madame CJ did her thing so long ago it's like a fairy tale. This is my real life. And this ain't no fairy tale. Or if it is, it's the part at the beginning, where everything is wrong for the princess, only in this one, that's just how the story stays. It don't go anywhere after that. You don't get it. That's not your fault, I guess. But quit thinking you can save me from something you don't understand. You ain't lived it. You can't even imagine it. Reading some articles about some lady doesn't cure anything. Not one thing. See you tomorrow," she said, heading toward the door.

"Wait!"

She paused, and I stood there for a few seconds trying to think of how to make her want to stay, make her want to talk. "My brothers are going to be waiting for me."

"Okay." I hurried over to my desk and pulled out a few protein bars. "Because I don't know what else to do."

"I'll eat them," she said, taking them. "Because I don't know what else to do either."

And she disappeared into the hall.

* * *

Kiana and Max fought a turf war over my brain space all day Saturday. I couldn't tell who was winning. I only knew for sure who the loser was: me. Anytime Kiana had the stage, all my stress hormones went into overdrive, and I kept trying to think of how to help her. I wasn't naive enough to think that building her self-worth would solve all her problems. Winning a Kiwanis Club contest wasn't going to help her when her mom was weaving down the hallway high and angry, trying to parent when she couldn't form a sentence. But winning it could be a foundation at least. It could be a bright spot.

Maybe.

She was right about my ignorance. What did I know, really? I knew some facts about her life. I didn't have even the slightest idea of what it felt like to be her. I'd grown up across the city but a world away. I'd been a debutante, for pity's sake. That was a far cry from living with a meth-head mother. But the only instinct I had was to try to get Kiana to see herself like I saw her.

When Max had the stage, my hormones went into overdrive too but not so much the stress ones. My mind ran down two tracks: *I want to kiss his face* and *What am I doing with him?* There were a hundred reasons someone would date him as long as that someone didn't need to stay near her mother.

But there was his smile to consider, the half one he gave when he was being mischievous, the slightly different one that appeared when he was thinking about something he liked, and the big, unreserved one that he broke out like it was the most natural way for his face to rest. It was funny that I'd assumed he was still his old surly self for the first few weeks after he'd moved back, but I could see right through that now. That was his uncomfortable face, and I regretted the weeks he'd had to sit at church feeling out of place.

There were other things to consider: his work ethic, for one. You didn't grow up in Jim and Hattie Guidry's house without a deep appreciation for hard workers. Daddy would have liked Max. Hard work was a part of him.

I couldn't overlook the melty thing that happened to me around him, the way my hands suddenly turned fluttery and my whole body buzzed with energy that couldn't find an outlet. Maybe that explained the electricity that danced along my skin wherever he happened to touch it. If I had to stand blindfolded in front of a hundred people and they could each touch me only on my shoulder for a half second, I would still know his touch because I would feel it like a heartbeat, a tiny throb wherever he made contact.

There was the kissing. He was so good at it.

And there was so much more. He showed up to church every Sunday and listened. He loved his family. He had good manners and was courteous to Mom. And even though he'd gone way off target with the whole "telling me to experience the world" thing, in every other way he'd been pretty thoughtful.

He was without doubt a good man. Such a good man.

And a good-looking one too.

Aargh.

He doesn't want to be here, I reminded the part of my brain that had wandered into another daydream of cooking a Saturday-morning breakfast with him while he made smiley face pancakes for a child I could almost imagine.

I erased the mental picture of Saturday-morning domestic bliss to go have real Saturday-morning breakfast with Mom downstairs. Mom, who was here now and needed me now.

I washed my hands so I could help her finish chopping veggies for omelets. She blinked at me and went back to chopping onions, but her gaze wandered to the window and out into the distance, and I knew she was lost in her own memories of Saturday mornings past with Daddy.

I wished they didn't hurt her, but I didn't know how to make it better. I wanted love like that, love so deep it could almost break you. Daddy had anchored her. She would be okay at some point. She was doing better than she had been for a long time. But even the sadness was a witness to how deeply they had been connected to each other.

"Mom? Max is coming for dinner tomorrow."

She blinked and cleared her throat. "Good. I like him, Lila Mae."

"I do too."

"You figured that out finally?"

"What do you mean, 'finally'? He's only been coming around for a couple of weeks."

"You've been gone on that boy since junior high, sweetheart."

"You knew?" I guess that was no surprise.

"Of course."

"Okay, I was gone on him then. But it's not like I've been pining for him the last ten years. I was pretty over it with the Princess Charmin thing. And he's barely been back. For sure not long enough to figure anything out."

"What's to figure?"

"Everything. If I should even date him."

"Yes."

"It's not that easy. We want very different things out of life."

"Does he want a family?"

"Yes."

"Then there's nothing to figure out. You're on the same page. The rest is details."

"But they're not shrimpy details, Mom. They're huge lobster details."

"Still details. It all works out."

I wanted to tell her how insurmountable the biggest detail of all was, that being with him meant not being with her. It meant leaving her with no one in her house, with one more separation, with one less person to pour her energy into. But I didn't want to add a layer of worry when she carried so much already, so I said nothing and glanced out the window. It was gray today, but it hadn't rained yet. "Would it make you too sad if we went and worked out in the yard? I think the pavers down to the lake could use some weeding." Sometimes it helped. Sometimes it made the fog thicker. She'd loved puttering out there with Daddy.

"I'd like that."

We finished making the omelets, and I told her about Kiana and not being sure how to help her.

It got me classic Hattie Guidry advice. "I don't want to tell you what to do, honey, except to love her and keep feeding her as much as she'll let you."

After breakfast, we spent a few hours weeding and telling stories about Daddy. A couple of times she teared up, but they were happy tears, and I think overall she missed him less because he had filled the afternoon.

I graded for a while, and she worked on her magnolia while we watched a house-flipping marathon on the home-improvement channel. I swear that TV was on for LSU games and HGTV and nothing else. At nine she went to bed, and I watched her go, sorry to see that her tiredness had given way to sadness again.

I was more certain than ever of one thing: she needed me here, and it didn't matter how much I wanted to be with Max. He was never going to need me like this. They were two objects trying to occupy the same space in my life, and only one of them could fit.

I wish I knew the right way to tell Max it couldn't be him.

Chapter 17

MAX TEXTED SUNDAY MORNING TO say he was going to another ward but he was looking forward to dinner. He couldn't have planned a more effective way to key up my anticipation to see him. Mom kept sending me knowing glances while we worked on supper together, me chopping a salad and her making biscuits. She had to repeat things two or three times, questions about how my day had gone or requests for tools out of the kitchen caddy on my side of the counter.

"As your grandfather would have said, you're as jumpy as a sinner in church. This is about Max, I'm sure."

I rolled my eyes, but she only smiled, and when the doorbell rang twenty minutes later and I jumped, she flat out laughed. "Why don't you go get it?"

I did, tugging down my fitted purple cardigan and wishing I had some wedge heels by the door to slide into before I answered it. The idea of arming myself with a few extra inches to face Max made me feel better. Too late now. I opened the door and stepped back in surprise when I found Brother Lewis and Bridger on my porch instead. Brother Lewis held a foil-covered lump in his hands.

"Hello," I said.

They were still dressed in church clothes. Brother Lewis cleared his throat. "Is Hattie here?"

"She is. Come on in." They stepped into the foyer and stayed put. "Let me go get her for you." I walked back to the kitchen. "Mom? The Lewises are here."

"What in the world?" She wiped her hands on her apron and hurried out to greet them. I followed her but only so I could go upstairs to grab a pair of wedges.

"Hey, y'all. What brings you by?"

Bridger studied the floor, and I swear it looked like he was trying not to smile, but it was his dad who answered. "You're on our new home teaching route. We thought we'd stop by and bring you a little something to make it official."

At dinner time? Hmm. I paused on the stairs and ducked down to watch. Brother Lewis handed Mom the loaf. "It's banana bread. We made it. It's dark. Sorry."

Mom took it liked he'd served it up on a silver platter. "Bless your hearts, you didn't have to do that."

Uh-huh, especially not at supper time. It was hard not to laugh.

"Hope we didn't come at a bad time," Brother Lewis said, sniffing the air. "Smells like we might have caught you right before supper."

"Perfect timing. I was telling Bridger's class today that I was making some smothered chicken tonight. Y'all stay and have some."

Ohhhhh. Now it was becoming clear. Showing up here at supper time was well-played. Good for Bridger. He was still looking too skinny. He needed some of Mom's cooking.

I scuttled the rest of the way up the stairs to put my shoes on and made it back down as the doorbell rang again, and this time it was Max. Even though I was braced to see him, when he smiled at me, I had to grip the doorknob for balance.

"Hey," I said.

"Hey." He leaned down and kissed me. "I should probably apologize for doing that. I'm not going to."

I stepped out of the way and waved him through. "Come on in." I followed him to the kitchen, introducing him to the Lewises, who were already seated at the kitchen table. The timer went off, and like we'd done a million times, without a word, Mom swept over to the oven to pull the biscuits out, and I grabbed the salad bowl and brought it to the table. Max went straight to the cupboards to set two more places.

"Coleman, would you bless the food for us?" Mom asked.

He said a short blessing, and within minutes, Mom was drowning in a flood of compliments for the chicken. It was especially nice to see Brother Lewis digging in, obviously really happy with the food. I wondered how long it had been since he'd been able to take joy from a simple pleasure like this. Probably a long time, but it didn't surprise me that Mom's chicken would do the trick.

After dinner, the men jumped up to handle the dishes and shooed us out to the living room. "I don't like this," Mom protested. "I'm going to have to come in and rearrange whatever it is you do."

"You won't, Sister Guidry," Max said. "I've been paying attention. I know where everything goes."

"All right," she said as I pulled her toward the living room. I sat her down in her arm chair and plucked her embroidery from her basket to set on her lap.

"Do that, Mom. Try to take it easy."

She winced a couple of times when she heard the dishes clink, but she stayed put. I mostly sat and stared into space.

"Mom? Tell Max I'm upstairs for a minute if he comes out." She nodded, keeping her eyes on her magnolia. In my room, I switched to shoes better suited for walking by the lake and made a stop by the side of my bed to send up a short but utterly sincere prayer. *Please, give me the strength to walk away.*

I went back downstairs, and uneasiness roiled in my stomach, making me wish I'd eaten less. I never liked these conversations, no matter which side of them I was on.

Max was bent over Mom's needlepoint as she explained what she was doing.

"Beautiful," he said, looking up and smiling at me.

"Thanks," I said, offering him a weak return smile.

His gaze sharpened, but instead of looking worried, his half smile appeared. "Would you be up for a walk down to the dock?" he asked.

"Sure."

As we crossed the backyard, he complimented the freshly groomed stone path. "Your mom said you guys worked on this yesterday. It looks great."

"Thanks."

"So you're a great teacher *and* a great daughter," he said, sliding his hand around mine like he'd been doing it forever. The fact that it felt so easy and right only made my stomachache worse. "Is there anything you can't do well?"

"I can't sing, I guess. Other than that, I've pretty much got it all."

"I believe you." He dropped a kiss on top of my head.

I should have slid my hand right back out of his, put distance between us, but we only had about a ten-minute walk to the pier, and then we'd sit and talk, and that would unravel everything, and we would never hold hands again, so I gave myself that last ten minutes.

He didn't say much, commenting on a scent or a sound every now and then, squeezing my hand when we heard a bird call he liked and I'd tell him what it was. That was about it.

It was so unfair that the very first boy who had ever made me imagine the possibility of romance, on the edges of this very lake, was the one I was going to have to break up with as soon as we reached the dock.

Too soon, we were there, and we slid our shoes off to dangle our feet in the water. I leaned back and listened to the frogs, out in full force in the warm spring night.

"You've been pretty quiet," he said, his voice so mellow it barely created a ripple in the mood. "Are you sorry you agreed to this talk?"

"Yes and no. I don't want to have it, but I know it needs to happen."

"You don't want to have it," he repeated, his tone thoughtful. "Maybe you should go first."

I settled my hands in my lap and stared down at them, white frog bellies twitching against my leg. Where was I supposed to start? I didn't know. I jumped to the end. "I don't think we should see each other anymore."

He nodded. "Okay."

"You're fine with that?"

"Oh, no, I disagree with you. That was an, 'Okay, I hear you.' And then I was going to think."

"About what? I just broke up with you."

A bummed-out expression clouded his face. The acting was about as good as when athletes did TV commercials. "Wait, you broke up with me? You mean you were my girlfriend for a while and I missed it? Man, I miss all the good stuff."

"Oh my gosh, stop. I didn't mean it like that."

"Then how did you mean it?"

"I mean that I'll keep working with you on the conference, but you should stop coming over for Sunday dinner and showing up at my classroom, stuff like that."

He nodded again. It was rhythmic, like it helped him think or something. When he stopped, he said, "Why?"

"For the millionth time, dating doesn't make any sense."

"Dating has never made sense to anyone. That's not a reason."

"Of course dating makes sense. You find someone you like, and you spend time doing things together, seeing each other in different situations so you know if you're compatible or not. Dating doesn't make sense for *us*. Like, none."

"Sure, if that's what dating is. But that's not what dating is. Dating is when I like you and you like me and we go do stuff together that we like, or even might like. And why shouldn't we do that?"

"You're being difficult."

"Yeah."

I shot him an annoyed look.

"What? Like I'm going to make it easy for you to dump me? No, ma'am."

"The longer we keep pretending we can work out, the worse it's going to hurt when we have to admit we can't. Why do this?"

"Hold still," he said. "You have an eyelash on your cheek." He leaned closer to look at it, and just like that he was kissing me again, sliding his fingers through my hair. I returned the kiss, murmuring a protest when he lifted his mouth from mine, but it was only so he could brush a kiss against my jawline, my neck, and below my ear in a spot I decided was now my favorite. He brought his lips back to mine, deepening the kiss the tiniest bit before leaning back. "That's why."

I stared out at the water. I had no answer to that.

"I know we haven't had deep spiritual conversations, and this isn't something I would normally ever think is any of my business, but is us not dating an answer to a prayer?"

"Are you asking me if I prayed about dating you? Yes." I was glad the falling dusk hid the heat in my cheeks. This conversation felt even more personal than the kissing had. "I'm not supposed to do it. I'm sorry. I wish I'd gotten a different answer."

He scrubbed a hand through his hair, a short staccato movement and the first evidence that he was growing frustrated. "I'm not mad at you. I'm confused, I guess. I asked too, and my answer was different. It means one of us heard what we wanted to hear, and I'm worried it's me."

"You prayed about whether we should be dating, and He said yes?" I asked, pointing up.

"Yeah. It was pretty clear, actually." Now he really did look confused. "What did you ask Him?"

It was a surreal conversation. I'd never prayed about any of my previous relationships, much less discussed any kind of personal revelation with them. But it didn't make sense to me either that we'd gotten different answers, so I told him. "I asked for the strength to walk away even though I don't want to."

"Oh." He was quiet for a minute. "And you got a spiritual confirmation?"

"Yeah."

"Like a thought in your head or a feeling? I'm not trying to be a nosy, I swear. I'm just trying to understand since I'm the one getting dumped."

"It was more like a feeling. Like as soon as I stood up, I felt kind of sick to my stomach."

He looked at me, confused. "How did you know that meant we were supposed to break up?"

"Because I really don't want to. And the fact that I felt so bad about it right away meant that . . ." I trailed off. It had been really clear in my head before I'd come downstairs. "If I wasn't supposed to break up with you, I would have felt happy because it would have meant I didn't have to. So the fact that I felt bad meant that's what needs to happen."

"I don't get it."

"It makes sense to me," I said, not sure if it really did anymore.

"Maybe we got different answers because we asked different questions. And I hate to even say this the way I'm about to say it because I don't want to say I'm getting the answers to questions for you or anything ridiculous like that, or that I do a better job of asking God questions, but—"

"Just say it," I said. "I promise not to take offense."

He rubbed his bottom lip a few times. "Here goes. It sounds like you told God what you wanted to do, then asked Him to help you do it. Did you ask Him what He wants you to do?"

I clenched my fists. "I don't have to ask everything. Sometimes it's obvious. This was a situation where I only needed to ask for the perseverance to stick with the clear choice."

"You promised not to take offense," he said. If his voice hadn't been so full of stress, I might have stormed off the pier.

I took a calming breath. "Sorry. To answer your question, there didn't seem to be a point to asking when I knew the answer. How did you ask Him?"

"I asked if this was the relationship He wants me in right now. He said yes."

"Like with words?"

"No. A feeling. But a clear one. Easy to understand."

"How is that even possible? We have no idea when you're going to get transferred out of here, and once you're gone, that's it. I'm staying here. You're not. The longer we're together before that, the more tangled up in each other we'll be. I think that's the actual definition of being too attached: all caught up in one another's strings."

"What if we did this as a no-strings-attached? Why don't you ask Him if he wants you to date me? And if He says yes, why not have a little faith that it'll all work out?"

"What if it doesn't?"

"I don't know," he said. "I decided not to worry about that when I got my answer."

I drew my feet up out of the water and wrapped my arms around my legs to make a comfortable perch to rest my chin on. "It's like you said though. I didn't ask the same question, so I do have a ton of worry." My voice was low, but he heard me and answered anyway.

"Would you ask? I don't know how this is supposed to work out, or even if it will work out, but I'm pretty sure either way we're going to learn something valuable from it. Maybe this isn't about getting married. Maybe this is about spending time together right now. Maybe it's about a lot more, but I figure if it is, we're not going to have to figure it out on our own."

He'd said marriage. He'd thought about it, then. Maybe that was normal for guys the way it was for girls. Mormon ones, anyway. It made me feel better to know it wasn't a factor only for me.

I closed my eyes and shut out the sound of the lake lapping against the dock, closed out the bright moonlight, and said a prayer even quicker and more heartfelt than the one in my room had been. *Should I be in a relationship with Max? Is this the right thing?*

I opened my eyes and peered down the lakeshore to the point where it curved around and disappeared into the darkness. There were no pangs in my stomach, no ugly pits. Instead, I felt an easy kind of quiet. Was this because I was giving myself what I wanted now?

"Lila? You mad?"

I lifted my head and turned back to him, leaning over to press a soft kiss against his lips. "You win."

"You'll ask?"

I shook my head. "I already did."

Max whooped and jumped to his feet, splashing slightly as his legs came flying out of the water. "Woo-hoo! *Yes!*" He did some kind of touchdown victory dance. "When can I take you out again?"

"Like my pawpaw used to say, in for a penny, in for a pound. Whenever you want. Other than nights where I have to grade until my brains fall out, my schedule is pretty open."

"Tuesday. We'll do something Tuesday."

He pulled me to my feet, and I wrapped my arms around his waist and peered up at him, tilting my chin so it would be easy for him to steal a kiss. "I kind of think you'd do your best convincing if you stayed out here with me for a little while."

"Lila Mae, I like the way you think."

Chapter 18

WITHIN A WEEK, THE GUIDRY house looked nothing like it had for the last two years. Where Mom and I had rattled around it alone, unable to fill up the silence on our own, now it was full of voices. It started with the Lewises showing up Monday night because Mom had invited them over for family home evening. She rushed around making pecan fudge for the treat afterward, her cheeks flushed and eyes bright.

I invited Max over, and we ended up with a sweet lesson from Brother Lewis about granting grace to others, followed by a boisterous game of Bananagrams, mainly because Brother Lewis played it like it was Balderdash, clearly making up words and then defending them straight-faced. It only got worse when Max copied his strategy. Mom hadn't laughed like that since Daddy died.

Max and I went out to dinner Tuesday night, and we ended up spending Thursday evening at my house watching back-to-back episodes of *Sherlock* and Friday night at his apartment, where he made me breakfast for dinner and then we watched a Sixers game on TV. It galled me to cheer for them, but they weren't playing the Pelicans, so I didn't feel like too much of a traitor.

Saturday was Jaimie Graceley's bridal shower. It was the first time in a long time I hadn't dreaded one of these things, mainly because I'd been too busy with Max all week to think about how much I didn't want to go. Plus, I'd get to hang out with Kate. I showed up early to help, and Jaimie squealed when I walked in. "Lila! I heard a secret about you. A good one!"

I did a quick sort through my brain to see what she might have heard but came up with nothing. "Tell me. I need some good secrets about myself."

"Don't act like you don't know. You and Max Archer are a *thing* now."

Uh-oh. "We're a *thing* now? What does that mean? What kind of thing? Can I guess? Is it plant, animal, or mineral?"

"Stop," she said, grabbing my arm and pulling me into the kitchen, where she stuck a paring knife in my hand and parked me in front of a pile of apples. "You know what I mean. Are you dating or not?"

"Did Kate tell you about this?" I clenched the knife in my hand. If Kate did tell, I wondered if it was wrong to stab a pregnant woman somewhere nonfatal, like her bicep.

"So it's true? Y'all are dating?"

"We go on dates, yes."

That made her squeal again. "Yay! Finally! We'll all be showing up to your mama's house for your bridal shower soon."

I was shaking my head before she even finished. "It's not like that."

But she ignored me. "I hope your wedding is in the next six months because Caleb and I want to start a family right away, and if I'm like Kate, I may have morning sickness and not be able to help you like you've helped me, and I would just feel terrible. Don't be mad if that happens."

My mouth was hanging open by the time she finished. There didn't seem to be any way to stop the tide of nonsense, so I didn't try. "Where's Kate?"

Sister Gracely swept in right then. "Upstairs having a little moment. She'll come down in a bit."

"Morning sickness?" I asked.

"Yes, but I think she's already feeling better. Do you mind slicing up those apples? I made a dip for them, and I didn't want to cut them too early and let them get brown."

"Yes, ma'am," I said, starting on my first apple. Just in time too because the doorbell rang again, and the rest of the wedding belles showed up to string puffy paper flowers and color-coordinated balloons everywhere. Staying in the kitchen kept me out of their path.

Twenty minutes and a dozen sliced apples later, Kate walked in. She'd freshened her makeup, but she wasn't a hundred percent yet. I'd have to keep an eye on her to make sure her color came all the way back. I hugged her, smiling at the way her drum of a belly pushed between us. "How's Jellybean?"

"Difficult." She rubbed her stomach, her smile belying any true annoyance. "Good thing I love him already."

"Did you tell Jaimie about Max and I?"

She shook her head. "But I can't promise my mom didn't."

I sighed. It had been only a matter of time before word got out anyway. "Guess this means I can sit with him in church tomorrow."

"People would talk more if you didn't."

She couldn't stomach the smell of food, so I spritzed the apples with lemon juice to keep them white and followed her out to help with the decorations while we caught up. Within an hour, the first official guests began arriving, and within another half hour, a sea of ladies in pretty spring dresses spilled out of the house and into the Gracely's beautiful yard. Bishop Gracely had obviously decided to make himself scarce, so there was no stopping the flow of the estrogen-fest. I loved it though. It felt kind of tribal, like the elders and the neophytes of an ancient clan all trading stories and secrets.

I helped serve up the food and entertained Kate's great-aunt Blanche, who always made a big deal about having driven in from Zachary, even though it was only a half hour away. Maybe that felt like an eternity when you were almost ninety.

After everyone was fed and chatting, Kate struggled to her feet and announced the games. Since I wasn't needed and didn't love party games, I melted to the back of the crowd near some distant Gracely cousins and watched. I wouldn't do games at my shower. I'd much rather do something ridiculously sentimental, like have all the ladies take turns giving me advice. And I would be all about the food. I'd want a brunch, maybe a crepe bar, with sweet and savory options. I thought maybe I'd do deeper colors though. I loved all the muted hues the current belles were using, but I wanted something richer because it was hard to imagine Max surrounded by pastels or—I froze with a stuffed mushroom halfway to my mouth. Whoa.

Whoa.

I'd imagined my own bridal shower and wedding colors a million times before. But I'd never thought about adjusting them for anyone specific.

I had just thought about my wedding to Max.

Whooooooooa.

I sat down, only half listening to the girls' chatter as they tried to guess which celebrity brides had worn which gowns.

Shouldn't I be panicked that I was thinking about Max in wedding terms? That wasn't "no strings attached."

But I *wasn't* panicked.

"Aren't you glad, Lila?"

I looked up, not sure what Jaimie had asked me. "I'm sorry, what?"

She laughed. "I bet I know what you're thinking about. Or make that *who*." That set Jorie and Hailey to laughing while the other two belles immediately turned to their neighbors to figure out what Jaimie meant. "I asked how the YSA conference is shaping up. Two of the belles met their fiancés there."

"It's coming together," I said. "We'll announce the details soon."

"It wouldn't be the same without you," Jorie said. "You've gone to every conference since I turned eighteen. It's weird for me to think I won't be going after this year. I'll miss it. Oh, I know! Del and I will chaperone next year."

Nothing like publicly getting called out as an old maid, even if Jorie hadn't meant it to be mean.

Kate caught my eye and grimaced. She cleared her throat, and all eyes turned back to her. "All right, ladies, it's time for Jaimie to open her gifts."

Once Jaimie had opened and exclaimed over two negligees and a set of Egyptian-cotton sheets, I decided the attention had faded from me enough to sneak into the kitchen and clean up. When I'd done enough to be useful, I escaped to my car, texting Kate before I drove off. *Cleaned in kitchen. Need to go home and grade. Feel better!*

Kate's replay was instant. *Jorie has always been an idiot. Love you. Come back in and eat some cake.*

I didn't answer, instead putting the car in gear and pulling away. I wasn't in the mood to celebrate anymore.

Chapter 19

JAIMIE'S SHOWER PUT ME IN an odd head space, and I didn't trust myself to stay cheerful or even rational around Max that evening. Instead, I crawled into my Lincoln High sweatpants and an LSU shirt, pulled my hair into an "I don't care" topknot, and swapped my contacts for glasses. Maybe that was why I wasn't super thrilled when he texted an hour later to tell me not to be mad but that he was standing on my front porch.

I went downstairs to open the door and found him looking way too cute in a sage-green polo and tan shorts, flip flops on his feet. In general, I liked a guy who made a more thoughtful shoe choice, but the rest of him was perfectly preppy, and I frowned. Not fair. I had such a weakness for a well-dressed boy.

"I said don't be mad. I brought you food."

"I'm not mad you're here so much as I'm mad that you look cute and I look like a scrub."

"You think I'm cute?"

I rolled my eyes at him. He grinned and leaned down to kiss me. "You're cuter. If you were my teacher, I would have a crush on you. Wait. I do have a crush on you."

"You think you're going to get through this door on charm?"

"Yes."

I stepped out of his way. "Come in."

I led him to the kitchen and helped him unload the bags. "What is it today? It smells ridiculous."

"I found a soul-food place and picked up some takeout. Red beans and rice and hot links."

"My favorite."

"I want to be your favorite. I'll bribe you with food all day long."

My stomach fluttered. He'd been saying things like that more and more—that I was cute or his favorite or he had a crush on me. My insides curled up and purred like a cream-fed kitten every time.

I fetched plates from the cabinet and slammed the door shut, setting them on the counter with a clatter. His eyebrow shot up. I didn't meet his gaze, but I silently dared him to say anything, coiled and ready to snap back with a response. He kept his mouth shut.

Oh yeah. He had sisters. He was no dummy.

I set the table while he transferred the food from the Styrofoam containers to serving bowls and brought them over. "I got enough for your mom too. She's not here?"

"No. She went over to Brother Lewis's house this afternoon to help him get some tomatoes started. She thought it might be therapeutic for him to learn gardening."

"It's getting dark. I'm surprised she's still over there." His voice held a hint of something I couldn't identify, a slippery feeling that disappeared as soon as I reached for it.

"I'm sure she'll be back soon. Unless she's decided that they're in danger of starving, in which case she'll take over their entire kitchen and feed them until they pop."

"Sounds about right."

I took a bite of the red beans and rice, but I was too distracted to enjoy them. I finished chewing and set my fork down. "You have kind of a tone right now."

Surprise flashed over his face. "Do I? Sorry. I don't mean to."

"'I'm surprised she's still over there,' and 'Sounds about right,'" I repeated in the exact same tone he'd used. "Are you getting at something?"

This time he was the one to set his fork down. "No. I'm sorry though. You said you wanted to work and have some space from me tonight, and I elbowed my way in. I'm going to take mine on the road to eat and let you get back to your work." His voice wasn't tight, and his movements weren't angry when he pushed back from the table and retrieved the takeout box from the counter, but my stomach clenched like it did when I had to confront a student about something.

"I wasn't trying to make you mad, I swear. It just sounded like you had some deeper thoughts about my mom, and I wanted to hear them."

"Maybe you aren't mad at me, but you feel mad at me. And I don't want to press my luck, so I'm going to take off." He packaged his food and walked back over to me. "To be clear, I'm not pouting and leaving. I'm also not going to stay here getting on your nerves. I'll see you tomorrow, okay?" He leaned down to steal a quick kiss before heading out of the kitchen.

I watched him go, frustrated with myself but frozen, not sure what to do. Hearing the front doorknob decided it for me. "Wait!" I said, running for the foyer. He was halfway out the door. "I'm sorry. I'm being a basket case. Why don't we finish dinner and not talk so my brain can unwind? Then I'll make a minicobbler, and while it bakes, we can go for a short walk. That should cure me."

He looked confused. "It's okay, Lila. I like you as much as I did twenty minutes ago, I want to kiss you as much as I always do, and I should probably warn you that I have every intention of sitting next to you in church tomorrow and holding your hand, but the last thing I want to do right this second is get in your way. Eat, refuel, get back to whatever you were doing. We're fine."

How had this Philly boy learned to speak so sweetly? It was like Daddy had trained him. I took a giant step back and pointed at the ground in front of him, on my side of the door. "Look, I made a safety buffer for you. You can step in that with no repercussions."

His half smile appeared. "Like this?" he asked, letting go of the door-knob and taking a step forward.

"Yes, that's good," I said like I was coaxing a puppy. I took another step back. "There, more safe room. Try another step. You can do it."

He took another step, this one bigger. "Lila?"

"Yes?"

"I'm a fast learner. I think I've got this down now. And that means if you don't take off running, I'm going to catch you. And then you're mine."

I widened my eyes and whirled around, heading for the kitchen—in extreme slow motion. His bag of food thumped to the floor about two seconds before he grabbed me from behind and lifted me up to plant kisses wherever he could reach—the top of my head, my cheek, my neck. I squirmed until he let me down, and I turned around and hugged him. "Sorry I'm being so moody."

"I get it. Stress morphs you into a porcupine."

I let go of him enough to punch him in the stomach.

He laughed again. "I'm still hungry. Can we go eat and not talk while you get to feeling better and then make cobbler and walk and then talk finally? I don't mean a serious talk either," he clarified. "I mean have a conversation with no subtext?"

I stepped back and zipped my lips. We took our seats and ate without a word, although every now and then we'd catch each other's eye and laugh.

It felt right to have him sitting there with me. Every time my head got involved, my anxiety over the future spiked, but when it was only about how it felt to be with him, any time, that wasn't confusing. That was clear. Clear like spring rain, clear like the lake outside. I remembered a GA talk, from Elder Holland maybe, where he said that if something was right when you asked about it the first time, then you shouldn't give in to the temptation to doubt that answer later.

Dating Max right now was the right thing. I laughed as he caught my eye again. No, there was no escaping this. If a small piece of me had wondered for ten years what those first glances under that rowboat had meant, how long would I be doomed to wonder about what might have been if I decided to walk away now? No, this was about trust. Trust in an answer to a prayer. Trust in Max.

Dinner was fast. By the time we both qualified for the Clean Platers club, I was so full I didn't want to think about dessert. "Do you think you're going to have room for cobbler?"

"Not for a week." He groaned and dropped his head in his hand. "The sad thing is, if there were more food, I'd eat it."

"I better hide my mom's in the fridge for her, then," I said, standing up to clear the table.

When he had the dishes washed and dried, he smiled at me. "Now we walk?"

"Now we walk."

I didn't want to go down by the lake. We'd never had a walk down there that wasn't fraught with some kind of emotion, good or bad. Instead, I led us down the driveway. When we reached the road, he took my hand and sighed, a small one, the kind of sigh I made when I caught a whiff of gardenias in the summertime or listened to the last notes of a Rascal Flatts song. It sent a shiver down my back. When did this boy not send a shiver down my back? Or flutter my stomach? Or weaken my knees?

He squeezed my hand. "Does talking through stress help you? Because I'd love to listen if it does."

When he'd shown up, I'd been dealing with Max stress, but it had dissolved, fog to his sunshine. "I'm a public school teacher. I will always be stressed. Do you know how many hours you're in for with that kind of offer?"

"Lay it on me. I want to hear it."

"Okay, but I need to confess something first."

"Uh, okay. Should I be worried?"

"No." I wasn't going to tell him I'd daydreamed him right into our future wedding. But I wanted to be honest in a non-scary way. "I want to tell you why I was stressed when you showed up. Don't run away screaming, okay?"

His only answer was to hold my hand tighter.

"The way I feel about you is my crazy Mia Maid crush times ten. Or maybe to the tenth power. I don't know. I like how that feels until I freak out about you leaving. Then I shut down. That's what was on my mind when you showed up. But when I don't think and I listen to my instincts instead, I'm calm. Like now."

Max stopped and turned to look at me, and I knew he was about to kiss me.

It was so . . . mmmmm. Good. So good.

He lifted his head far enough for his words to feather over my lips as light breaths. "I don't want to make you feel calm," he said. "Far from it." And he kissed me again. When he let go and stepped back, "calm" had turned to a riot inside me. He laced his fingers through mine again and started back down the road. We walked long enough for my breathing to settle almost back to normal before he spoke.

"Whatever this is between us right now is definitely how I felt ten years ago to the tenth power, not times ten. It's weird and not, which makes no sense, but that's how it feels. It's awesome. What I know for sure is that this is going to work out. We'll work through the details."

His certainty washed over me, and I grinned into the dark. When I told Mom about this, she was going to smile like she hadn't in forever.

"Max? You did kind of have a tone when you were talking about my mom being over at the Lewises. Not a bad one, but I can't figure it out exactly. What were you thinking?"

His shoulders rose. "I honestly don't know. Maybe . . ." He trailed off, his voice thoughtful. "Maybe I watched too many Hallmark movies to shut my sisters up, but it seems like it would be pretty awesome if your mom and Brother Lewis turned into a thing."

"Whoa," I said so quietly I didn't even realize I'd said it aloud until Max pulled me against him.

"Oh, man, I'm sorry, Lila. I was thinking out loud, trying to figure it out, that's all."

"It's okay." I was too dazed to know if I was telling him the truth. Mom and Brother Lewis? No way. She was barely starting to smile without a flash of pain in her eyes, and it had taken her two years to get to that point. She wasn't even close to jumping into a new relationship after being married to my dad for almost thirty years, and Brother Lewis's grief was much newer than hers. Besides, even if both of them were ready for romance, he was nothing like Daddy. Brother Lewis had always been plain-looking, quiet, and steady. I couldn't imagine Mom would ever be up to dating again, but if she was, she would choose someone handsome, with charisma.

"No, seriously, I'm sorry. I feel like I've ruined the mood."

"Which one? I've had about seven since you showed up."

He laughed. "That's true."

"Don't make me punch you."

"Go right ahead. I'm here to tell you the truth, and the truth is that you've cycled through a new mood about every ten minutes tonight, and I love that you let me see all of them, and I'm not going to apologize for noticing them."

"Can we stop talking about me?"

"Sure, whenever you do, you egomaniac."

"Too far, too far."

"Truth hurts."

"I have two brothers. I'm a dirty fighter. You better watch it."

"I'm not even a little scared."

"It's too early in our relationship for you to have lost your awe of me."

He scooped me into a hug that lifted me off the ground and spun me in a full circle before setting me down again. "Now *that* is never going to happen."

"Max? You're kind of the best."

"Take it back. I wanted to say it first."

I grinned and leaned into him.

"So tell me what's stressing you out that's *not* me."

"Conference. And work."

"What's stressing you out about the conference? Everything on the list is getting done, right?"

"Yes. But I keep worrying about all the things that could go wrong. What if we don't sell enough tickets to cover the cost of the *Creole Belle*? What if everyone thinks our ideas are lame? What if we can't find any awesome speakers? What if we can't get the service project done? What if—"

He held a finger over my lips. "It's going to be fine, I promise. Bishop Gracely says it's pretty much the same enrollment every year, maybe a little higher the last two years, and if those are the numbers we get, we can definitely pay for the boat, no problem."

"I don't relax very well. I won't feel better until we get the paid registrations."

"I know I can't make you not stress out, but I think it's great that you care so much."

"You're not witnessing me being great as much as you're witnessing me being totally neurotic."

"Lila?"

"Yeah?"

"Take the compliment."

"Thank you. I *am* great."

"Good job. Talking about the conference isn't going to help you feel better. Noted. What about work? What's stressing you out there? I mean, besides the fact that your entire job is dealing with teenagers all day."

"Kiana."

"Something wrong with her?"

"Yes and no. She's excited about her project idea, but she's hitting a brick wall in other ways, and I don't know how to help her."

"What kind of brick wall?"

"She came in the other day, and it almost broke my heart to see her so happy." He tilted his head at me, an "I don't quite get that" tilt. "It's so hard to make her smile like that. I realized she doesn't get to feel that very often, and it killed me."

"I can't even imagine that. It's hard to think that people have long strings of hard times punctuated with rare good things and not the other way around."

"You and I are privileged," I said. "That's something I've figured out. Living on a tight missionary budget for eighteen months is not the same thing as having to go to a food pantry a couple of times a week and still skipping meals. I don't know if either of us could ever really understand that."

By now we'd wandered almost a mile away from my house, even at our slow pace, and I turned the corner that would send us winding back toward home. "Kiana doesn't expect much out of life. And then, when she finally comes in and gets all excited about something—" My voice hitched. I hated even remembering what had happened next.

Max hugged me and rubbed my back. "Hey, shh. It's okay. What happened?"

I sniffed a few times, trying to pull myself together. "It went very wrong, and it's all my fault."

Chapter 20

He held me away from him and waited until I looked up to meet his eyes. "Tell me," he said.

I took a shuddering breath. "She found a way to do her project. It's a performance piece, but she doesn't want to dress up like Madame CJ Walker and do a monologue. She wants to use quotes and documentation from original resources to tell the story of CJ Walker's empire, but she wants to make it real for her classmates. So she told me her idea, and"—I swallowed, disbelieving that I had ever said this once, much less that I had to repeat myself—"I told her it couldn't be done."

Max's expression didn't change while he patiently waited for the rest.

"I thought I'd always be the teacher to tell them they could do whatever they put their minds to. And then the second I talk a student into stretching herself, I'm the first one to tell her she's gone as far as she can go."

"I have a hard time imagining you as a dream killer. I guess it's possible that you're a horrible person and I'm too dumb to see it, but I'm going to need more information to decide. What did you tell her no to?"

"Awesomeness. I said no to awesomeness. Her ideas went way beyond the scope of what I expected. She wants to recreate CJ Walker's life but with a modern setting against a contemporary backdrop and use multimedia elements. She'd be staging an entire one-woman show, but there are so many elements, and she doesn't have the resources or the technical know-how to put it all together. So I had to tell her the thing everyone else in her life tells her: lower your expectations." I tugged my hand out of his so I could jam it through my hair, so frustrated by the situation that the energy clawed its way out any way it could, as if yanking my hair out by the roots was going to help anything.

"I don't know. Everyone tells you that you're going to walk into the first year or two of teaching with stars in your eyes, sure that your dedication and belief in the kids will be enough and that you'll figure out pretty quick that it isn't the case. I always thought that was so cynical. Drove me nuts last year when all the old teachers would give me this condescending look when I would talk about how excited I was for an upcoming lesson or about a student breakthrough. They would be like, 'Yeah, yeah, we'll see how long that lasts.' And I was sitting there thinking, 'No way. I'm not going to be like you. I believe in these kids.' And here I am, not even at the end of year two, and I'm like, 'Quit dreaming so big, kid.' This sucks so bad."

"I can fix this," he said. "I bet you anything I can fix this. All you need to do is break it down like a work project. Assess resources, delegate, all that. This is totally doable."

I took a step away from him. I could almost hear gears grinding in his head as his business-school learning engaged and went to work on the problem. Maybe I should have been ecstatic that he was so willing to rush in and help, but it bothered me. I wasn't even sure why. Maybe it was his "All you need to do is . . ." Like I hadn't thought it all out before I'd had to crush Kiana's vision. Did he think I didn't understand project management?

I took a deep breath.

"Uh-oh," he said. "That's the sound my mom makes when she's trying to hold on to her patience."

I hesitated. He'd been nothing but awesome, showing up to feed me, going on a walk to hear me out. I wasn't going to be mean now. "I think I might have a frustration hangover from about a million things right now. Are you okay if we call it a night? I'm worried that I'm going to end up pitching about a half dozen more fits about things that don't matter."

"Sure," he said, his tone flat. Ouch. "Are we almost back to your house?"

"We're a few minutes out." We walked in silence, although I slipped my hand into his again so he would know I wasn't mad. I didn't know what I felt, exactly, but it wasn't anger.

He gave me a hug on the front porch and headed for his car. I walked through the house and down to the lake, making my way to the pier to sit and think. I hated that I kept shutting down as if I were figuring out the same thing about Max and me over and over again.

What had he done wrong, really? He'd asked to listen to my problems and had had the nerve to suggest solutions. That was what I was going to get upset over? I lay back on the pier and stared up at the sky.

Max was too impressed with his own intelligence and life experience, and as much as he thought I was trapped in a box of limited perspective, he was just as distinctly trapped in his. But it didn't make him a bad person. And I guess the positive side was that he had a lot of confidence in himself and his ability to get things done. I could respect that.

I still didn't like him sweeping in to be like, "I can fix this for you." What would I have wanted instead? Sympathy? Yes. And I would have been fine if he'd said, "Maybe I can help you brainstorm." Not, "I can fix this for you." And definitely not, "All you need to do is . . ."

But that boy was right to trust his brain. It came up with good stuff. And I didn't want to stand in Kiana's way if there was a way to solve this. I got up off the pier and walked back to the house. Time to hitch up my britches and work some stuff out with Max like a grown-up.

But tomorrow, when I'd rested on it.

For now, I sent him a text. *Sorry I was so weird. Think I figured out my mood. Thanks for trying to help. Would love to hear your ideas at dinner tomorrow.*

I went back to work on my grading but sent a whole stack of papers flying trying to grab for my phone when it went off an hour later. It was Max. *Sorry I was being the supreme idea overlord. Stoked I'm not kicked out of Sunday dinner.*

I smiled. *My mom would be mad if I banned you.*

Max's reply was instant. *I get that. I would be mad if I couldn't see your mom.*

Hey! And ME!

You? Well . . . sure.

You're so going to pay for that.

Can't wait.

* * *

After Sunday dinner we found ourselves driving Bridger home instead of walking down to the pier. Maybe because Mom had said, "Would you gentlemen like to walk down to the pier with me?" and Brother Lewis had said yes at the same time Bridger had said no. And they had both glared at each other. Mom had looked like she was about to drop the invitation when Max had whispered to me, "Don't be mad," before offering to give Bridger a ride home, which Bridger accepted. Brother Lewis and Mom both looked pretty torn as to what they were supposed to do, but Max had pushed back from the table, his keys already in his hand.

The Lewises lived about fifteen minutes away, and Max talked video games with Bridger all the way there. Bridger was tense and angry but too well-trained to be flat-out rude, so he answered Max's questions, and we survived the drive.

After Bridger climbed out of the car, I looked over at Max. "Why did you tell me not to be mad?"

He drummed his thumbs against the steering wheel a few times before he answered. "After I left last night, I called my mom because I had the feeling I'd screwed up somehow, but I wasn't sure how. She had some thoughts."

He'd called his mom for advice? My innards melted like ice cream in July. "What did she say?"

"Um, well, if I understood her right, I probably need to ask you a question instead. What did I do to upset you last night?"

"When you jumped in trying to solve the Kiana problem, it made me feel like you weren't giving me credit for having considered all the available options, like I don't have the ability to think through all of that myself. I have a bigger ego than I thought. Sorry you got caught in it."

He sighed. "No, I'm sorry. I'm a hardwired problem-solver. I like to pretend it makes me a good leader, but mostly it makes me that Michael Scott guy on *The Office*. Did you ever watch that show?"

"I tried a couple of times, but I kept wanting to punch Michael Scott in the face."

He smiled. "I bring that out in people sometimes too. My mom was like, 'Listen, Max.' And I said, 'I'm listening.' And she was like, 'No, that is the wisdom: Listen. To her. To other people. To a hammer, *everything* is a nail. You're a hammer.' So I'm going to work on being less of a hammer. Then maybe I can level up as a human."

"Oh, man, your mom is smart."

"Yeah," he said on a breath powered by tiredness and frustration.

I rubbed his arm. "Hey. Hammers are incredibly useful."

"Sometimes. But they're not exactly finesse tools."

"Maybe not, but the thing is, your mom was right that I was upset because I wanted you to listen. But when I calmed down, you know what I wanted?"

"Cobbler?"

I squeezed his arm in a mock threat for the teasing. "Stop ruining the moment, Max."

"We're having a moment? I love moments. I'll shut up now."

"What I wanted when I calmed down was a hammer to help me nail Kiana's problem. *Help* me, not do it for me."

"Got it. So can I help? And how can I help?"

We'd reached a red light, and I couldn't help myself; I pulled his head down to meet mine for a fast, hard kiss. "You're a fast learner. That's hot. Yes, you can help. Let's go home and brainstorm."

At home, Brother Lewis's car was still parked in front of the house. Max nodded at it. "You okay with that?"

"With what?"

He shook his head. "Nothing."

"Don't 'nothing' me. There's nothing going on. My mom made Brother Lewis into a project, that's all."

"Okay."

His tone was totally unconvincing, but I let it drop in favor of setting us up at the coffee table with my laptop. I poked my head into the kitchen while I waited for it to boot up.

"Are they back yet?" he asked when I came back to sit down by him.

"No. And don't even try to make anything out of that. It's just a walk to the pier."

"Uh-huh. Like the ones we take. Alone."

"Max . . ."

"Fine," he said, holding up his hands in surrender when he heard the lava in my voice. "We were going to talk about how I can help you with Kiana?"

I let him change the subject and clicked through a few web pages about Madame CJ Walker to give him an overview of who she was, explaining Kiana's concept for her project as I went.

"I can't believe we didn't study her in business school. She's the original Mary Kay."

I squinted at him. "How do you know Mary Kay?"

He held up three fingers. "Sisters, remember?"

"Right. But yes, that's pretty much what she was doing."

"It's so cool that she rewarded the women who were helping their communities as much as she rewarded the ones who did a lot of business. She was leveraging the TOMS Shoes business model a hundred years before it was trendy. If there's anything that could make me jump to a different company from Taggart, that would probably be it. It's crazy that with the way business and social trends are running, Taggart hasn't tried to do more philanthropic outreach."

"So you want to switch to a company with a social conscience?" Hope, that stupid, fickle bird, twittered in my chest.

"I need to stick with what I'm doing so I can learn and get the experience I need. I'm more hoping that I can move up enough to do something about aligning Taggart with a progressive operating model."

"Why not switch to a nonprofit organization? I'm sure there are tons of them dying for someone with a brain like yours."

He shook his head. "I love the business world. I love the challenge and the competitiveness and the innovation. I like that there's immediate feedback in the numbers you can crunch to measure the job you're doing." He broke off and shook his head. "Man, I told you I have a massive ego. It probably makes me a weak man, but I thrive off of winning, off being the guy who does the best job on a team. I'm hoping that doing my best with Church callings builds up my karma since I don't do it in my work."

"You don't have to apologize for that. If everyone wanted to be a teacher, the world wouldn't work. Some of us have to train you future CEOs for balance."

"You should probably drop the mic and walk away now."

I grinned at him, and he reached over to pull me into a hug, tucking me into his chest. "I like you. A lot."

I nestled my face into his neck, inhaling his delicious Max smell of soap and a light trace of spicy aftershave. "Ditto."

"Yeah?"

"Totally." It should have scared me to say it, much less feel it. But it didn't. And I stayed right where I was until I heard the french doors open to let Mom and Brother Lewis in.

"Thanks for taking Bridger home," Brother Lewis said when they found us. He cleared his throat. "I apologize for him being difficult."

I smiled at him. "It's okay. I deal with that age all day long. He's a good kid."

A hint of gratitude shaded his return smile. "Thanks for saying so. It's been a hard couple of years for him. For both of us."

I nodded. "Brady was the same age when my dad died. It gets better. Not easy but better. You add a hard age to losing a parent, and I'm telling you, Bridger is doing awesome, considering."

"That's what Hattie said too."

"She's a smart lady," I said.

"That she is," he said, glancing over at her.

Her cheeks reddened at the compliments. "You don't have to butter me up. I already fed you."

"And it was fantastic," Brother Lewis said. "The only reason Bridger comes out of his room on Sundays is so he can get supper here."

"Then let's get him out again. Y'all come next week too," Mom said, walking him to the door and closing it after exchanging polite good nights.

"It's good to see you looking relaxed," Max said.

A soft flush colored the top of Mom's cheekbones. "It's nice to be relaxed for the first time in forever."

She headed back into the kitchen, and I turned back toward the laptop, but Max's gaze pinned me, his eyebrows lifted like I'd told him the sky was purple.

"What?" I said.

He shook his head. "Nothing. Tell me more about Kiana's project."

I spent the next twenty minutes explaining it all—her research, how she wanted to present it, why I didn't think it was possible. Even repeating it put a sick feeling in my stomach. After I'd gone through all the information, Max leaned back against the sofa and stared into space. He was quiet so long I wasn't sure what to do. Was this how he thought? Should I give him space?

I rose from the couch, but he gave a slight start and reached out for my hand to pull me down beside him. "Sorry. I faded out, didn't I?"

"It's okay. I didn't want to distract you, but I did anyway, huh?"

"I'm glad. I might have some ideas, but I need to think about it for a day or two. Does that mess you up?"

"Not at all. You're already way farther along than I got with this."

This time it was him who got up from the couch. "I better go. I have to go home and make some family phone calls before I cash out for the night."

"You calling your mom?"

"And all my siblings."

Aargh . . . more melting. "Do you do that every week?"

"With my brothers and sisters, yeah. I talk to my mom more than that though. Probably every day, actually."

Puddle. I was one big ice cream puddle on the floor. Somehow I made my puddle legs support me as I walked him to the door. He gave me a good-bye kiss that was even better than peach cobbler, and I shut the door behind him. I leaned against it, thinking for a minute. When he'd shown up three months before, I'd thought I'd known all his flaws and had wanted nothing to do with him. Then I'd learned those flaws were the kind a boy could grow out of. And it was all stuff I could live with.

Live with. LIVE with. Like in a marriage.

I'd made my choice. I just hoped I could live with it too.

Chapter 21

KIANA SAT IN MY CLASSROOM Tuesday afternoon, her face a locked vault, but her hands wouldn't stop moving, first twisting a piece of scrap paper into an impossibly tight spiral, then tracing an ink drawing someone had done on the desk during the day. Southside Boys graffiti, a budding gang in the neighborhood. Davonte Lackey, then. I'd make him clean it off tomorrow and give him a pad of blank paper to work on instead—as long as it wasn't gang tagging.

"Don't be nervous," I said.

"I'm not."

I narrowed my eyes.

"Just because I don't want to meet some dude you want to bring in don't mean I'm nervous. It means I don't like it."

Oh, man. My completely nontraumatic upbringing was getting in the way again. How many times had this kid had to speak to strange adults she didn't know in situations where the stakes were much higher? How many times had an authority figure signaled some new, unwelcome change in her life? Cops. Social workers. Other teachers. I knew from her file she'd dealt with all of them—often because of her mother's choices.

"Kiana, I'm an idiot." She drew her head back in a "what are you talking about" move. "I thought it would be cool to surprise you with some good news about your project, but this is stressing you out, isn't it?"

Her eyebrow went up. "I don't really like surprises."

"I'm sorry. Here's what's happening right now. I told my friend Max Archer about your idea for your presentation, and he wants to help you with it."

"You said it wasn't doable."

"I didn't dream as big as you did, and I should have. I think Mr. Archer has some ideas, if you want to hear them."

She gave me the eye. "He your boyfriend?"

The question shouldn't have caught me so off guard. This was how high schoolers defined things, and I should have been ready for it. But instead, the question put me right back in high school. I felt ridiculous saying he was my boyfriend, but there was absolutely nothing else to call him. I struggled to find an answer, like "Yes" or "No" had suddenly become the most difficult words to pronounce. Max chose that moment to walk in with a beat-up backpack slung over one shoulder. His light-blue button-down shirt with the cuffs rolled up to his elbows and his polka-dotted tie juxtaposed against the backpack that had obviously seen him through college was insanely attractive. I couldn't even explain it.

"You her boyfriend?"

Kiana had gotten tired of waiting for me to answer.

Now I'd have to kill her. "Kiana, that's not appr—"

"Yes," he said, holding out his hand for her to shake. "I'm Max."

"You can call him Mr. Archer," I said, keeping a straight face, even though it wanted to rearrange itself into a Velveeta grin. "He's going to talk over your presentation with you. See if you like his ideas." He'd called me the night before to discuss it with me, carefully working through each element I'd worried about and coming up with an idea so ingenious that if I could have crawled through the phone to kiss him, I would have.

Max pulled out his laptop. My loop-de-loop stomach switched from celebrating our status update to nerves for Kiana's reaction. Would she see the vision? Max didn't have any concern on his face. "Lila says you want to create a backdrop that you can use with a multimedia presentation. She described what you want to do, and I think I understand it. What do you think the obstacles are?"

I relaxed a tiny bit. I'd made a big deal on the phone with him about how he couldn't think of himself as a coach telling her what to do. He had to be more of a counselor, pulling answers and information out of her, helping her see connections between things.

"It's going to be expensive. I don't have none of that equipment and no money to buy it."

Max nodded like he was considering this for the first time and typed something on his laptop. "I'm going to set up a flow chart so we can start figuring out how to solve all this. Is that okay with you?"

"What's a flow cart?" He angled his screen so she could see it, and her face cleared. "Oh, that's like mind maps when we have to do prewriting for essays in English."

"Exactly. It'll help us organize information."

"Go ahead then."

"Thank you," he said, not even cracking a smile. As easy as that, he'd made her feel like she held the reins. Magic.

Piece by piece, they broke down the elements of Kiana's project. Her expression grew more dazed as it became clear to her exactly how complicated her idea was. But it was also becoming clear to me as I listened to it all that she was right. She was so right. This was the way to do it. Max's face reflected only deep thought, like he was working out the math that explained why the universe kept expanding.

A half hour later, her project idea had been disassembled and strewn across dozens of boxes in Max's flow chart. Kiana had shrunk in her chair as if she were too tired by the magnitude of it to even sit up straight anymore. I looked away, staring instead at the bulletin board we'd put together, the display that was supposed to inspire young minds to discover history and change the world. This was how it happened—moments like this with students where if you could break through to them, everything truly could change. Max was about to present the plan that could change everything for Kiana.

No. That wasn't right.

He was about to present a plan that could let Kiana make everything happen for herself. I didn't know if she had enough fight left to believe it. I held my breath as he moved his laptop aside and folded his arms in front of him. "I'm a businessman," he said. "I bet you wonder what that has to do with history."

"Not really. Madame CJ was a businesswoman."

I let my breath out and smothered a smile. This was going to be okay.

"Exactly," Max said. "The fact that CJ Walker was such an incredible businessperson made me wonder how she would solve this problem. But you know her better than I do, so I'm going to ask you. Let's say Madame CJ needed to do a presentation for a bunch of investors in her company. And to do that presentation, she needed to really blow them away. And let's say she had all the ideas and talent in the world, but there was no way she could afford the equipment she needed to do her idea up right. What would she do? Borrow it?"

Kiana considered this and gave a single slow shake of her head. "No. No, she wouldn't have had much luck with banks because she was black and female. When CJ needed money, she made it."

"How about if you do the same thing? Start a business so you can afford all this stuff."

This was the linchpin right here. I'd been skeptical at first, but he'd said something I couldn't shake: "Nothing will teach her the lesson you wanted her to learn from CJ Walker like walking in her footsteps will. If she starts a business to pay for everything she needs, she's going to end up with a great presentation for sure, but it won't be her dreaming about the possibilities anymore. She'll be living them. She'll learn some skills that are going to take her way past this project."

I'd argued about the short amount of time she'd have to work and the cost of getting a business started and the difficulty she'd have trying to work while dealing with all the craziness at home. But he'd settled me down with a quiet request. "This is what I do, Lila. Trust me. Please?" So I'd texted him this morning when Kiana had agreed to meet with him, and now, as I watched him work with her, my heart folded even more of him inside it.

"I don't know anything about business," Kiana said, her energy dropping again.

"You've never been to a business or shopped at a business or watched a show that had a business in it?" Max asked.

"Yeah, but that doesn't make someone an expert."

"Having a consultant helps, and I'll be your consultant. Are you willing to try brainstorming with me?"

I'd seen this look on Kiana's face so many times before. It was the point at which she was wavering, deciding if she had the energy to give to caring about something we were discussing in class. Usually she shut down again, but when she let go and dove in, she was spectacular.

"All right, Mr. Business. I'll brainstorm."

I couldn't help it; I cheered. "Yes, Kiana! Yes!"

"Simmer down there, Miss Guidry. Writing down ideas don't pay bills."

Max grinned. "Brace yourself, Kiana. We're about to amaze ourselves. Let's talk about what you can do for a business."

"Marketable skills. That's a thing, right? I don't have those."

"Everybody does. We're going to figure out what yours are. Let's start by listing all the things you like or that you're good at."

"I like TV. I like reading. I make good fried chicken. Go ahead, Mr. Business. Tell me what we're supposed to do with that."

"Nothing yet. Talk to me some more. What other kinds of things do you do?"

For the next ten minutes, he pulled answers out of her, mostly flippant ones, about her talents, skills, and interests. I could see how some of them could lead to a job for her but not a business. She liked learning but not school. She read a ton because, even though she liked TV, they couldn't pay their cable bill, so they didn't have it at home much, but library books were free. She kept her brothers busy at home with the broadcast channels they could get without cable and a steady stream of movies checked out from the library. She loved the library and the park. She liked clothes but couldn't afford them often. She liked cleaning her house. That one startled me, but I sensed it came from a need to have some control over her environment.

When he'd pulled a long list out of her, he turned the screen to face her again. "You want to come over so you can see too, Lila?"

"Yeah, Lila. Come see," Kiana said.

"That's Miss Guidry. To both of you."

"Yes, ma'am," they said in unison, and both of them busted up.

"I can tell I'm going to have to separate you. Y'all both know it's impolite to gang up on someone like that." I settled down in a desk where I could view the screen with them. The screen was full of bullet points.

"What do you see here that could be a business?" Max asked her. She pointed to "likes to clean house."

"I could do a housecleaning business."

He nodded. "Yes. But can you find enough clients fast enough within walking distance of your house to earn the money in time?"

"Nope. Nobody around has money to pay someone for that."

"What else?"

"Can I be a professional TV watcher? That sounds like a good gig."

"No, because if that was a job, my little brother would already be doing it," I told her.

"You kind of take the fun out of stuff, Miss Guidry."

"Aw, man, and I thought I was the fun teacher."

She sniffed. "You're all right."

"What about books?" Max asked. "You have so much book stuff on here. There has to be a way to make that pay."

"Maybe she could get paid for reviews," I suggested. "Wait, no. I don't think most reputable sites would pay for reviews because it wouldn't be ethical. It's probably a great way to score free books though. Librarians always want to know which books teens like. I bet if you set up a book review blog or YouTube channel, you'd have all kinds of authors wanting to send you free books."

"That's going on my list," Kiana said.

"What list?"

"My list of stuff I'm going to do. I'm putting it right after getting paid for watching TV."

"All right, smart aleck. Max is right. Let's go back to talking about books. How do you make money from books?"

"Write them," Max said.

"I have a couple friends who majored in creative writing. I'm going to guess based on their experiences that it's a very long road that doesn't pay well."

"Probably."

"Bookstores," Kiana said. "As much as they're always charging for books, they must be rolling in the dough."

"You think that's bad, you should see how much it costs when you get to college," Max said, even though I was making a slicing motion across my throat. I didn't want him scaring her with stories of how expensive college could be. "Even the used textbooks are expensive."

"You have to buy your own schoolbooks at college? Here you only have to pay if you lose it, and half these fools take theirs home the first day, stick it on a shelf, and don't look at them again until the last day when they gotta bring them back. Dummies. I always hope whoever had my book the year before was a dummy, because that's how you get the books that still look good."

"Wait." Max stared at Kiana, but he wasn't exactly looking at her. He had disappeared in his head somewhere, like he had on my sofa Sunday night. Kiana shifted uncomfortably, and I held up a finger to indicate that she should wait a minute. Sure enough, he blinked and came back to us. "What if you set up a business buying and selling used textbooks?"

She shrugged, unimpressed. "It's hard to get over to LSU. Even with the buses, I don't want to always be dragging big, old, heavy textbooks everywhere."

"Think online. You'll still need to make some trips to the LSU bookstore to look at their used books to see what they're selling them for, see if you can find those books online for less, and then sell them online yourself."

She frowned at him. "Sounds kind of boring. And besides, I barely figured out that selling schoolbooks was even a thing. Who knew people would want to buy stuff like that?"

I laughed. "I don't think anyone wants to buy them. They *have* to buy them."

Kiana's fingers got busy again, this time drumming the top of her desk. "Have to, huh?" Only this time, instead of sounding appalled, she sounded thoughtful. "'Have to' is good for business, right?"

A small smile tugged at Max's lips, even though he was half distracted clicking around on the Internet. "'Have to' tends to be very good for business, yes."

"I like getting the new books from dummies, but if I had to be buying those things? Uh-uh. I'd be buying the cheapest, most beat-up books I could find, no question."

"Look at this," Max said. "This is an online search for textbook prices. I picked this accounting book, and it costs almost a hundred dollars new. If you buy it used, in poor condition, it's still twenty-five dollars."

"Crazy," Kiana muttered.

"Maybe, but it's the kind of crazy someone's making money off of. May as well be you." He clicked through the different copies for sale from different vendors, having Kiana write down the range in prices for books listed in the same condition from poor to excellent. When they'd gathered data for a few different kinds of books, he sat back and regarded her. "You like math as much as you like history?"

"I don't like history," she said, glaring at me and refusing to give me a crumb. "I hate it less than other subjects."

I smothered a smile.

"Do you hate math less than other stuff too?" he asked, his patience unshaken.

"I guess."

"Then wrap your brain around the numbers you wrote down, and see if you can come up with an angle for a business. I'll let you think about it while I step outside with Li—Miss Guidry for a minute."

"You know what the word *euphemism* means?" Kiana asked with a sly grin. "Because I do. You go right ahead and 'step outside.' I'll do math."

"Kiana!"

Max laughed and pulled me out of my seat and to the hallway. "You can't kiss me here," I whispered.

"Settle down, Miss Needs-Some-Loving. That's not why I brought you out here. I have an idea I want to run past you."

"Hit me."

"What would you think about me arranging some financing for her that she'd have to pay back? I know there are organizations out there that do microfinance-type loans, and she's going to need some money to buy some of the equipment she needs. Why not set this up so it's an ongoing income stream for her, a business she runs herself, where she can pay for her project, keep doing the business to pay for the loan, then keep it open as long as it benefits her?"

"That's a pretty big financial obligation. I was thinking about trying to find a grant, plus a donated laptop, and all that."

"Are you going to be able to find a grant in time? She needs to start making money now, and we can connect her to someone who can make the loan immediately. It's an obligation, yes, but I had to take this whole microfinance class at Wharton, and it's fascinating what kind of a difference it makes in lives. Wouldn't it be better to have her work for it? Wait, public school teachers are usually Democrats, right? Are you about to yell at me for my conservative ideals?"

I pinched him. "I'm a registered independent. I vote with whoever has the best ideas. This is a really good one. But I'm still worried that we don't understand the kind of chaos that runs her life, and I don't want to put her in a position where she's ruining her credit right out of the gate because forces she can't control wreck her ability to do this business."

"I get that. But microfinance loans are typically geared with highly favorable terms for the borrower and are pretty generous in forgiving debt. If something goes wrong, I'll personally guarantee the loan so it can't bounce back on her, but let's not tell her that, okay? I think she has to feel like this is all on her to pull off, that we're only here to point her in the direction of possibilities, not to save her."

"You're really excited about this."

He shrugged, but the casual gesture didn't fool me. His body almost hummed with energy. "This is fun. Doing any job day in, day out can feel like a grind. This takes me back to business school and sitting at the edge of possibility each time we planned a project to take the world by storm."

"All right. I say we do it."

"Cool. I'll go explain it to her right now."

By the time Kiana left another hour later, she looked dizzy, but she'd also rationed out more smiles than usual. She'd figured out where she wanted to tackle the textbook resale business, and she'd committed to writing a business plan based on some templates Max showed her. By the time Max walked out to go back to work for a couple of hours, it was all I could do not to wrap myself around him and beg him not to leave, or if he did, to take me with him.

He'd slung his backpack over his shoulder and glanced toward the door. "Am I allowed to hug you good-bye before I leave?"

"Maybe you're not allowed to leave."

"Now, there's a change I like. You're usually trying to throw me out of somewhere."

I glanced toward the door before getting high enough on my tiptoes to steal a lightning fast kiss from him. "No more throwing you out, I promise."

His eyes darkened, and he slid his arms around for a hug that was probably longer than it should have been for as many students as were still on campus. I didn't care. "Promises like that make me want to promise that I'll never leave, but I really do have to go back to work."

"Go," I said, stepping back. "I understand."

He dropped a kiss on my forehead and walked out with a wave. I walked to my desk and settled behind it, grinning. Even though our meeting was ending, the air vibrated with new beginnings.

Chapter 22

IT MIGHT BE BORING TO say, but I love routines. There is a comfort and security in knowing what to expect. My classroom ran better with routines, and so did my life. But I'd never had a routine as good as the one Max and I had fallen into. He and the Lewises were a part of every Sunday, and Monday nights too sometimes, if Mom decided to have family home evening. Sitting together at church had gone from feeling like a major commitment to the way church was meant to be spent. During the week, we were at each other's houses most nights, him plowing through work stuff while I graded. My favorite nights were when I had to plan a new lesson and he helped pull together whatever crazy props or supplies I needed to make the lesson happen or when he was bouncing ideas for work off me or asking me how I'd deal with an office conflict he was experiencing.

A couple of nights each week we worked on stuff for the singles conference, which was going awesome. It only took four days to sell enough tickets to ensure we could cover the cost of the boat.

Routines were helping Kiana big time too, especially the routine of working on her book business with Max. The money was coming in steadily, something she wasn't used to, and it was good to see her almost relaxed. I had a feeling she'd dealt with too much chaos by seventeen to ever relax all the way.

I was definitely relaxing though, for the first time in what felt like forever. Even the belles didn't drive me crazy. When Jorie started in on why she absolutely had to have walnuts in her chicken salad sandwiches at her bridal shower and not almonds, I not only didn't roll my eyes, but I also didn't even think about rolling my eyes. And when Lacie had her bridal shower two weeks later, instead of counting down the number of presents she had to open before I could help clean up and leave, I made mental notes about which things I'd want too. And it didn't freak me out or make me sad.

When I came home afterward and found Mom arranging a bouquet of lilies that was elegant in its simplicity, I smiled. It was an arrangement she used to do for us for dinner at home.

"I love them," I said, sliding onto a stool at the kitchen counter to watch her work.

"Hey, sugar. How was the shower? Did Lacie make you crazy?"

"No, she was all right. The food was good. They did the most darling petit fours with Tiffany-blue fondant and made them look like miniature gift boxes. They were almost too pretty to eat."

"That does sound precious. How clever."

"I'm going to have to remember that."

There was a short pause. "For what?"

"It seems like something worth remembering."

Mom picked up the vase and examined it from a couple of angles before she lowered it enough to peer over the tops of the lilies. "Like maybe for your own shower someday?"

"Sure," I said, hopping off the chair and heading to the fridge. "Someday." I looked for a cold bottle of water.

"Someday soon?" she pressed.

I found my bottle of water and closed the fridge, heading out of the kitchen as I said, "I have no idea."

"Lila Mae, you stop right there. If you're filing away petit-fours ideas in your head, you must also have some inkling that you'll need that information soon. Set yourself down and talk to me."

That was a tone I hadn't been able to disobey since I was a kid. I made my way back to the stool. She nodded in satisfaction. "How's it going with Max?"

"He's good."

"And how are y'all together?"

"Good." I couldn't help smiling. "Great."

"He makes your heart happy," she said with a soft smile. "That's how I used to look after a date with your daddy."

My heart did a double-thump, one happy, one sad. "I think I'm falling for him, Mom."

"I think you should, not like things like this can be decided. They just happen." She pushed the lilies aside and leaned on the counter, stretching her hands out to take mine. "I like him for you. Y'all are good together. I hear you planning that conference and talking about your work and laughing." She squeezed my hands. "I hear you *laughing*. I love that. Let yourself fall, baby girl."

"I always thought it would be scary to realize I'd found the person I wanted to spend the rest of my life with. But it doesn't feel scary at all."

"What does Max say?"

I deflated a tiny bit. "Nothing yet. Nothing like 'I love you,' anyway."

"He will. It's all over his face."

"It *feels* like he's almost saying it all the time. That's good for now."

"That's better than good. That's everything. If he's speaking louder with actions than words, you hang tight. Those words will follow."

"I can't believe I'm talking about being in love with Max Archer. Who would have ever thought?"

She raised her hand, her smile growing pleased. "He's always gotten under your skin in a way no one else has. Y'all just needed to grow up a bit to appreciate each other."

"I really do, Mom. He's such a good guy. He reminds me so much of Daddy. Max is so on top of things, and he's really invested in doing any job he's in charge of right. He's got Kiana's head so full of ideas for her book business that she's almost more interested in that than she is in CJ Walker. I love it. The business will do her more good in the long run than the history will, that's for sure. But if she can meld what she learns from both of them? She's going to be unstoppable. And he's been amazing with the conference."

She straightened. "Are you ready for it?"

"Just about. The Denham Springs Stake Relief Society has been amazing to work with on the Friday-night barn dinner after the service project. Max has the workshops and speakers all nailed down. Our stake is helping to put on dinner Saturday, so I know it's going to be good."

"You better believe it. President Gray asked the Plaquemine Branch to come in and make y'all a jambalaya supper. They know what they're doing. And our ward is doing desserts. It's going to be delicious."

"Two weeks to go. That flew. Max keeps waiting for me to freak out, but I have so much faith in him that it's easy to breathe and leave it to him. There are two things that make it hard to be in charge of something. If I feel like I'm the only one who cares about an outcome, that's hard. But Max wants this to be as good as I do, and he's willing to put in the time. The other thing is if you have to work with someone you can't please, but we're so supportive of each other, it's a big ole love fest. It's kind of nauseating."

"It's perfect," she said, her eyes a little misty. "That's how it's supposed to be. Well done, Lila Mae. Well done."

I rounded the corner to hug her. "You and Daddy were the best teachers."

"I wish that for you, honey. I hope that's what you find with Max."

It didn't even make me queasy to say it. "I think I have."

Chapter 23

"ARE YOU READY FOR THIS?" Max squeezed my hand as we stood at the foot of the *Creole Belle*'s gangplank.

I stared at the boat, lit up and glowing in the falling dusk. I squeezed back. "So ready."

"Good." He stepped onto the gangplank and made sure he had a good grip on me as I followed in my four-inch heels. "We've got an hour to check it all out before everyone starts showing up."

Mrs. Chapel met us on the promenade deck. "Good evening, y'all. Would you like to inspect everything?"

"Yes, ma'am," Max said, and I smiled. It was a reflex now, the ma'ams and sirs, as much a part of his vocabulary as mine. Miss Chapel toured us around, and my nerves keyed up with each passing minute. It was excitement, not anxiety; there was nothing to be anxious about. The *Creole Belle* staff had handled their end of things beautifully. I dawdled at the deejay booth. He was my second biggest worry of the night. Dancing with a bunch of Mormons when an inappropriate song came on was almost as awkward as watching a TV show with Mom when a sex scene happened.

"Can I check the playlist?"

"Sure." He flipped his laptop screen around so I could scroll through it. "Nothing to worry about," I said, shooting a relieved smile at Max.

He scanned it and fist bumped the deejay. "Thanks, man."

"I got you," he said, smiling as he slipped on headphones to test his equipment.

"What was that for?" I asked as Max drew me toward the banquet table.

"Nothing. Just thanking him for doing a good job."

It sounded like they were talking about more than the playlist, but I let it go. With Max, anyway. Butterflies kicked up in my stomach as I wondered if

Max had made a special song request. I tried not to let my imagination run away with me, but I was already halfway into a daydream of us out on the dance floor, swaying together, lost in the music of what would become "our" song, trying and discarding different sound tracks for the dance . . .

"Good idea. Sound good to you, Lila?"

I blinked. "I'm sorry, what?"

"Mrs. Chapel recommended that we eat now, or we might be too busy overseeing everything to eat later."

"I can almost promise it," she said. "I'd hate for you to miss out on this. Our chef is amazing."

We took our plates and worked through the buffet line. Max sampled a little bit of everything. "Quality control."

"Good thinking," I said with a straight face. I stuck to the catfish cakes with spicy rémoulade and some gorgeous grilled vegetables, and we took our seats.

Max took one bite of the blackened chicken alfredo and did his food happy face. "This is ridiculously good." He gave Mrs. Chapel a thumbs-up, and she smiled before turning back to the catering staff to give them instructions.

We finished our dinners, eating quickly so they could reset our spots, but when Max pushed back from the table and held out a hand to help me up, he took his time drawing me into a long hug. "We did it."

"You're amazing," I said. "This conference has been spectacular because of you."

He lifted his head to stare down at me. "No. I only executed orders from the best general I've ever worked under. You're the amazing one." He glanced around the deck and toward the still-empty gangplank. "Hold on." He let go of me and hurried over to the deejay, who smiled and nodded. When he came back to me, he held his hand out. "May I have this dance?"

Right on cue, music spilled out of the speakers, and Mrs. Chapel nodded to one of the crew. A second later, the lights on the deck dimmed. Max walked back, a slow, intentional walk and the look in his eyes made my heart pound harder with each step he took toward me. He was it. I'd finally found my one, and when Etta James sang the words, "At last . . ." from somewhere deep inside her soul, I slipped my hand into his and melted, everything disappearing but the soft light, the music, and Max.

He held me close, no fancy ballroom moves, just swaying that carried away pieces of me until I was a billion separate atoms humming with electricity.

I leaned into him and absorbed it all, floated in it, drowned in it, came alive only to find that every sense was tuned to him as he leaned down to kiss me, a soft kiss, a promise. He tucked my head beneath his chin and let the song play out. We were barely even moving anymore, even though Etta James was filling me all the way up inside, the deep joy of her song capturing what I had become with Max.

As the last strains of the song died out, Max's heartbeat sped up, a distinct change in rhythm I could feel right away with my head pressed against his chest. As connected as we were at the moment, it didn't feel like nerves. The energy between us shifted toward anticipation. The deejay had put on "Can't Help Falling in Love with You," and instead of finding Elvis corny like I usually did, it was perfect. Max threaded his fingers through mine and pulled me over to look at the river and the lights winking to life on the other bank.

I leaned on the railing and soaked it all in, but Max leaned next to me and called my name, his voice soft as the river breeze. "Lila Mae." His face was serious, and my stomach rolled with the light slap of the waves nudging the boat.

"Hi."

He smiled. "Hey." He reached up and wound a tendril of my hair around his finger, letting it slide off again. "This song was my request."

I was going to swoon. Flat-out, weak-in-my-knees, pass-out-from-happiness swoon.

"You're the reason I came here to Baton Rouge. You've been in the back of mind ever since the night with the lightning bugs. It doesn't make any sense. I know that. But I thought maybe coming down here and finding you would put it to rest. I thought we'd go out, and I'd see how normal it all was, and I'd break the spell."

This time he straightened and slid his fingers into my hair, around to the back of my head in a way that always sent tingles down my spine, and pulled me up for another kiss as sweet and soft as the one he'd given me while we'd danced. He leaned his forehead against mine, his eyes closed, and took a deep breath. "I can't break the spell. I don't want to. I love you, Lila."

I wrapped my arms around his waist, and stayed there, listening to the strong, sure thump of his heart. It didn't even scare me to look up after a minute and say, "I love you too."

He squeezed me tight.

I reached up to touch his lips. "Say it again."

"I love you." His eyes softened, and he dipped down for another kiss.

"I love you back."

He held me for a couple of minutes, and his heartbeat twined with the last notes of the song. Finally, he sighed. "The last thing I feel like doing is running a dance right now."

"But we're the kind of people who do even the stuff we don't like." I slipped out of his arms. I missed him, and he was only a foot away from me. "Should we go be grown-ups?"

He grimaced. "Yes."

We walked around the pilot house back to the bow where the dinner was set up. The deejay winked at Max, who grinned back at him before he glanced over at the gangplank. "Just in time." A group of six was about to board. He squeezed my hand again. "I'm so glad I'm doing this with you."

"The dance?"

"The everything."

"You're killing me."

"I know. It's the best kind of worst, isn't it?"

"Yeah." I glanced around as a crewman examined the boarding passes for the newcomers. "When we came here to check it out for this dance, I had no idea this is how the night would go. I figured I was doomed to run around checking on details while everyone had a night full of romance and moonlight."

"Don't forget the detail about how I'm madly in love with you, okay?"

My cheeks heated, but I stood on tiptoe to press a kiss near his mouth. "That's not a detail. That's the headline."

"Funny you say that, because it's exactly what I think about you."

Before I could answer, the first group was on the deck, exclaiming over the boat and the table settings, laughing and chattering about where to sit.

"Game time," I said, and Max shot me a smile. I used to think it was hinting that he had a secret, but now I knew it.

He dropped a quick kiss on my forehead before going over to greet the newcomers.

For the rest of the night, we found each other as often as possible in between handling questions. We'd opted not to sail because the rental fee was so much more affordable if we stayed docked, but it was still perfect. Before long, every table filled with guys and girls in their best suits and semiformal dresses, sprinkles of sequins and costume jewelry sparkling in the deck lights. Conversations and bursts of laughter rolled off each table, and when the catering staff began to remove empty plates, the deejay changed the music to something upbeat, and a few girls drifted out to the dance floor. By the next song, the floor was full, and Max came to find me. I looped my arm through his as we watched the dancers. "We did it."

"We're awesome."

I burst out laughing. "We are. I can't wait to see what we cook up next."

His forehead furrowed, and he looked like he was about to say something more serious, but the song changed again to a pop tune that had nearly worn out my radio the year before, and a cry went up from the crowd. I looked over to see Jorie coming right for me. "Dance," she said, grabbing hold of my wrist and pulling me away. Max shook his head and smiled. "You come too!"

And we spent the rest of the night like that, jumping into the crowd on the fast stuff, reconnecting like magnets for the slow ones, and taking turns handling logistical issues in between. By the time Max walked me off the boat, I had my high heels in my hands, and when we reached the end of the gangplank, he swept me up and carried me to his car. "Don't want you walking on this asphalt in the dark," he said, his voice low.

"Sure, that's why you picked me up."

He stopped and stole a hard kiss before walking again without a word.

"Are you going to do that every time I'm sassy?"

"Yes."

I let out a happy sigh. "And to think, my mom was always telling me my mouth was going to get me in trouble, like it was a bad thing."

He stole another kiss when he walked me to my door twenty minutes later.

"I don't want to go in," I said. "It means the best night of my life is over."

He drew me into his arms. "I guess that's our first disagreement because I feel like this is the beginning of everything."

I nodded, suddenly too overcome with happiness to find words. After several minutes, he peeled his arms away and stepped back.

"Max? I love you."

His huge grin showed up. "I love you too."

"See you at church."

He drove away, taking a piece of my heart with him, and it didn't scare me one bit.

Chapter 24

"KATE?"

She rolled to her side to look at me. "Yes, sweetie?"

"I think I'm superstitious."

"Okay." She pressed pause on the movie. We'd unfolded her living room sofa bed and put in *10 Things I Hate About You*, popped more popcorn than a theater of people could eat, and hunkered down in our pajamas for a girls' night while David was off doing his National Guard training for the weekend. Max was on a site visit at Taggart's Houston plant to look at how they were streamlining their shipping process, so it was a perfect night for Kate-time. "What are you superstitious about?"

"Everything is so good right now. It can't last forever. I'm waiting for something to go wrong."

"That's not superstition. That's your anxiety talking."

"Really? Then why have I worn the same pair of—"

"Don't say underwear! In the name of all that is good and right, do *not* say underwear because it will kill me to end our friendship, but that's too disgusting to still love you."

"I was going to say socks."

"That's not much better. I might have to kick you out and not hang out with you again until my stomach feels better."

"You have a baby in there. When does it ever feel good?"

"Jellybean bothers me less than the idea of you wearing nasty, weeks-old socks. How long have you been wearing them?"

"Twenty-two days. Ever since the night Max first said he loved me."

"That's so gr—wait. You wouldn't have been wearing socks to that dance." She looked over by the door. "You wore sandals here, no socks."

"When I said socks, I meant earrings." I touched the pearls in my ears. "I wore these on the boat, and now I don't want to take them off."

She hit me with a pillow. "You're the worst."

"But that's superstitious, right? I'm afraid to take them off in case it makes everything go wrong. Right now, everything is going so right. Kiana is killing it with her textbook business, and she's already made enough to buy the materials she needs. It won't be long before she repays her loan for the laptop, and the school will loan her the projector, so she doesn't have to buy that. And Max? Is perfect."

"No, he isn't."

"You don't like him?"

"I like him, but no one's perfect."

"You're right. He's got his faults. But he works on them. So I guess that makes him perfect for me."

"You guys are so good together it makes me want to puke."

"Everything makes you want to puke."

"No, that stopped a few weeks ago. Now it's just you two."

"It can't last, right?"

"What? This honeymoon phase? No. But that doesn't mean you aren't always going to have a great thing. Do you think that's what you're heading for? Always?"

I rolled over to stare at her living room ceiling. "Yes." I clapped my hands over my face when she squealed. "This is so crazy," I mumbled.

"No, it's not! You said it. He's perfect for you. And he's lucky to have you. You don't need those earrings for luck. This is real." She started humming the wedding march.

"Shut up." I pinched her, and she giggled while she reached to unpause the movie. "Hold on," I said, struggling to sit up. She started to as well, then grunted and stayed where she was. "I've been so sure this would work, so sure I followed a prompting when I got into this relationship, but I'm getting nervous. I think that's what my obsession with the earrings is about. It's getting real. No, this *is* real. But it can't go like this indefinitely. I've seen how hard he works. He tells me about how happy his bosses are with him. He's going to get promoted and transferred. Then what?"

Kate shrugged. "Then he takes a better position in this office and stays. You're way better than a promotion."

"What if he resents me?"

"Nothing you've said about him makes him sound like he's the kind of guy who's going to resent you. Are you really afraid of that?"

"Yeah." It had become a slowly snarling knot in my chest, this fear that he would stay for me, pass up bigger opportunities, and eventually hold me responsible for not having the career he'd planned out for himself.

"Hey," Kate said. "Stop the crazy worry spiral you're doing. You are totally worth a change in his future plans. If he loves you, staying here with you to have a life together is going to feel like a privilege."

I wanted to believe that, but I wasn't sure I was a good consolation prize for losing his future CEO status. As if I'd conjured him, my phone vibrated and flashed his name on the caller ID.

Kate smiled at it. "Go ahead," she said. "I'm honored to be second place now."

"He usually texts. I want to make sure nothing's wrong."

She waved for me to get on with it.

"Hey," I said, climbing off the sofa bed as I answered.

"Hey yourself. You and Kate having a good time?"

"Always. What's up?"

"Well . . ." And already I knew the rise and fall of his voice well enough to hear that he was trying to play it cool. "How would you feel about going out for a fancy dinner with me tomorrow after I get back in town?"

"How fancy?"

"Maison Lacour?"

My heart kicked into double time. "I could make that happen."

"Good."

"Is this a special occasion?"

"I think you're worth a dinner at Maison Lacour every night."

"Nice dodge."

"I might have a surprise."

I could barely hear myself over the blood pounding in my ears. I was on the balls of my feet, almost dancing with giddiness, but I kept my voice even. "I love surprises. Sounds like a good night."

"Well, I love *you*. You make every night a good night. Pick you up at six thirty?"

"Sounds good. Love you."

"Love you too. Bye."

"Love you!" Kate repeated in a syrupy imitation. "I love *that*! I love hearing you say 'I love you' to a boy who deserves you. Hooray!"

"If you love that, I'm about to blow your mind. He's taking me to dinner at Maison Lacour tomorrow night, and he says he has a surprise for me."

Her jaw dropped. She didn't breathe for a couple of seconds, and then she sucked all her air in as a huge gulp. "*He's going to propose!* He's totally going to propose." She sang it. "He's going to propose!" Then she climbed off the sofa and did an off-balance pregnant sashay. "Lila's getting married, Lila's getting married!"

I grinned. "Maybe."

"You so are! Don't take those earrings off. You were right about them! Now. Let's talk about what you're going to wear."

We spent another hour goofing off before she got tired and I left. Even though it was past ten, I was too wired to sleep when I got home. I was going to slip down to the lake for a walk, but Mom was in the living room. "Hey," I said. "I thought you'd be in bed already."

"Couldn't sleep," she said. "Sometimes you know before you lay down. I decided to work on the magnolia."

"It looks beautiful." She smiled at me for the compliment, but it wasn't an all-there smile. "Are you okay?"

This time she blinked, and I got her full attention. "I'm fine, sweetie. Why?"

I settled down on the couch. "I don't know. You don't look sad, exactly. But you kind of do. Sorry. That doesn't make sense. Were you thinking about Daddy?"

She set the embroidery hoop down in her lap and patted it, staring at the floor in front of her for a long moment. "Always. I was thinking too that it feels like the last two years of my life since he died somehow disappeared on me. I sleptwalked through them. I got Brady out on a mission, but I barely remember it. The flower shop has been running itself, but orders are starting to fall off. I was thinking that your daddy would understand how I've felt, but he wouldn't like it. I don't think this is how he would want my life to be."

"Of course you've been sad, Mom. You lost the love of your life. No one gets over that. Your kids are doing fine. And Daddy absolutely knows how you feel. You shouldn't feel bad about anything."

"I don't know about that, Lila. I don't know. I've never been one to sit and let life pass me by, and that's exactly what I've been doing."

I glanced to the fireplace mantel where our last family portrait hung. We'd taken the picture out by the lake, Daddy in a charcoal sweater that looked beautiful with his prematurely gray hair. A twinge of panic slivered through my chest like I was about to lose him again. "What are you saying? That you're going back to work?"

"Among other things. I'm restless. I need to be more creative again. I was talking to Coleman, and he said he's taking fiddle lessons and it's been helping him deal with losing Debbie because he can't think of anything but the fiddle when he's trying to learn. None of my usual activities has really helped. I need something new."

"He doesn't know, Mom. It's not the same for him. He doesn't get how it is for you."

She gave me a startled look. "He understands almost better than anyone, don't you think?"

"No. He doesn't get how much you loved Daddy. So few people get a love like that. And he got to say good-bye. You didn't. It's not the same thing. It's not."

She looked away and bit her lower lip for a minute. It wasn't something she did much. When she looked at me again, she wore the same expression she used to get when I'd come home complaining about mean girls when I was in fourth grade, like her heart hurt for me. She'd tell me that she loved me, that I'd get through it and one day understand it was a bump in the road. Seeing that look on her face now almost made me queasy, but I wasn't sure why.

"I feel pretty understood by Coleman. And I understand him too. It's watching him handle his grief with so much grace that's made me realize how poorly I've handled mine. I got twenty-eight happy years with your father when some people don't even get one like that. I'll never stop missing him, but one of the things I learned being married to him is that each day is a gift, and we should use our gifts to bless each day."

Tears sprang to my eyes. I'd heard him say that so many times.

"Oh, honey," she said, hurrying to me on the sofa. "I didn't mean to make you cry."

"I miss him," I said, melting into her hug.

She scooped my legs across her lap and held me tight. "I do too. More than ever. That's what I'm figuring out. I went numb because I couldn't have survived if I didn't. But having a friend like Coleman, watching him let the grief in, he takes the bad so he can also feel the good. I haven't done that enough. I'm trying to wake up, Lila. I'm trying to wake up."

I stayed in her hug for a full minute before I sniffled and drew back to meet her eyes. I forced out a question that tried to choke me. "Are you and Brother Lewis dating?"

Her cheeks looked exactly like a magnolia would have had I rouged one of its petals, and the tightness in my throat grew worse.

"We're . . . friends," she said carefully. "Even that feels strange, to be friends with a man who isn't your father. I didn't mean Coleman when I was talking about waking up in my life." The color in her cheeks didn't fade though.

"What do you mean, then? You're going to start fiddling too?"

She smiled, the pink fading. "Very funny. No. I'm going to start by being involved with the floral design at the shop. And I want to do other things too. Go back to volunteering at the women's shelter, for sure. I can't believe I let that go." She used to teach floral arrangement classes there. For the first time, I detected a glint of tears in her eyes before she blinked them away. "I don't know. If Coleman can take up fiddling at over fifty, I bet I can find a new hobby to throw myself into too."

I cleared my throat. "How about a wedding?"

"I'm sure I'll get a lot of those at the shop."

"I was thinking mine."

"Sure, honey. That's my dream to do, but I'll get plenty to—" She broke off, and her eyes widened. "You're getting married?" She grabbed my hand to check for a ring.

I tugged it away from her, laughing. "Maybe. Probably? I think yes. Max wants to take me to Maison Lacour tomorrow to talk to me about something important."

"Oh, baby, that makes my heart so happy." She hauled me back into her hug, laughing and rocking us back and forth. "I always had faith in that boy. I knew he'd be smart enough to hang on to you."

"We're hanging on to each other. I can't imagine ever letting him go."

She leaned back to frame my face in her hands. "Isn't it wonderful?"

"Yes. He makes me so happy."

"Then he makes *me* happy. What are you going to wear to dinner?"

I burst out laughing at her exact repeat of Kate's question. "Want to help me pick?"

She hopped up off the sofa and pulled me up. "Absolutely. There's no way I can sleep now!"

Chapter 25

"HE'S HERE," MOM SAID, PEERING through the curtains.

"Don't stand there like that!" I sat on the sofa, trying to play it cool, but she'd been stuck to the window watching for him.

"I'm too excited."

"I know, but I don't want to weird him out with you pressing your face all up against the glass."

"I'm doing no such thing," she said, but she backed away to stand at the door instead, her hand on the knob, ready to fling it open the second he knocked.

"Mom . . ."

"Oh, hush."

A moment later, the knock came, but Mom's lips moved in a silent, slow count to ten before she opened it. "Hey there, Max. You look like a Macy's ad," she said, and he did. He was dressed in a crisp black suit, slim cut, with a gray-striped dress shirt and black tie.

I stood up to hug him, and he broke into a smile. "You look gorgeous."

I'd picked a dress of deep-plum lace over a flesh-colored shell that skimmed the top of my knees. "Thank you. My mom's right. You look great too."

"You made a beautiful daughter, Miss Hattie."

"You're too sweet. Y'all will be the most beautiful couple in that restaurant tonight."

"Thank you, Mom." I hugged her and walked with Max out to the car.

"I have something really cool to tell you," he said when he buckled in on his side. "I think if Kiana holds it together with this textbook business, she should be paid up by a month after the competition, and the rest is all hers. If she stays at this pace, she's going to average $500 a month. But I think

I figured out a way that she can increase that big-time without a ton more effort. I can't wait to tell her."

"That's awesome. But maybe—"

"Wait, can I guess what you're going to say?"

I fought a smile. "Go ahead."

"Maybe instead of telling her, I can help her figure it out herself?"

"Exactly," I said, reaching over to squeeze his leg. "You'd make a good teacher."

"I could never do what you do. I always knew there had to be a level of skill that made some of my teachers better than others, but watching you, I see that it's more than that. You're talented the way concert pianists and ballerinas are talented, and there's no way I could do it." He reached over to thread his fingers through mine and settled our joined hands on the console between us. "Have I told you lately that I love you?"

"Not since yesterday."

"Boyfriend fail. I love you."

"I love you too."

He stole a stoplight kiss. When the car started moving again, the conversation went back to Kiana. The competition was in two weeks, and her project blew my mind daily. I'd hoped she would catch a vision, but she was producing something far beyond anything I could have dreamed up. She'd gone to talk to the drama teacher, Mr. Bell, about how to build a set, and the industrial-design teacher about using his students and the school shop equipment to make what she needed. She'd gotten the home ec teacher, Mrs. Cooper, to use some of her senior students to make a costume for Madame CJ Walker that blended modern and historic styles.

The kids in my class were paying attention to the process, asking her every day for updates or more information about Madame CJ. "Do you know last Friday she told my class she wasn't going to tell them any more about Madame CJ until she did her presentation? She said if they wanted to know before that, they'd have to look it up themselves."

"Ha. Sounds like her."

"Even better was how she said it. She told them, 'I ain't your Netflix, trying to entertain you. This is more like an HBO production, and y'all are going to have to shut up and wait.' It was awesome."

We were laughing when we pulled up to the restaurant, whose lights were already shining in the dusk. A hostess in a black cocktail dress greeted us and directed us to a plush bench while she checked on our table.

The delicate silk wallpaper and dark wainscoting made me smile. "I haven't been here since I was sixteen. It's as beautiful as I remember."

"You've been here before?" Stress flashed over his face. "Oh, man. This isn't where everyone comes for prom and stuff, is it? When they're trying to be fancy?"

I smiled. "I don't think so. I came here with my parents as a sweet-sixteen birthday celebration dinner. I have nothing but good memories here. That's when they gave me this," I said, touching the pearl pendant I'd worn to match my earrings.

"Oh, good. I can live with that."

The hostess walked up. "Thank y'all for waiting. Your table is ready."

We talked about the decor and the dinner choices when the waiter brought our menus, but I couldn't imagine trying to get any food down. There would be no room for it when so much extra electricity filled me, but I managed to request the night's special, blackened redfish.

All the way through the artichoke-heart appetizers and the delicious fish, I held up my end of the conversation, but everything Max said sounded like it was coming from a distance, muted under the thrum of my adrenaline and the electricity while everything else around us sparkled with extra clarity: the glint of crystal on the other tables, the flash of light off silverware, the soft clink of forks against fine bone china.

Finally, the waiter cleared away the entrées and set a dessert menu down. I picked it up and ran my finger over the linen cardstock. "Seems like you can't go wrong with bread pudding," I said.

"Mmm," Max murmured, but it wasn't a sound of anticipation, as in "sounds delicious." He sounded as distracted as Brady did when I tried talking to him during an LSU football game. He reached over and took the menu from me, setting it down before taking both my hands in his. "Hey." His voice was low and husky and sent a strong current down my spine.

"Hey yourself."

"I wanted to talk to you about something."

I fought to keep my nerves steady. "I'm listening."

He propped his elbows on the table, lifting our joined hands so he could brush kisses over my knuckles. "I love you."

"I love you too."

"I never thought when I came back to Baton Rouge that it would end up being one of the best experiences of my life, especially not after the disaster it was ten years ago."

"Things change. Cities. People."

"I've definitely changed. I think that's why we work, you and I. You've always been awesome. I had to grow up enough to meet you at your level. I'm so lucky you gave me a second chance."

"I'm lucky you came back and took a shot at one."

He leaned forward to press a soft kiss against my lips, then settled back again. "I've set and achieved a lot of goals in my life. Every one I've gone after, to be honest. Some of them were hard, but none of them has scared me like coming after you. But we're here. *You're* here. And this thing we have, it's the best thing in my life, and in a way that's crazy. Maybe you've figured out that I thrive on being the best at things, like my job."

I smiled. "I've noticed."

"It sounds corny, but I feel powerful when I smash a goal and move to the next one. With you, it's different. I feel peace. And that sounds boring, but it's not, I swear. It's more like this feeling of being whole." He groaned and broke eye contact, staring up at the ceiling like he wanted to climb into it, but we were still holding hands, so I squeezed his.

"I get it," I said, my voice softer than the murmuring diners around us, so he had to lean forward to hear me. "I understand. Completely. I didn't feel empty before, but now I feel more than I was."

"Yes," he said on a sigh. "That." He lifted one of my hands to press a kiss into my palm this time. I felt the touch of his lips all the way down through my toes. "In a life I was living not too long ago, bringing you here to tell you about my promotion would have been all about celebrating the new job, but now it's about celebrating it with *you.*"

I froze. This was about a promotion, not a proposal? I tried to keep the shock off my face, but he stopped smiling. "Whoa, what's wrong?"

I shook my head and withdrew my hands from his so I could drink some water and dab at my mouth with my napkin, stalling for time to pull myself together. "I'm fine," I said, and my voice held steady. "Tell me about this promotion."

Max didn't answer. He sat back, but he didn't relax. His eyebrows wrinkled, which meant he was problem-solving, and before I could think of another change of subject, his eyebrows straightened at the same time, and he couldn't have looked more horrified than if he'd knocked his water into my lap. "I'm an idiot," he said in barely more than a whisper. "I'm such an idiot."

I stifled the impulse to crawl under the table. "I don't really want to talk about this, but I'd love to talk about dessert. I think we were saying bread pudding?"

Max didn't answer for so long that I had to force my eyes up from the menu to meet his. He wasn't looking at me though. He was staring at the tablecloth and chewing on a corner of his lip. "Bread pudding?" I tried again.

"I need to run out to my car for second." It was like I hadn't even spoken. "I'll be right back. Excuse me."

He pushed back from the table and bolted for the door. I stared at the dessert menu for another five minutes, but that was practically a Jurassic era as the words turned into nonsense squiggles in front of my eyes. I couldn't set it down though, because I would never be able to figure out what to do with myself if I let it go.

By the time Max walked back up to the table, I had aged fifty years, but when I forced myself to look at him as he slid into his seat, he looked exactly the same as he had when he'd walked out. How was that possible?

"Hey," he said, and it came out as a bark of sound. He cleared his throat and tried again. "Hey, you. I'm about to make the biggest jerk of myself ever, but promise me you'll let me explain?"

He was saying it was going to get worse. How could this get worse? I had no control over the direction things were taking either way, so I nodded.

His forehead cleared slightly, and he reached into the inside pocket of his suit jacket to pull out—

Oh, dear Daddy and all his angel friends . . .

A ring box.

A RING BOX.

Chapter 26

He set it on the table between us. "This isn't how I planned to ask you. I want us to have a talk about all of that, to make sure it's what you want too—"

"It is." I couldn't help myself.

A grin broke over his face. "Yeah?"

"Yeah."

He laid a hand on the tablecloth, palm up, inviting me to take it. I slid my hand into his without hesitating.

"I'm only showing you this box because I wanted you to know I've been thinking about this for a while. And you can be sure I'll be asking you soon, but until I do, can you pretend I didn't show this to you? And forget that I was a total idiot not to realize how it would look when I brought you here? And promise to be surprised when you see that box again?"

I eyed it. "Can I look at it?"

He snatched it off the table and tucked it back into his jacket pocket. "No way."

It was hard not to pout, which I knew I should be embarrassed about, but I didn't even bother hiding my disappointed sigh.

Max smiled. "I'm feeling better about how it's all going to go when I pull that ring out next time."

"I don't even know what you're talking about. Rings? Weren't we talking about your promotion?"

His grin stretched wider. "That's exactly what we were talking about."

Oh my heart. Would there ever be a time when that smile didn't turn me into goo? The waiter stopped at our table again and inquired whether we had decided on dessert. "Bread pudding," Max said, and I managed a teasing smile back even though Fourth of July and New Year's collided in my chest and stomach as I considered that at some point soon, this beautiful man was going to ask me to marry him.

The waiter left, and I nudged Max's foot beneath the table. "Your promotion?"

"Man, Lila. It came faster than I expected. I'm so stoked. I start in two weeks, and it's going to be awesome. I'll be a senior manager over manufacturing. It's going to mean some trips to China." He leaned forward, his expression anxious again. "Just to be clear, I don't *want* to travel away from you for work. If anything, I'll be spending a lot of time finding reasons not to."

That set off more flutters in my stomach. He was planning his future around *us*. I was an *us*, an us that was going to become permanent. "That's the great thing about teaching. I almost never have to travel unless I'm chaperoning a field trip, but at worst, that will be for a week once a year when the kids take their Washington, DC, trip."

"Do you think it's going to be hard to transfer your credential?"

"What do you mean?"

"I don't know how credentials work between states. Will Texas take your Louisiana credential? It seems like they would since you're neighbors."

Everything inside of me froze again. "Why are you talking about Texas?"

"Because the promotion is in Houston?" The bewilderment in his voice was no match for the confusion trying to claw its way through my insides.

"You didn't say that."

"I didn't?"

It was definitely not a detail I would have missed. "You're saying you're moving to Houston in two weeks?"

"Yes. They're putting me up in a corporate housing complex until I can find a place of my own. I was going to see how soon you could come out and apartment hunt with me. I'm not in a rush. I know you need to finish the school year, but that's over in a month, so I thought we could do it then."

All my supper threatened to make a grand reentrance, and I fought the nausea with a deep breath, then another. "I can't move to Houston."

"I know not right away, but if we did an August wedding, that's three months." Color reddened the skin over his cheekbones. "Is that enough time? I can wait longer, however long you need."

"This . . . It's not about time. It's about distance. I can't move to Houston. I thought you'd gotten the promotion at the office here. My whole life is here. I can't leave."

The waiter showed up right then to set a gorgeous plate of bread pudding in front of us and drizzle it with crème fraiche.

"Thank you," Max said, his voice subdued. The waiter smiled and left. I didn't touch my spoon.

"You can't, or you won't, leave Baton Rouge?" Max's words were quiet but clear enough to hear the hurt lacing them.

"Both. I've told you that from the very beginning."

"I know. I guess I thought things might have changed."

"And I thought you had changed your mind about staying here now that you've seen a different side of Baton Rouge!"

"And I thought that if you felt for me like I feel for you that you would have changed your mind about leaving, about being with me even with all the crazy demands my career is going to make on me."

Tears pricked at my eyes. How was it possible for us to get to this point when we'd both been so clear about what we wanted in our futures? "This is what I was afraid of from the beginning."

He'd been picking at the dessert, not eating it, but I jumped when his spoon clattered to the table loudly enough to turn heads around us. "Are you going to turn this into 'I told you so' right now? You said you got the same feeling I did, that we were supposed to see where this relationship ended up."

It took a supreme effort not to jerk back like I'd been slapped, but that's what the anger in his voice and eyes felt like to me. "I'm not saying I told you so. I'm saying if I'd listened to my instincts, we wouldn't be in this mess right now." The press of tears clogged the back of my throat. An ugly cry wanted to come out in a wracking sob that I couldn't start in this restaurant. I steeled myself to shut down every emotion and focus on the immediate goal of getting out of the room; it was a skill I'd honed in the classroom, the ability to keep a tight lock on my feelings so I didn't lose it with the kids. "I'm going to the ladies' room. I'll meet you up front?"

Max's hand was in the air to signal for the check before I finished the sentence.

I collected my purse and bolted at the fastest walk I could manage and still look dignified. Every time the conversation tried to replay itself in my head while I touched up my lip gloss, I forced myself to think of test questions about the Clinton era instead.

When I walked back out, Max offered me an uncertain smile and slid his fingers through mine, twining our hands together as he pushed open the restaurant door. Every slight friction between our palms and fingers triggered pangs in my stomach.

My friend Anna taught a creative-writing elective across the hall from me. She always said "somehow" is a story killer. If a story ever says something happened "somehow," like a hero is caught in a deadly trap but in the next scene he has somehow escaped, that author flat-out didn't know what they were doing so they couldn't explain it. And if they couldn't explain it, it was because they were trying to force impossible events into the plot. I'd been trying to force impossible events into my life. "Somehow" was my story killer too. Somehow this was all supposed to work out.

Not really, as it turned out.

We drove in silence. No, not silence. His tires were loud against the asphalt. Why had I never noticed that his tires were so loud on asphalt? My fingers twitched to turn on the radio and fill in the quiet, but we'd always turned it down so we could talk. Turning it up would be another admission that there was nothing else to say.

Max drummed his fingers against the steering wheel. "I hate this."

I jumped at his machine-gun burst of frustration. His jaw set in a hard line, his hands now tight against the wheel, his knuckles glowing white in the streetlight filtering in. I turned back to stare out of my window, tall oaks flying past, marking the time until I could climb into my bed and let out the wall of feeling pressing against the back of my throat and eyes. Except Mom would be home, waiting, happy. Expectant.

A tear slipped out. What was I supposed to say? *I almost got engaged. Then we realized neither of us had listened to each other about the most important things, and that's no way to start a life. So now I guess we're not going to do that.*

I wiped the tear away, glad it had fallen on the cheek facing away from Max, but he sensed it anyway.

"Hey, hey, no," he said, reaching over for the hand I'd folded across my stomach, as if that would calm me. He signaled a turn into the empty parking lot of an elementary school and stopped the car, turning in his seat and hauling me toward him. I melted into him, the smell of his neck and the slight whiff of starch in his collar so familiar that it ached. Nothing would hold back the tears now.

"Don't," he whispered. "You're killing me. We're going to fix this. I know it looks bad now, but we'll figure this out."

I leaned into him, loving the way his arms tightened around me but hating that I couldn't ignore the hollow feeling growing in my chest. I pushed against him and settled back into my own seat. "How, Max? How do we fix this? Neither of us is willing to give up the one thing that's more important to each of us than we are to each other."

He sucked in a sharp breath, but he didn't argue. "I can't derail everything I've ever planned for. I thought your mom would be happy if we got married."

"She would be. If we got married *and* I stayed here. All her pieces aren't put back together. If I were the kind of person who could leave her here on her own, I wouldn't be the kind of person worth marrying. And it's not just that. Moving away would be pulling a huge part of my heart out and leaving it behind forever, only coming back to visit a piece of myself."

"But staying here means undoing my life, unraveling it totally, settling for less than my dream."

Now *that* was a slap. "No one's asking you to settle."

"That's not what I meant! Believe me, I know I would be the luckiest man on earth if you married me. But at the same time, I've had a clear sense of purpose for as long as I can remember, a total certainty of what I'm meant to do. And it's not just a career goal—it's the path God has been pushing me down for years. I can see it. Staying here as a middle manager for Taggart isn't going to get me there. It feels wrong to throw away this opportunity. I'm torn between two things that I'm equally sure I'm supposed to do. I don't know how to solve that."

I pressed my hands into my eyes and kept my palms there for a couple of minutes until I was sure the tears had stopped. "I would never, ever ask you to make that choice. I love my career as much as you love yours. I understand, and I'm not mad. I'm just so, so sad this isn't going to work." The tears welled out again anyway, and Max leaned over to press his lips against my forehead.

"No, please don't. Please don't. We need to sleep on this. It feels impossible now, but we'll figure this out."

I nodded. I didn't agree, but I didn't want to be trapped inside this bubble of pain with him anymore. "Okay. We'll talk again tomorrow, but right now, I'm wrung out. I better get home."

He started the car, relief easing the stress lines that had appeared around his eyes for the last few minutes. I wished I could believe my own words, but I knew a lost cause when I saw one. I couldn't even think about the misery this was going to translate to in the weeks and months ahead. I had to focus on the incredibly difficult conversation waiting for me when I got home. That felt impossible enough.

Chapter 27

MOM FLEW OUT OF THE kitchen. "Tell me!" she demanded, grabbing my arms to stop her momentum. When she straightened, she froze. "No."

"No what?"

"No to whatever or whoever put that look on your face. No to Max. No to everything."

I burst into tears, and she had her arms around me faster than a bass could snap up a worm.

She pulled me over to the sofa and tucked herself into the corner of it. I don't know how long she sat there patting my back, but by the time I tapered down to the full-body shudders I hadn't experienced after crying since I was a kid, I felt like I'd been gouging my eyes with pinecones. She squeezed me and let go. "I'm going to get you a glass of water and a box of tissue. I'll be right back."

She disappeared into the kitchen and returned with Kleenex, and she was wearing a clean shirt from the dryer, switched out for the damp silk blouse I'd sobbed all over.

"He didn't propose?" she asked, handing me the water and sitting back down.

"He almost did. He showed me the ring box. But that's not what he'd meant to do tonight." And between exhausted shudders, I explained how it had all gone down, omitting the huge detail that she was my biggest reason for staying.

She rubbed my back. "It's hard for someone who didn't have a problem leaving his home behind to understand why that's too hard for you. There's nothing wrong with folks settling down in places different from where they grew up, but for some people, their roots run so deep that pulling them up will kill them. They'll never survive the transplant. I think you would eventually," she said, brushing my hair back from my forehead. "You're a strong girl, Lila Mae. So strong. And I'm proud of you. But there's no question that you couldn't uproot without some massive trauma. I can understand why you would hesitate."

"There's no hesitation. I didn't consider it for a second." I gathered my hair up, claustrophobic from its weight. I looked around for a pencil, but Mom had a knitting needle in my hand before I could grow too frustrated. I wove it through the bun and breathed a sigh of relief at the cool air on my neck.

"Are we mad at him?" she asked.

"Yes. But also at me. And the situation." I flopped back against the sofa and closed my eyes, willing everything away. "I'm maddest at myself. I saw this coming and walked into it anyway. Why did I do that?"

Mom didn't say anything for so long that I had to peek to make sure she hadn't fallen asleep. She was watching me. "Why did you do that?" she repeated. "That's a good question to ask yourself."

"I don't know." It was a groan straight from the pit in my stomach.

"You need comfy pajamas and a good night's sleep. Go on up to bed. That'll fix you up better than anything."

"Max seems to think we're going to wake up and this'll be better too. It won't."

"So he's not mad?"

"No. I don't know. He's frustrated but thinks this will work itself out."

"That makes you the only holdout."

I didn't want to argue with her or defend myself. Unless she had the whole picture that I did, she would wait for this to blow over and for Max and me to straighten ourselves out. But she couldn't see herself the way I had for the last two years. I didn't want her to know how hard it had been to hold her together, and she definitely didn't need to know that not following Max to Houston was more about keeping her together still than it would ever be about roots. "I'm going to leave my phone with you. Kate will probably text. Will you tell her what happened and let her know I'll catch up with her tomorrow?"

"Of course, sugar." She stood and pulled me up, giving me a hug and a pat on the bum to send me toward the stairs. A half hour later, when I'd washed the dried tears and makeup from my face and changed into some LSU sweats, Mom didn't say a word when I knocked on her door and climbed into her bed and cried until sleep overtook me.

* * *

I went to Mom's ward in the morning instead of mine. I called one of my counselors and asked her to handle the day and spent the afternoon back in bed reading a book about the slave trade in South Carolina. Exactly twenty minutes after our ward would have ended, the doorbell rang, and I had no doubt it was Max. Mom's muffled voice floated up, and I dragged myself out of bed to save her a trip up to get me.

I slunk downstairs in my sweats and caught my breath when I saw him standing in the foyer. This was why I hadn't wanted to see him; the only thing that had ever hurt more than this was watching Daddy's casket lowered into the ground.

"Hey," he said, his eyes soft with concern. "How are you?"

I swept my hand down to indicate my amazing post-breakup Sunday-afternoon couture. "Awesome. Super on top of my game."

"I was—" He broke off whatever he was going to say. After an infinite minute, instead of opening his mouth again, he opened his arms. I could have resisted a tractor beam more easily. I was inside them in two seconds flat, his hug warm and familiar as he tucked me against him. I tightened my arms around his waist, making him my life preserver in a sea of feelings trying to drown me. I didn't know how long we'd stood there. At some point, he shifted his weight on his feet, and it broke the spell enough for me to pull back over his murmured protest. "Let's walk. It's warm. I'll go barefoot with you."

He slipped his shoes and socks off at the deck doors and rolled his pant legs up. Mom had disappeared, maybe into her room, to give us some space to figure things out. When we got down to the rock path leading to the lake, I slid my hand into his, and he sighed like our clasped hands were the thing that let him breathe again.

He didn't speak again until we'd reached the lakeshore. "I don't know if I've ever been this miserable."

"Sorry."

"It's not your fault."

"Isn't it? I'm the one who won't agree to leave."

"And I'm the one who won't agree to stay."

Neither of us spoke again until the pier. A new energy crept in between us—a noisy, uncomfortable buzz. When I let go of his hand to settle myself at the end of the dock, I didn't reach out to take it again.

"Is it *won't* leave?" he asked, breaking a silence as thick as the humid air. "Or is it *can't* leave?"

"Can't."

"*Can't* makes this all so much harder than *won't*."

"Maybe. I don't know. *Won't* implies a choice. *Can't* is about things I can't control, things I have no choice in. I can't leave my mom. I feel like you won't stay. It makes me angry on top of sad. Am I wrong to feel this way?"

"It's not a choice for me either. I can't pass up this promotion. It could permanently change my future, and I have way too much college debt to walk away from something like this."

"Even if that means walking away from me? From us?"

He dropped his elbows to his thighs and buried his face in his hands. "You're the one who won't take a gamble on us. Marrying you, raising a family with you, all makes me even more sure that I need to take this job. It's because it's *not* about me for once. Suddenly, I'm thinking in real terms about kids, about providing for them and making sure they'll have the opportunities I did, about taking care of all of you."

"Please stop," I whispered. The pain of imagining the family we couldn't compromise to make tore through me. It was an evisceration.

"I can't," he said, straightening to look at me. "I can't give up on us. Please don't give up on me. Please, baby." He reached out a hand and threaded it through my hair, drawing me close enough to brush a kiss against my lips.

It hurt worse than anything.

I placed my hands on either side of his face, brushing my thumbs over his cheekbones before I pressed a kiss against his mouth and let go. "I can't leave her." I stood and walked halfway up the dock before I stopped and turned to see him on his feet, staring after me. I loved him. I loved him so much. But the fact that he would ask me to turn my back on Mom made it the tiniest bit easier to turn my back on him.

* * *

I'd been saved by my students more than once, and Monday was the clearest illustration of the fact that it had been total ego to think I was saving Kiana. In the same way that throwing myself into my work had let me swim through the thick sludge of grief after Daddy died, throwing myself into the last-minute prep for Kiana's presentation kept me afloat in the pain trying to swamp me.

Max had disappeared without another protest. I'd gone straight up to my room from the dock, and Mom had sensed enough not to ask me about it before I'd left for work this morning.

Kiana bounced into the room, wound up and overflowing with words. She wouldn't need a protein bar to bribe her to life this morning. "Miss Guidry, I gotta show you something. I have a new idea."

"If I remind you that you already have an amazing project you need to present in less than two weeks, is it going to stop you from trying to throw something else into the mix?"

"Nah. Now listen." She pulled some earbuds from her backpack and thrust them at me.

"Like, literally listen?" I took them from her.

"Yeah, like literally."

I adjusted the earbuds while she fiddled with her phone. "You ready?"

I nodded, and a second later, a hook-heavy beat filled my ears, followed by rapid-fire lyrics. It took me a second to realize I was listening to an intricate rap about . . . "Hamilton. This is from the musical," I said, finishing my thought out loud.

Her face fell. "You already heard of it."

"I've listened to the soundtrack a million times. If I win the lottery, I'm going to use the money to go to New York and see this on Broadway."

"It's dope. And it gave me an idea. I listened to this thing all day yesterday, and I'm going to write a rap into my project. Don't worry, I can get it done. And my brother Andre? He's only thirteen, but that kid comes up with beats like you never heard. He's going to help me."

I pulled the earbuds out, sad to part ways with Alexander Hamilton. "If you think this is what your project needs, go for it. One question: what are you going to do about the time?" The rules set a strict limit for how long the presentation could go. Any presentations that ran over would be disqualified.

"I'm taking a bunch of the slam-poetry sections out and turning them into this rap and keeping the time the same."

An original score with barely over a week to pull it together? It sounded impossible. I smiled. "That sounds amazing. I can't wait to hear it."

"You gonna love it, Miss Guidry." She called that last part over her shoulder because she was making her way toward Tasha Miller. Interesting. They weren't close friends, and I hadn't seen Kiana go out of her way to talk to Tasha before, but now she was waving her arms and thrusting the earbuds at her. A smile spread over Tasha's face as she listened.

I made it through the day by teaching like a woman possessed. My students would never see such a forceful presentation on the Gulf of Tonkin

Resolution again in their lives, but throwing myself into it kept me functioning all day.

Brother Lewis and Bridger came over again for family home evening, but when Max texted me, I left Mom and the Lewises in the middle of a game of Scrabble where Bridger, the ringer, was whupping both of them.

I went upstairs to read the text. *I don't know how to do this.*

That made two of us, and that was exactly what I texted him. *I don't either.*

Are we done?

I stared down at the question. We didn't feel finished, but there was literally no way to move forward. When I didn't answer, Max texted me again. *I don't want to be done.*

I tapped out an answer. *I don't think we have a choice.*

How can loving each other not be enough? For either of us?

My only answer was to curl up and cry.

Chapter 28

Kiana quivered. Her lips, her arms, the bangs across her forehead all trembled like end-of-autumn leaves in a November wind. She was pacing, the shaking stopping as she mouthed her lines over and over, then she stood still, and the trembling started again.

She had paused in front of me and was now holding out her brown leaf hand. It shook like mine did when I skipped lunch, but I couldn't fix this with a granola bar. "How I'm gonna stand out there and say anything when I can't even keep my hand still?"

I reached out and took it, wrapping both my hands around hers. "I don't know how you're going to do this." Her eyebrows flew up. She'd clearly been expecting a different pep talk. "I don't know how you do anything, how you get yourself to school every day, how you get your brothers out the door, how you run a business now, how you made all this happen. But you do it. So no, I definitely don't know how you're going to do this. I just know that you will because that's what you do. You dig down, and you find something, and you make it happen every time. And when you figure it out, explain it to me because I could use a big old dose of whatever your secret is."

Her hand tightened around mine. She nodded, and the quivering stopped.

"You're up next." The two students on stage were doing a mock debate about the merits of Louisiana having thrown off Spanish rule in the eighteenth century. It was thoughtfully researched and well-prepared. "Have you been watching these other projects? They all did good work, but none of them has the pure, raw spark of genius that lights yours up. Not even close. You saw it in class."

A small smile broke out on her face. She'd presented her project yesterday, and they'd nearly lost their minds in the cheering. It had gotten so loud that Mrs. Santana across the hall and Mr. Deng next door had both come running over to make sure everything was okay. Mr. Deng had left with an annoyed shake of his head, but Mrs. Santana had grinned at the whooping, cheering class and shot me a double thumbs-up before racing back to her own classroom.

"I'm going to sit in the audience now. I can't wait to see their reaction. You've got this." I gave her a quick hug, just long enough to feel her stiffen and relax, before I hurried out to the auditorium. Man, if ever a kid needed more hugs, it was that one.

Mom smiled when I slid in next to her, and I leaned over her and patted Kate's belly. "For good luck," I said.

She rolled her eyes. "I'm not the Buddha."

The seat next to her sat empty. It was hard not to stare at the spot where Max should have been. He'd become the master of the empty seat. He hadn't shown up at church yesterday, and even though I'd known he wouldn't come around for dinner, his unset place at the table, his chair pushed in with no air of waiting had made it impossible for me to choke down more than a few bites of the roast Mom had made.

Bridger had been happy to eat extra helpings to make up for my pitiful efforts, but I hadn't even stayed downstairs for Mom's pecan pie. That might have worried her more than anything else she'd seen me do all week. Every part of my life suffered from the Max-shaped hole in it.

As I leaned back in my padded theater seat, I caught Mom watching me. "He won't come even for this?" she asked.

I shook my head and clapped as the debate onstage finished and the presenters took their bows. Max had tried to convince me to let him come over for days, but by Thursday he'd quit asking, and by Saturday he'd stopped texting all together. "It's fine. Kiana's next."

The curtains closed, and a murmur of interest rippled over the audience. No one had started with a closed curtain so far. The murmur changed to confusion, then worry as nothing happened. I tried to peer up into the control room. The Kiwanis Club had rented the theater at the performing arts high school for the competition, and I didn't know how much the different venue was going to throw the drama kids Kiana had recruited for handling the technical stuff.

A moment later, a series of lights clicked on and off, ending with the large spotlight coming on and staying on. The curtain opened and showed Kiana's simple set washed with cool-blue light. She stood in a long muslin skirt and shapeless blouse, a drab muslin scarf covering her hair. As her gaze fixed on the ground, I held my breath. I'd seen her rehearse this several times. If she could hold herself together, the prize was hers.

"I was born for more than this," she said, staring at the almost barren stage around her. And just like that, she had them, every last listener drawn in. *Who was she, and what was she born for?* I could almost hear the question in the way Mom leaned forward, caught up in Kiana's spell.

"My name is Sarah Breedlove, and though the war ended two years before I was born, I can't honestly tell you I have felt one day of freedom. I grew up under the tyranny of my brother-in-law, married at age fourteen to escape him, and now, at twenty, I'm a widow and a mother making a dollar a day taking in wash. It's not enough to hold body and soul together, much less a mother and her child." Suddenly her head shot up, and she stared out at the audience instead, her gaze defiant, her shoulders drawn back, and her bearing proud. "But I done told you I was born for more than this."

A heavy but simple beat started, one her brother had put together for her, and the rap Tasha had helped her revise, Hamilton style, poured out of her, a monologue of longing and steely desperation. Mom's fingers bit into my arm, but I stifled my protest when I realized she didn't even notice she was doing it, all of her attention on the stage, caught up in CJ Walker's story. "I'm the child of slaves/life tries to keep me chained/but I rise above/ and I'll use my pain/My daughter deserves better than the start I got/ When my last rites are spoken/she will know I fought/To be more, Live more, do more with my life/to show her that there's a point to this strife."

Kiana's delivery was raw and fierce—angry, desperate words rapped out of an angry, desperate place. The rap ended, and immediately the stage went dark except for a single rectangle projected onto a blank space on her set. A video played, with Kiana narrating about how Sarah's scalp bothered her and she dealt with constant skin disorders. "We are poor," Kiana explained. "So few of us have indoor plumbing. We can't afford it. We don't get to bathe often, and the soaps we can make or afford are full of harsh chemicals, like lye."

A shot of a pile of hair filled the screen. "That's mine," she said. "It's falling out. My daughter Leila worries about it, pats the bald patches on my head and asks if it hurts. Every spare cent I have goes to making sure Leila gets her schooling. I have nothing left for fancy tonics. But my brothers, they own a barbershop. And I've been asking questions. I've learned so many things about caring for African hair, and mine is getting better. So much better, in fact, that I'm going to work for Annie Malone, selling her hair care to my neighbors and friends."

The video cut off at the same moment the spotlight came on to reveal Kiana on the stage again, now in a trim, long black skirt and tailored white blouse. A new beat began, a lighter beat with a horn-heavy Dixieland jazz hook, as Kiana began a new rap about becoming an expert in working with black women's hair, about how she could sell honey to bees, about how Charles Joseph Walker, a smooth-talking newspaper man charmed her into marriage, and she became Madame CJ Walker.

She continued to switch between rap monologues and video clips as she changed outfits and spun out Madame CJ Walker's story, how she expanded her empire and trained other women to become beauty experts and gain their own financial independence. When Kiana appeared in front of the set after the final video montage, the audience gasped. She'd been slipping her other costumes on and off over her regular street clothes, ducking behind the set during video montages for the quick changes. Now she stood in her own clothes, discount store jeans and a T-shirt that had been washed too many times to look anything other than worn out.

A new beat came on, this one starting slow with a melancholy piano hook playing over it. "I wasn't born to privilege/I live in North BR/Ain't no silver spoons or German cars/Schools are falling down/homes are doing worse/Some say my street number ain't an address but a curse/Crime stats are high, opportunities low/but I'm not, because I look around and know." The music stopped, and her backdrop lit up again with a series of images: a snapshot of her good test scores, blank scholarship applications, buildings on the LSU campus. She stared straight out into the audience, her chin up, her stance firm, like an MMA fighter taking the ring. "My name is Kiana Green, and like Madame CJ Walker, I was born for more than this."

The guys in the control room killed every light but the spotlight shining on her, and the audience went crazy. Mom wiped her eyes before applauding, and Kate just kept saying "Wow, wow, wow" as she clapped. People were climbing to their feet to cheer, and the applause rolled toward Kiana in a wave of sound. Her jaw dropped slightly as she took it in, more and more people rising to their feet. A smile peeked out for a second before her expression crumbled and she dropped her head into her hands.

"Bless her heart, is she okay?" Mom called over the audience thunder.

I nodded. "I don't think anyone's ever given her so much at once. I'm going to go check on her."

Mom nodded and leaned over to explain to Kate while I slipped into the aisle and out to the hallway to make my way to the wings. Kiana was barely coming off the stage, and I held out my arms so she could walk into them. "You did it," I said, the applause still thundering. "They want you to do an encore."

"How do I do that?"

"Go out and take another bow." I turned her by the shoulders and gave her a push. She cast me an uncertain look, and I nodded. She stepped back out, and the applause surged. This time she grinned and waved, bowed a couple more times, and ran back to me. Jamarcus was working the curtains, and as he drew them closed, Sadie and Tasha ran out to get the set. Kiana's brother had run her laptop and projector, and they'd all practiced until they could each set up and take down their part of the show in ninety seconds flat. "I need to get out of the way back here, but I'll see you after the show." I gave her another quick hug and headed back to my seat for the last time. Four people still stood clapping, and I recognized her grandmother and little brothers. They kept clapping until the next presenter was announced.

It'd been an expensive night on a teacher's salary, almost a hundred dollars in tickets to get all these people here, but it was so worth it for Kiana to feel the support she deserved. I didn't mind a single ticket I'd bought— except for one.

Max's absence at church had surprised me, his absence at dinner had made me sad, but his absence on Kiana's night infuriated me. I pulled my cell phone out as I sat down and sent him a terse text. *You owe me $10.*

Maybe he'd realize it had been for the ticket to see Kiana and feel like the worm he was for missing it. I kept my phone in my hand through the remaining six presentations, but it never went off.

I understood avoiding me, but Kiana hadn't deserved to be shut out because Max and I had broken past fixing. He may as well have ground my last bits of hope beneath his heel.

After the last presentation, the emcee announced a brief intermission so the judges could make their determination. It was Kiana's to lose. No one could touch her. The presenters all came down to the audience to wait for the results in their reserved section, and Kiana stopped by my seat. "Mr. Archer asked me to give you this," she said, handing me a ten-dollar bill. I whipped my head around. "Where is he?"

"He had to go," she said. "He didn't tell you he was leaving?"

She'd be even more shocked to hear he'd never told me he was here. "No, but thanks for passing along the message. Better get to your seat,"

I added as the lights dimmed in warning. "Looks like they're fixing to announce the winners."

Her expression went blank, her familiar I-don't-care face, and before I could tell her not to stress because I was sure she'd won, she was already moving down the aisle at a sauntering, indifferent pace toward her seat. The emcee stood again and thanked everyone, introduced the chapter president from the Kiwanis Club, who gave a short speech, and then cleared his throat. I could see Kiana's shoulders tense from ten rows back.

"Third runner up is 'The Myth of the Red Stick' by Patrick Bordelon, Catholic High School. Second runner up is 'St. Denis and White Chief in Dialogue' by Whitney Nguyen, Baton Rough High School."

This time Kiana's shoulders slumped. She thought she'd lost.

"The winner of the five-hundred-dollar grand prize and the privilege of representing Baton Rouge at the state level is Kiana Green, Lincoln High School."

The room exploded again, and Kiana spun around in her seat to stare at me, her mouth half open. I laughed and waved for her to go onstage to accept her trophy and check. "That's you," I mouthed, pointing. "Go, go!" And watching her float up the steps, tugging on the hem of her shirt like she was making sure it was real and she was there, not dreaming, I escaped Max's oppressive weight for a few precious moments.

Chapter 29

MAX DIDN'T TEXT. OR CALL. But Thursday morning, I woke up to an e-mail.

To: Lila
From: Max
Subject: Excuses
Hey. I'm sorry I've been MIA. I don't know how to deal with what's going on between you and me, so I've stayed away, thinking maybe that would save us both some heartache. I had to go to Houston this past weekend so I could find a new apartment, and I need to go back this weekend so I can sign a lease and pick out some rental furniture and all that stuff. I'd put it off, but I'm supposed to start in the Houston office a week from tomorrow, and I just want to have as much settled as I can before I do that.
Sorry I didn't say hi on Tuesday at Kiana's program. It's hard. That's all. I don't have any good excuses.
I don't know why I'm telling you this. Sorry it didn't work out.
Max

I sat up in bed and read the e-mail again, trying to process what I was seeing. *I had to go to Houston so I could find a new apartment.* The words made me want to throw up. He needed to stay. I needed him to stay. I needed him, period. And even knowing all of that, he could still leave.

To: Max
From: Lila
RE: Excuses
I'm thankful that you showed up for Kiana, but I hate that you can't do it for me. Don't give up yet.
-L

I didn't know why I said it. I shifted uneasily against my pillows. I didn't want to give him false hope, but the guilt was nothing compared to the sense of wrongness that the thought of letting go gave me.

He lit up my caller ID a minute later, but I deferred the call. He followed up with a text. *Please talk to me, Lila.*

That one I answered. *Let me think. And pray. A lot, probably.*

I dressed for work, and besides first period, where the class tried to convince me to spend the whole time celebrating Kiana's win, I robot-walked through my day. I drove home and fought a bone-deep weariness all the way. This was what had tried to overtake me after Dad had died. This was what had drowned Mom from the second he'd stopped breathing.

Friday was only tolerable because I got an e-mail with directions from the Kiwanis Club for the state competition: it would be at the old state capitol in three weeks.

After work, I walked into a wall of familiar scents and sounds at home. Mom was cooking up shrimp, and Brother Lewis's low voice rumbled over the sound of Harry Connick Jr's first album playing on the iPod. Mom's laugh spilled out of the kitchen, then trailed off, and I sighed. Bridger must be giving them one of his surly looks. He'd gotten better, but he was still a teenager, and he couldn't let go of *all* his attitude, or it would shake the balance in the universe.

I wanted nothing more than to drag myself upstairs, but I decided to run interference between Bridger and the grown-ups for Mom's sake. I turned to the kitchen and froze in the doorway. There was no Bridger in sight, only Mom wrapped in Brother Lewis's arms, kissing him.

I gasped, and they broke apart.

Mom's hand flew to her mouth. "Lila Mae."

"Sorry," I said, not knowing what else to say before I whirled and headed for my room like I should have done when I got home. I lay on my bed and stared at the ceiling, not even sure how to handle all the emotional input of the last two weeks. A few minutes later, Mom knocked and let herself in.

"Hi, honey."

"Hey, Mom.

"You don't sound mad."

"I'm not mad."

"Then how are you feeling?"

"I have no idea. Numb."

She walked to my bed and sat at the foot of it. "Are you disappointed?"

"About you and Brother Lewis? No. I don't know what I feel. I'm not upset. It's just weird."

"Because he's not Daddy."

"Because he's not Daddy."

She plucked at the blanket a few times. "I thought you knew how things were going with us, but when I saw your face in the kitchen, I realized you've had no idea. I should have been more direct with you, but I couldn't figure out how to bring it up."

"It's front and center now." I scooted up so I was leaning against my headboard and grabbed a pillow to hug to my chest, like it was going to anchor me in place while the ground beneath me floated away. "What do you want to say?"

"I like him." She took a deep breath. "I've been worried you would hate the idea of me dating again. Or, at the very least, be uncomfortable with it. I'm so sorry I didn't sit down and talk this out with you."

"I don't hate the idea of you dating, but it was super uncomfortable to walk in on you making out with Brother Lewis."

"Lila Mae!" Her cheeks turned pink. "Don't be tacky. We were not making out."

"I would have thought it was weird even if it was Daddy. Kids don't like to think of their parents kissing for any reason."

"Especially when your mom is kissing someone you're not used to?"

"Especially then."

She nodded and went back to plucking at the blanket, her gaze far away. I hadn't seen that distant look in her eyes for several weeks.

"You okay, Mama?"

She blinked at me. "Yes, sweetie. Just missing your dad."

I felt guilty for being glad to hear that, but I pressed anyway. "Even with Brother Lewis?"

"Yes. And he misses his Debbie too. But I don't love your father any less because I'm enjoying my time with Coleman. Nothing could make me love Jim less."

"Where is this going with Brother Lewis, do you think?"

"I don't think either of us is in a rush to figure it out. Especially not me. I have too much on my plate. Did I tell you I scheduled new classes at the shelter? And Loralee Hilldean wants me to do her daughter's wedding."

"Wow. Are you up for that?" Loralee Hilldean was on the society pages of the *The Advocate* at least twice a month.

Mom's eyebrows shot up. "Have I been so out of it lately that you think I can't handle it?"

"You've been out of it since Daddy died. But yes," I said, testing the words to make sure I spoke the truth. "Yes, I think you can handle it. I know who I got my grit from."

"You've been so patient. But I'm here now. I promise. I'm not going to disappear on you. All the worst holes in my heart are knitting back together. I'll be fine." The idea that her heart was whole made me burst into tears. "Oh no, oh, sweetie, what's wrong?" she crooned, even as she pulled me into her arms.

"I'm a mess. I don't know." But I did know. I was so happy to see her coming back to me, but the fact that my heart was in tatters struck me again with a new ache. "I'm glad you're going to be okay," I finally managed to sniffle into her neck.

"I am." She rubbed my back for a while and then leaned back to hold my face between her palms. "I'm going to be okay, and you are too. I have faith."

"Mom? If I went to Houston, would it break your heart?"

"It seems to me your heart is broken right now, and *that's* what's breaking mine at the moment. I know you've been worrying over me, but it's my turn to fuss over you. Baby girl, you're meant to be with Max. If you're saying no to him for my sake, don't. I'll hate it if you leave, but at this point, I'm going to hate it more if you stay." She hugged and rocked me for a few more minutes before she kissed my head and stood. "I need to go check on Coleman and make sure he's recovered from his shock."

I picked up my phone when she left and pulled up Max's number, hesitating before opening a text. *I'm doing my best to change my mind, but it's so hard to think about leaving. I need to spend a couple of weeks trying to say goodbye to this place before I know if I can do it for real.*

His response was immediate. *What can I do to make this better?*

I gave a laugh-sob. Be a less ambitious, talented guy who didn't get promoted? But that wasn't Max's character, and I knew that above all, this decision had to be mine alone, without any persuasion from him so I could never hold it against him in the future. If we still had one. If I could see it his way. If I could learn to see my daydreams coming true somewhere else.

I sighed and answered him. *I need to survive the end of school. I need space, but I promise I will think about this constantly. I'm going to try to make this work. I promise.* I hit send and waited for his answer. It was almost an hour before it came.

Okay. I love you.

It only made me cry again.

Chapter 30

"Miss Guidry, did I do something to make Mr. Archer mad?"

I froze until I was sure I could dig into this with Kiana without crying. I'd made a decision, but I couldn't think about it until school was done next week. I drummed my fingers against a stack of papers on my desk. "Of course not. Why would you think that?"

"He e-mailed and said he can't come tomorrow night."

She meant her scholarship competition. "I'm sure he'd come if he could, Kiana. But he's in Houston."

"It's okay. But you're bringing your mom and your friend again, right? I need my audience."

"I'm bringing them, plus a couple of extra," I promised. Brother Lewis had surprised me the night before by asking if he and Bridger could come. Even Bridger had looked interested, so Brother Lewis had gotten them tickets.

"All right. See you in the morning. You for real going to make me take my final?"

"Yes, for real. We're reviewing in class tomorrow."

"You mean playing games? I'm down."

"They're games with a point."

"No complaints here. See you in the morning."

I managed not to cry until I got home, where I watched a home-flipping episode that happened to be filmed in Baton Rouge, and it set me off. I needed to be with Max, but I needed to feel how hard it would be to leave these roots of mine behind if I was going to tell him yes with any conviction, so I watched every second of the show, listening to the familiar accents and devouring the familiar scenery. I went to sleep with cucumbers on my eyes to bring down the puffiness, and when I got up Friday morning, it seemed to have worked. That was good because if the cucumbers hadn't worked, I'd have had to use Kate's old pageant trick of putting Preparation H on any telltale bags.

First period looked more like sugared-up kindergartners than high school juniors. After the fifth time of threatening to shut down the final-review version of *Jeopardy!* and give them worksheets instead, I dropped one of their history textbooks on my desk with a satisfying boom. "What has gotten into y'all? You need to straighten up and fly right."

"Sorry, Miss Guidry," Chauncy Tremonton called. "We're excited for Kiana's thing tonight. Hard to concentrate."

"You're going?"

"Yeah," he said, and a number of kids echoed him.

"Wait, raise your hands if you're going to be at Kiana's competition."

"Oh, we wouldn't miss this," Jamarcus said, grinning, and Tasha Miller smacked his arm.

Kiana looked uncomfortable. "Can we do the review, please?"

I nodded and put up the next question, but I held on tight to the feeling of being full of happy tears for the first time in a long time.

Kiana stopped by on her way home after school. "What you wearing tonight, Miss Guidry?"

I blinked at her. "I don't know. A dress, I guess."

She looked down at the ground. "You think I can win?"

"I know you will."

She nodded and looked up but past my shoulder, not meeting my eyes. "If I win, I'm going to call you up with me. If you really think I can do this, maybe you could wear something extra nice."

She was making herself more vulnerable than she'd ever allowed herself to be, asking something from me for the first time of her own free will. Darn those happy tears again. "I'll wear my nicest dress, Kiana. I'm that sure."

She smiled, but it wobbled. "I got this?"

"You got this."

I hesitated to ask my next question, but I wanted to be sure there wasn't anything more I could do. "Is your mom coming this time?"

She smiled, a tiny crescent full of sadness and relief. "She took off again. It's been quiet without her. And good. I would worry too much if she was there."

"You sure?"

Her smiled grew a little bigger. "I'm sure. I got who I need." She waved and left, and I packed up, knowing I would be too on-edge to concentrate until she held the grand-prize trophy.

I killed time with Mom in the garden for a couple of hours before she shooed me off to get ready. Up in my room, I hesitated before I pulled out the lace dress I'd worn on the night when everything had gone wrong with Max. It was the nicest one I had, and Kiana deserved that.

I managed a few big, loose curls in my hair and went downstairs to find Brother Lewis working a Sudoku book next to Mom while she embroidered. It was still weird to see him there, but it didn't stir up any bad feelings for me, and that was a good step. Bridger was busy on his phone, but he nodded at me when I walked in.

"I'm going over early to help Kiana. See y'all there."

At the Old State Capitol, the parking lot already buzzed with parents and contestants in everything from Sunday best to costumes, all streaming toward the check-in table in the grand lobby beneath a gorgeous stained-glass ceiling. I verified that Kiana hadn't shown up yet, and I waited for her, but it didn't take long.

She walked in five minutes later with her grandmother and brothers and rushed over to me. "I was going to get sick, but I realized you would make me do my show anyway, so I'm going to skip the puking."

"Good plan," I said. "Let's get you official."

We got her name lanyard and a sponsor pass for me and went to figure out who to talk to about getting her set from her uncle's car to the stage. The next two hours were a blur, but the program started right on time. When the lights changed for Kiana's presentation, third to last, I'd seen enough to be wildly impressed by the creativity and intelligence of high school students from all over Louisiana, but there was still no doubt Kiana had outdone them all.

Her energy crackled, and the audience took a familiar collective breath and leaned forward with the same tension the audience had the night she'd performed in the city competition. I caught sight of a few of my students sprinkled through the audience, and when Kiana's scene faded to black at the end, they were the first on their feet to cheer for her, though the entire audience was right behind them, roaring their approval.

Kiana had done it again!

I swept my eyes over the crowd for the twentieth time tonight, wondering if Max had snuck in again, but he hadn't. I should have begged him to come. Kiana deserved that. I clapped extra hard to make up for his absence.

The last two students performed, then the audience got an intermission while the judges conferred. Kiana rushed up the aisle from the contestant section and launched herself at me, almost tackling me in a hug. I held her tight. "You are everything, baby girl. That was so good."

"I couldn't have done it without you, Miss Guidry. You're staying until they announce the winners, right?"

"Of course."

She stepped back to squint at me and nodded. "Good dress. I hope we win."

"*You'll* win," I said. "You did this. And if you win, don't call me up there with you. I can't take credit for something that came straight out of your brilliant brain."

"Let's not pretend you and Mr. Archer aren't a big reason why."

Jamarcus called to her from halfway down his row, and Kiana took a half step toward him, her face eager, before she stopped and scowled. "That fool can come to me if he wants to talk." She marched down the aisle the other way to where Tasha and Sadie sat, jumping up to squeal when she reached them. Jamarcus frowned, then shrugged and climbed over his rowmates to make his way to Kiana. I smothered a smile. She had him good, and she might be just what he needed.

"I see why your mother kept bragging on you," Brother Lewis said when I sat back down. Kate and Mom sat between us, but he leaned over to make sure I heard him. "You're a gift to those kids."

"It's exactly opposite," I said, smiling at the compliment. "But thank you."

I watched the judges, heads together down at the table in front of the stage. I couldn't concentrate on conversation with Kate or anyone else. Nerves churned my stomach. Kiana had done the best job. Not only was her performance electrifying, but her research was flawless too, and she'd done a better job than anyone else of drawing a modern-day parallel. But there was no question she lacked some of the polish of the finalists from the private high schools, and I didn't know if that would hurt her with the judges.

"Excuse me, ladies and gentlemen," one of the judges said into his microphone. "We've reached a decision. Please take your seats."

A flurry of action exploded as everyone hurried back to their places, and when it settled down, the judge gave a speech about the importance of preserving our heritage and taking critical, thoughtful looks at our past. Finally, he cleared his throat and began the announcement.

"Third place and a $1,000 scholarship goes to 'The Carville Curse' by Paisley Hannock from Newman School in New Orleans." The room exploded in applause. She'd done a fascinating presentation of an oral history she'd taken from survivors of Louisiana's leper colony.

"Second place and $3,000 goes to 'Creole Creativity: Art from Conflict' by Aiden Batiste of Caddo High School in Shreveport." More applause, but I couldn't clap because I'd curled my hand around Kate's, gripping her so tightly she squeaked.

"Sorry," I said, letting go. She took my hand back and patted it.

"She's got this, Lila. She's got this."

"First place and winner of the $5,000 scholarship goes to . . ."

I squeezed Kate's hand even harder.

"Kiana Green of Lincoln High School in Baton Rouge."

The room went wild, and at least thirty of us went wilder than everyone else, screaming our joy as Kiana went up to accept her prize. We clapped and hollered all the way through her accepting her trophy and check, all the way through the pictures they had her take with the judges and other contestants, and all the way until she finally came down from the stage. Jamarcus grabbed her first, picking her up to swing her around, but I was right there after him to get my hug.

"I'm so proud of you, Kiana!" I shouted, and several of my first-period kids waiting to congratulate her burst out laughing.

"Thank you!" she shouted back, and I stepped out of the way so everyone else could get to her.

"Thank y'all for coming," I said when I got back to my guests. "I'm going to stay for a while to make sure she's able to get everything loaded back up, but I'll see you back home."

Mom shrugged. "It's probably a mess trying to get out of that parking lot right now. We might as well wait until it clears up."

"Me too," Kate said.

"It's not an LSU game. I think you'll be fine," I said.

"We should wait." That was Bridger, and we all turned to stare at him. He shrugged and looked back down at his phone.

I shrugged and sat down, asking Kate about Jellybean to pass the time until Kiana was ready to go back and start wrangling her set. Dixieland jazz played from the speakers as the high school kids and their supporters congratulated or consoled each other. Fifteen minutes later, I was all caught up on Jellybean, but Kiana was still surrounded by her classmates, even though most of the room had emptied as people had drifted downstairs to the rotunda.

A loud screech sounded through the PA system as the jazz stopped, replaced by feedback. The whole room turned to the front, and there at the podium stood Max.

Chapter 31

A MIDDLE-AGED WOMAN I DIDN'T recognize stood next to him wearing an expression like he'd handed her a puppy she didn't know what to do with. She eyed him like, "Cute, but what now?"

"Are we good, Kiana?" he asked.

"We're good!" She gave him a high thumbs-up, not looking the least bit surprised to see him.

"Thank you all for hanging around," he said. "Sorry it took so long, but I didn't want to steal one second of Kiana's spotlight."

"Hurry up!" she called. "I couldn't hardly think about my monologue because I was so nervous for this. Ain't no spotlight stealing. Get to it!"

What in the world . . . ?

Everyone laughed, and he smiled and slid his hands in his pockets, his gaze landing on me. "Hi, Lila Mae."

My hand floated up and managed something like a wave.

"Can you come on up here?"

Jamarcus materialized, gently taking my shoulders and pushing me toward Max. "Uh-uh, Miss Guidry. You're going." I didn't meet Max's eyes when Jamarcus deposited me next to him, but there was no way I would have argued with Jamarcus taking me exactly where I wanted to be. Though it felt a little too naked to let my longing for Max show on my face with so many witnesses.

"Hey," Max said away from the mic so it wouldn't pick up the soft syllable.

"You're killing me right now," I whispered.

"In a good way or a bad way?"

"I'm dead, so I'm not sure, but I think good."

He shifted back toward the mic. "Kiana and I have had a few talks over the last few weeks when I've checked in on her business," he said. "And

Lila Mae Guidry comes up all the time. Kiana has gone on and on about how much Lila has helped her, but I knew that already. I saw it myself. Lila knows the way things should be, and she has an unwavering commitment to making it happen. You should hear it from Kiana too."

Kiana was on the stage in ten seconds flat. "Good thing you listened about the dress, huh?" she whispered and startled a laugh out of me. She cleared her throat and stepped up to the mic. "I'm here as a character witness."

"We know Miss Guidry is great," Tasha called out, laughing.

"Not for her. For him," Kiana said, pointing at Max. "All those things he's been saying about Miss Guidry and how she sticks stuff out, that's true about him too. Only he forgot it for a little while. But he's remembered now. A couple of days ago, Mr. Archer called up my grandmama and had a long talk. Then he got me on the phone, and the next thing I know, I'm hired as a managing supervisor in his new office."

"What kind of offi—" I started to ask, but Max only smiled and shushed me.

"That's after he already helped me start my own book business. Next month, I'm paying our rent with my own money." Her chest puffed at this, and her classmates sent up a raucous chorus of cheers. When it settled down, Kiana turned her head and spoke straight to me. "People mess up. Mr. Archer knows he did it twice, but he asked me to come and remind you that he's fixing this way faster the second time."

She climbed down from the stage, and Max spoke again. "Next, I want to introduce you to Mrs. Brenda Lorris, a receptionist at the firm of Hargrove, Dirks, and Betten. I asked her to tell you a story."

She took the mic and cleared her throat, going slightly red when it made the mic squeal. "We're an architecture firm. A few months ago, we got a call from Mr. Archer, asking if we had a scale model of Baton Rouge. I told him that we did, and he told me he needed to borrow it that day because it was an emergency. I told him it wasn't available to loan. He offered everything he could think of to get me to agree, including a deposit that must have included every penny in his savings, and I still told him no. Then he told me the truth. He said it was for true love, that giving his sweetheart her city on a platter was the only way he could show her how he felt when he was afraid the actual words would make her run. And so I gave him the city model."

Another cheer broke out of the crowd, and my heart hammered faster than their hands could clap. He'd said that all the way back then?

"And believe you me, I got that deposit too." The crowd laughed. "But that's not all," she continued. "He called me at home about three hours ago after tracking me down on the Internet. You better believe I'll be doing some changing on my privacy settings." More laughter. "Anyway, he said this time he needed *me* to win his true love because he'd used all the wrong words, so he couldn't be the one to do the talking. It would have to come from other people and from his actions. Miss Lila," she said, smiling over at me, "I don't know how he did you wrong, but I've never seen anyone work so hard to make something right."

"Amen!" Kate called. *I knew about this,* she mouthed.

Max patted Mrs. Lorris on the back and gave her a gentle nudge toward the watching crowd. Now it was only Max and me. Every part of me wanted to smile at him, but all I could think about was . . . *what office?* What was Kiana talking about?

He reached behind him and pulled a letter from his pocket, holding it out toward me. I unfolded it, noticing the Taggart letterhead. I scanned it and gasped. "This is a resignation letter."

He nodded. "Yeah. I'm staying on for a few more months so I can keep a steady paycheck while I open my new business, but yeah, it's a short-term thing. I'm staying, Lila. I'm staying, and I'm investing in this city, opening a new business in Kiana's neighborhood, putting some of those kids to work. And I'm investing in us."

"No!" I shouted, and his hand froze in his pocket. "No," I repeated more softly. "You don't have to do this. I was going to give myself a few more days to be sure, but I know. Just looking at you, I know. I'll go to Houston. I'll go wherever you are."

I heard a loud Kate-like sniffle. I couldn't look at her, or I'd cry. Again. But Max was shaking his head. "I'll be done with Taggart in mid-December. How do you feel about a Christmas wedding?"

Intense joy broke over me, but before I could open my mouth, he was digging a familiar ring box from his pocket and going down on one knee. "I'm sorry I got lost, Lila. I was staying on my career path because it's the only vision I've ever had for myself until the future that you showed me, the one with us together. When I went to Houston and checked out my new apartment and office, instead of being excited, it all felt wrong. It meant nothing without you. So I came back and tried to figure out how to make my life work here."

I had to break in. "I don't want you giving up what you wanted for me."

"But *you* are all I want. And instead of feeling like I'm settling by staying in middle management at the office here, I've decided to throw myself into the only thing that's come as close as you do to making me excited to be alive, and that's developing young entrepreneurs. So I'm opening a temporary labor agency where we can hire people out of a community that's willing and ready to work if they're given the opportunities, and when we've got great workers, we're going to start listening to their ideas for their own permanent businesses, and we're going to figure out how to help them pull it off."

"We?" It came out as a question as I tested how it would sound for us to be whole again.

"We," he repeated. "If you'll have me." He opened the box. "Will you marry me?"

Nothing could have held the words back now. "Yes, Max. Yes, yes, yes!"

The shouts were thunderous, and Max jumped up to sweep me into his arms. "I need to always be with you," he said. "And if this is where you want to be, then it's the only place I want to be too."

"I love you," I whispered, since he wouldn't have heard me even if I'd used my full voice over the cheering, but his eyes softened, and I knew he'd gotten the message.

As Etta James's silken voice crooned the opening notes of "At Last" around us, Max leaned down to kiss me, and I fell in love with him all over again.

About the Author

MELANIE BENNETT JACOBSON BUYS A lot of books and shoes. She eats a lot of chocolate and french fries and watches a lot of chick flicks. She kills a lot of houseplants. She says "a lot" a lot. She is happily married and living in Southern California with her growing family and more doomed plants. Melanie is a former English teacher, who loves to laugh and make others laugh. In her downtime (ha!), she writes romantic comedies and cracks stupid jokes on Twitter. She is the author of eight previous novels from Covenant.